T
FAMIL

'Light-hearted gem of a tale'
Current Crime

'Chatty, cosy and very readable'
The Times

'High-spirited and very well done'
Birmingham Post

'Contains all the ingredients one could
wish for in a well-concocted mystery'
Boston Evening News

Books you will enjoy
from Keyhole Crime:

THE
FAMILY VAULT

Charlotte MacLeod

KEYHOLE CRIME
London · Sydney

First published in Great Britain 1980 by
William Collins Sons & Co Ltd

Copyright © Charlotte MacLeod, 1979

Australian copyright 1982

This edition published 1982 by
Keyhole Crime, 15–16 Brook's Mews,
London W1A 1DR

ISBN 0 263 73789 6

Set in 10 on 10 pt Times

Photoset by Rowland Phototypesetting Ltd
Bury St Edmunds, Suffolk
Made and printed in Great Britain by
Cox & Wyman Ltd, Reading

for Nate
with Thanks

According to Moses King (*King's Handbook of Boston*, first edition 1878) the Athens of America didn't have much of a history during its first hundred years or so; although Mr King did note that various Bostonians were murdered, hanged, imprisoned, put in the stocks, fined, whipped, or placed in cages for one reason or another. As time went on, however, things livened up. Beacon Hill became an area especially rich in history and legend.

The author makes this point to emphasise that her present chronicle of Beacon Hill belongs strictly in the category of legend. There is no Tulip Street on the Hill. There is no church, so far as she knows, that ever had a ruby-studded extraneous corpse turn up in one of its graveyard vaults. There is no character who bears more than a coincidental resemblance to any actual person living or otherwise, no incident that ever took place except in her imagination. Since she has gone to the bother of making up this whole story, she sincerely hopes it will be accepted and enjoyed as fiction from start to finish.

CHAPTER
ONE

'Who did you say you was going to dig up?'

Sarah manoeuvred herself a bit farther upwind. He seemed a sweet old man and she didn't want to hurt his feelings, but she wasn't used to people who breakfasted on Schlitz.

'We're not actually planning to dig up anybody,' she explained for the third time. 'At least I hope we're not. We're just going to ask the people who have charge of the cemetery to open one of the vaults and make sure it's in decent condition, so that my great-uncle can be buried in it.'

'How come?'

'That was his wish.'

She couldn't very well explain to a total stranger that Great-uncle Frederick had vowed he wouldn't be caught dead with Great-aunt Matilda, who had already pre-empted their assigned space in the more recent Kelling family plot at Mount Auburn Cemetery in Cambridge. She didn't quite know how she'd fallen into conversation with this down-at-heel old man at all, except that the cemetery was such a dreary place on a bleak November day, and there was nobody else to pass the time with. Cousin Dolph should have been here an hour ago, but he was still nowhere in sight.

Her new acquaintance was intrigued. 'Mean to say anybody can get buried here that wants to?'

'Well, no,' Sarah had to admit. 'All these old cemeteries around the Common have been declared historic sites, as I expect you know, so nothing is supposed to be disturbed. However, that particular vault over there by the wall belongs to our family, so we can't be stopped from using it if we choose.'

Nobody had so chosen for the past one hundred and forty-six years, but Great-uncle Frederick could safely be counted on to make a pest of himself to the last. In a way, the change of plans was going to work out for the better. Instead of a tedious funeral procession snarling traffic all the way across the bridge from Boston to Cambridge, the pallbearers would simply carry the casket out the side door of the church, directly into the ancient burial ground.

Sarah only hoped somebody would have sense enough to close those ornate cast-iron gates. There'd be crush enough without tourists thinking Great-uncle Frederick's internment was one more sightseeing attraction on the Freedom Trail. Cousin Dolph was probably still on the phone, recklessly piling up toll calls during the high-rate hours, rounding up the clan. It was useless to hope any of them would stay away. There wasn't a Kelling alive, except herself, who didn't adore a family funeral.

They'd all troop back to the house afterwards, expecting to be fed. How in heaven's name was she to manage a spread for that crowd when the week's grocery allowance was already spent? She'd have to talk Alexander into letting her stretch the budget for once, although that might take some doing. For such a gentle man, he could be remarkably inflexible about money. It was odd to be reasonably well-off in one's own right, married to a rich husband, and still never have an extra cent in one's purse.

The old man was still talking. Feeling guilty because she hadn't been listening, Sarah dug into the pocket of her sagging brown tweed coat and pulled out a couple of bite-sized Milky Ways. They were on sale this week at the supermarkets. Knowing how she liked them, Alexander had bought a bag and tucked a handful into her pocket to surprise her. Being so many years older than Sarah, he tended sometimes to treat her like his child instead of his wife.

Her new acquaintance shook his head. 'Thanks, miss, but I'm not s'posed to eat candy. I got the sugar diabetes, see? Got to watch what I eat. An' drink.'

He chuckled as though there were something funny about his affliction, blowing another gust of malt in Sarah's direction. She took another sideward step and put the titbits back in her pocket. He noticed.

'Hey, look, don't let me stop you. I never did go much for them Milky Ways anyhow. Even when I was a kid, my teeth was no good for chewin' nothing except maybe soup and mashed potatoes. Hershey Bars, now, I could eat them. They went down easy. I bet I ate a million Hershey Bars before the doctor told me to lay off the sweet stuff. Back in the Depression, you wouldn't be born then I don't s'pose, they used to sell 'em three for a dime and they was about the size of a cedar shingle. Yeah, I sure did like Hershey Bars. You go right ahead and eat your Milky Ways. Won't bother me none.'

Not knowing how to get out of it, Sarah unwrapped one of the little bars she didn't want any more and crammed it whole into her mouth, to get the business over as quickly as possible. Naturally Dolph arrived while she was struggling with her chewy mouthful, and of course he'd brought an entourage: a respected member of the Historical Society, an official from the Boston Parks and Recreation Department, and a foreman from the Cemetery Division. Dolph scowled at her bulging cheek.

'I don't see why Alex couldn't come.'

Sarah gulped down the awkward confection. 'I explained when you phoned that he'd already taken Aunt Caroline down to the Eye and Ear for her checkup. There was no way I could get hold of him.'

In fact, she could have tracked down her husband easily enough. The world-famous Eye and Ear Infirmary of Massachusetts General Hospital was within walking distance of their house, and Mrs Kelling well-known to the staff. Sarah hadn't bothered because she was heartily sick of having the entire Kelling tribe use Alexander as their odd-job man.

'Anyway,' she went on, 'I'm more closely related to Great-uncle Frederick than he is. Aunt Caroline wasn't even a Kelling.'

Until a generation or so ago, Kellings had often chosen their mates from among their third, second, and even first cousins, partly because they were a close-knit group and partly because it kept the money in the family. Nobody had seen anything remarkable about Sarah's parents having sprung from different branches of the same family tree. Nor did any relative think it inappropriate for the only child of that union to be joined in lawful wedlock to her fifth cousin once removed when he was almost forty-one and she a new-made orphan not quite nineteen years old.

After the marriage, Sarah had gone on calling her mother-in-law Aunt Caroline as she'd always done. Younger Kellings generally addressed any older connection as Aunt or Uncle, otherwise titles became too confusing. For a long time now it hadn't mattered what anybody called Caroline Kelling, as Dolph was pointing out with his usual tact.

'Can't think why Alex keeps throwing money away on doctors' bills. Caroline's stone blind and stone deaf, and there's not one damn thing they can do about it.'

Sarah didn't bother to answer. Dolph's companions were beginning to fidget. She took it upon herself to lead the group over to the vault, noting with amusement that the man who liked Hershey Bars was not far behind.

'Too bad you people didn't give us a little advance notice,' the Cemetery Division foreman was grumbling. 'Hinges are probably rusted out.'

He made great play with a long-nosed oilcan, then hauled out a bunch of huge old iron keys and selected the one tagged 'Kelling'. 'This ought to be it. Provided the lock still works.'

To his own apparent surprise, once he had pried the small brass medallion that covered the keyhole loose from its bed of moss and corrosion and managed to push it aside, he succeeded rather easily in fitting the key to the hole. The lock turned. The man from the Historical Society caught his breath.

'After all these years,' he murmured, 'we're going to see—'

'Nothing,' snorted the foreman.

The door had opened on a solid brick wall that blocked the entire opening. Cousin Dolph was beside himself.

'Damned bureaucratic interference! Who in hell ever gave anybody permission to stick that thing up? Now what am I to do? All the arrangements changed, Aunt Emma coming all the way from Longmeadow, and we can't get into the vault. I wish to Christ Alex were here!'

'At least he'd know how to take the wall down,' said Sarah, trying not to laugh.

'Take the wall down, that's it! Never should have been put there in the first place. You,' Adolphus Kelling thrust his Yankee beak within an inch of the foreman's more comely nose. 'Get a pickaxe or something.'

'Just a second, Mr Kelling,' the man from Parks and Recreation intervened. 'Ralph here and myself are delighted to co-operate with you on account of your uncle's distinguished military and civil record.'

Great-uncle Frederick had fought well with Black Jack Pershing and been a successful public gadfly for many years afterwards. Family opinion held that Bay Staters sent their short-fused fellow citizen to Washington on one commission after another simply for the relief of getting him away from Boston. Even now, it appeared the doughty local son was not going to rest in peace without one last struggle.

'However,' the young official was going on, 'Ralph and I can't take it upon ourselves to authorise any demolition. I'm afraid this will have to go through channels.'

'How long will that take?'

'In such an unusual situation, I really can't say. I expect we'll have to dig into the archives—'

'The hell you will! Look here, young man, any fool can see this brickwork is no part of the original vault. The blasted mortar isn't even dirty. Probably some nincompoop put it up during the Bicentennial, scared a tourist would pinch our bones for a souvenir. Now you listen to me and you listen straight. I've broken my back to get this funeral lined up the way Uncle Fred wanted it. Everything's scheduled for tomorrow morning at ten o'clock sharp. And if you think I'm going to undo all I've done and squat beside a stinking coffin for the next five years while a bunch of bureaucrats squander the taxpayers' money trying to make up their minds whether a man has a right to be buried in his own family vault, you can damn well think again.'

Sarah knew Dolph would be furious if she didn't back him up. She was glad that for once he had reason on his side.

'I'm sure my cousin is right about this wall. My own

father helped to make the arrangements when this cemetery was declared a historic site, and he made very sure we'd always be able to use our vault if we chose to. And we certainly can't use it with that wall there.'

'Damn right. Good thinking, Sarah. So let's get cracking.'

'Excuse me,' said the now deeply perturbed young man. 'I think I'd better call the office.'

He disappeared in the direction of a phone booth and came back looking relieved. 'I guess it's okay, Mr Kelling, provided you're willing to sign a note saying you'll take the responsibility. Got a pickaxe, Ralph?'

Ralph had not, and was properly chagrined at not having brought what he'd had no reason to expect would be needed. After a bit of discussion, he and his colleague went to borrow one from some workmen over near the Parkman bandstand while Dolph fulminated to the man from the Historical Society, whose name was Ritling.

Sarah wished her cousin would shut up. The city people were being a great deal kinder about this affair than the family had any real right to expect, especially in view of the last-minute planning and this latest contretemps about a wall that shouldn't be in the way. She eased her tired legs against one of the ancient gravestones and stared at the offending brickwork. She'd have sworn she knew all there was to know about that vault. Back when the historical sites issue first came up, her father had thrashed over the subject at meal-times until he'd put her off her food, but he'd never once mentioned that the vault entrance had been bricked up. Was it possible he never knew?

There seemed no reason why it should have been, except that body snatching to get corpses for medical students to dissect was still not unheard-of back when the old vault was abandoned for the more spacious lot at Mount Auburn. Surely, though, the erecting of a barrier to keep out grave robbers would have been noted in the family annals, which Walter Kelling knew backward and forward. Anyway, Dolph was right about the brickwork's not looking all that old.

Whoever did the work knew his trade, at any rate. The bricks were unusually small, in a nice proportion to the size of the opening, which was only about four feet square. They were laid in an intricate pattern of interlocking diamonds which Sarah had seen somewhere else but couldn't place offhand. To while away the waiting, she took out a notebook and began to sketch the opening, drawing in each separate brick with careful attention to detail.

Alexander would be interested. Bricklaying was one of his unlikely talents. He'd taken courses in various manual skills, mostly at the Centre for Adult Education over on Commonwealth Avenue. Learning to do odd jobs around the house used to be his sole excuse to get away from Aunt Caroline once in a while. One might think that having some time alone with his wife would be an even more legitimate reason, but Alexander didn't seem to go along with that idea. She tightened her lips and went on sketching. She was adding a not very flattering portrait of Dolph when the men came back with the pickaxe.

'Mr Kelling,' said the foreman, 'would you care to do the honours?'

'With pleasure.'

Cousin Dolph picked up the implement, studied it curiously, hefted it once or twice, then brought it down with a mighty wallop. The entire wall gave way. He stumbled forward into a mess of brick and mortar.

'Are you all right, Mr Kelling?'

Pleased with his feat, Dolph brushed away the men who rushed to help him. 'I'm fine. Didn't know my own strength, that's all. Damn shoddy construction, though, I must say. Good God, what's that?'

Ritling crowded in beside him. 'Why, it's—' He rushed off among the gravestones and began to retch.

The Cemetery Division foreman was clearly disgusted with this weakness. 'What's the matter? Vaults are made to hold bodies, aren't they? Here, let's have a better look.'

He took a butane lighter from his pocket and shot a candle of flame into the cavity. Sarah, wondering what the to-do was about, peered over his shoulder. A gust of beer told her that her new-found friend was right behind.

She'd been braced for something nasty, but not for what she saw. On the stone floor of the vault, sprawled as if it had been thrust in with no regard for funerary decorum, lay a body. It must have been a woman's. The flesh was rotted away, but the skeleton was still encased in the mouldered remains of an hourglass corset and a crimson skirt. High black boots with frisky red heels held the leg and foot bones together.

But what had turned Mr Ritling's stomach and would haunt all their nightmares forever after were the tiny chips of blood-coloured rubies that winked flashes of burning scarlet from between the grinning teeth.

CHAPTER
TWO

'Christ on a crutch!' gasped the old man with the breath. 'It's Ruby Redd!'

'You know her?' Dolph Kelling turned on him like a charging bull. 'What's she doing in our vault?'

'Dolph, don't be ridiculous,' Sarah protested. 'He didn't put her there.'

'That's right, miss. I won't say me and Ruby was ever any great buddies, but I'd never of done a thing like this to nobody. So this is where she disappeared to.'

Suddenly conscious that he had become the centre of attention, the old man stepped back, mumbling, 'I didn't mean to butt in.'

'We're tremendously grateful that you did,' Sarah urged. 'Please don't go away. Can't you tell us more about this—Ruby Redd?'

'She was a—well, she called herself an exotic dancer.'

Cousin Dolph's bulgy eyes took on a knowing glint. 'My God, I remember Ruby Redd! Jem and I used to drop in at the Old Howard every so often, to watch her strut her stuff. She had a sort of Gold Rush routine, supposed to be a dance hall queen on the Barbary Coast, or some damn thing. Always wore that black corset affair with a pair of knockers bulging out over the top the size of watermelons. Sorry, Sarah, but damn it, you're a married woman.'

'All right, Dolph. So that's why she had those rubies in her teeth? Wasn't there a real dance hall girl once who did the same thing with diamonds?'

'Stands to reason she stole the idea from somewheres,' muttered the old man.

'Why? Was she a thief?'

'Ruby was a lot of things, but mostly mean. Meanest woman I ever run acrost in all my born days, and that's sayin' plenty, though I suppose I shouldn't be speakin' ill of the dead. Funny, I can't seem to take it in that's Ruby layin' there. Got to be, though. I lived in Boston all my life, and I ain't never seen anybody else struttin' down Washington Street with a grin on her puss like a row of taillights on a wet night.'

'How long ago did she disappear?' Sarah asked him. 'Those plastic boots look like what girls have been wearing within the past few years.'

'Gosh, I couldn't say about the boots, but Ruby's been gone a long time. Maybe 'fifty or 'fifty-one it was. I'd been tendin' bar at Danny's for a good many years by then, I do know that. Danny Rate's Pub that was, right near the Old Howard. I knew the girls, see, because a lot of 'em used to drop in after the show. Nice kids, most of 'em. Snappy dressers, all but that Ruby. She never wore nothin' but that costume onstage or off, with a ratty old sealskin cape over it in the wintertime. I dunno where she got them boots, some theatrical costume place most likely. You can tell they ain't real leather, they'd o' rotted away by now, I should think. Anyways, I wouldn't of asked and she wouldn't of told me. Ruby wouldn't give nobody the time o' day unless there was a buck in it for her. Besides, I never had much time to stand around chinnin', we was always busy after the show. I bet I served you guys a few times. Prob'ly conned me with fake ID cards, too.'

'I shouldn't be surprised,' grunted Dolph Kelling, by no means displeased to be cast as a stereotype of flaming youth. 'So now we know who she is, what do we do with her? This vault's got to be cleared out pronto.'

'We'll have to call the police,' said Sarah.

'What for, damn it?' He turned to the man from the Cemetery Division. 'Can't you just open one of the other vaults and shove her in there?'

'Not on your life, Mr Kelling. Nobody's going to

convince me this Ruby Redd walled herself up in here and committed suicide. There's no statute of limitation on murder, and I'm not sticking my neck out. As you said, this is your family vault, so that makes her your responsibility.'

Pleased with himself, the man backed away and fished in his pocket for a smoke. Dolph tackled the other official.

'Well, you're in charge here. Do what you have to and make it snappy.'

'Sorry, Mr Kelling. As Ralph so properly pointed out, the contents of the vault belong to you. I think this young lady's suggestion that you call the police would be your wisest course of action.'

'Oh, the hell with it! Sarah, since you're so determined to turn this unfortunate incident into a public scandal, go phone Station One. And don't say I didn't warn you.'

Unexpectedly, Mr Ritling caught Sarah's eye and winked. 'Shall I go, Mrs Kelling?'

'No,' she replied demurely, 'why don't you stay and take notes? After all, we are adding another chapter to the family history. Try to think of it that way, Dolph. Oh, and I'm afraid somebody will have to lend me a dime for the telephone. I came away without any money.'

'I got a dime.'

The old man who had mixed drinks for Ruby Redd came to the fore again, taking Sarah's arm and steering her among the gravestones. She was touched by his gallantry. This was probably the most excitement he'd had since Danny Rate's Pub went the way of urban renewal.

Behind them, the foreman slammed shut the tall iron gates. The man should have thought of that sooner, Sarah could hear Cousin Dolph telling him so. She'd never before realised Dolph was quite such a pompous jackass.

As events turned out, she didn't need the old bartender's dime. They were heading for the phone booths near the subway entrance when a police car pulled up at the stoplight. Its driver held up traffic to hear their story, made a highly illegal U-turn, and pulled up on the sidewalk close to the ornamental palings. Sarah led the officer over to the vault. It wasn't until the policeman was trying to take down the particulars of the grisly find with Dolph Kelling, the foreman, Mr Ritling, and the man from Parks and

Recreation all talking at once that she realised her self-appointed escort had quietly melted away.

She didn't blame the old man for leaving. If she'd had any sense, she'd have gone with him. It was rude, silly, and entirely typical of Adolphus Kelling to make her do the dirty work. He'd go gassing around at the funeral, no doubt, about how he'd tried to hush things up for the sake of the family, but young Sarah had insisted for some ill-judged reason on getting them embroiled in a three-ring circus.

Sarah realised that she honestly didn't care what the family thought of her, and that, in fact, it was some time since she'd quit caring. This new feeling of detachment could not have come at a better time, since it helped her to get through what turned out to be a extremely sticky day.

Adolphus Kelling had obviously assumed that they need only tell their story for the bedizened skeleton to be whisked away to some discreet hiding place and the vault got ready for its part in the scheduled obsequies. He could not have been more wrong.

After an enthralled examination of the ruby-studded corpse, the young officer got on his car radio to notify headquarters of this fascinating break in the monotonous round of muggings, traffic accidents, armed holdups, and drunken brawls. From then on, pandemonium was let loose. Crowds pressed against the wrought-iron fence. Television cameramen struggled for angle shots of the glittering skull and were shooed away by lieutenants of Homicide trying to determine how Ruby Redd got to be Ruby dead. Reporters pestered for statements. Sarah, brought up to be courteous, was politely answering questions when she became aware that microphones were being poked at her face.

'Why did your Great-uncle Frederick want to be buried here, Mrs Kelling?'

'I'm sure my cousin could answer that better than I,' she hedged. 'I expect you might say it's because he had a strong sense of history. Don't you agree, Dolph?'

'Yes. Well put, Sarah. A strong sense of history. The Kellings have always had a strong sense of history.'

Dolph was off and running. Sarah managed to slip away

from the newshounds and check on what was happening at the vault. Somebody had asked why she thought the Kelling vault had been selected as the hiding place, and she'd said she had no idea. It wasn't the biggest or the best-hidden from the street. It wasn't the easiest to get at, being close to the church and far from the gate. She supposed it just happened to be the one somebody was able to open. No, the caretaker hadn't had any particular difficulty unlocking the door. Yes, those primitive old locks would probably be simple enough to jimmy if one knew how. She wouldn't have the faintest idea, herself. One would have to ask—she'd stopped herself just in time from saying, 'my husband'. This was not the time or place to advertise that Alexander had also taken a course in locksmithing.

The Homicide people worked as meticulously as archaeologists, photographing the skeleton from various angles, packing up as much of the mouldering costume as they could salvage, making especially sure not to overlook any ruby chips that might have fallen out of the teeth. It was a long time before they completed their task. Sarah was chilled to the bone, half-starved, and desperate for a ladies' room before the police showed any inclination to let the Kellings go on with their personal business.

'This old man who said he knew the woman,' somebody asked her for about the sixth time, 'where did you say he went?'

'I didn't say because I don't know,' she replied somewhat waspishly. 'He was with me when I went out to call for help, and he wasn't when I got back. I don't remember seeing him go off because I was talking to the policeman.'

'How long was he here?'

'I couldn't tell you. He was in the cemetery when I got here, that's all I can say.'

'Did he say why he was in the cemetery?'

'Oh, I doubt if he had any particular reason . . .'

'How did you happen to start a conversation with him?'

'As I recall, he made some remark about the weather, then asked me if I was a tourist. I thought he might be hoping to get a tip for showing me around, so I explained about having to meet my cousin. Then we chatted a bit, to kill the time. I'd got the impression my cousin wanted me to meet him right away, but as it turned out, I had quite a wait because he stopped to do some other business first.'

Dolph had taken it for granted, of course, that Alex's wife had nothing better to do than hang around a chilly graveyard waiting on his convenience.

'Did this old guy know the vault was going to be opened?'

'Not until I told him, if that's what you mean. Even then, I'm not sure he grasped what it was all about. He kept asking me whom we were going to dig up. I didn't know what was happening myself, until my cousin phoned this morning, and I don't believe he did, either, till shortly before he called us.'

The man from Homicide turned to Dolph. 'Is that right, Mr Kelling?'

'It is correct,' Dolph replied sourly. 'As to whether it's right, I leave you to decide. I'd naturally assumed Uncle Fred would want to be buried at Mount Auburn with the rest of us. I made all the arrangements, put the notice in the papers, called the relatives, went over to see Uncle Fred's lawyers first thing this morning, and got hit straight between the eyes with this outrageous codicil. That gave me roughly twenty-four hours to undo everything I'd done and do it over, and now this infernal trollop has to get herself planted in our vault! Hardly seems decent to go on with it now.'

Dolph sputtered a while longer, then sighed, 'Well, it's what Uncle Fred wanted, so I suppose we'll have to go ahead with it come hell or high water. Haul away the bricks and sweep up the rubies, eh? Gad, what a situation! Sarah, do you think Alex is back yet?'

'No, I don't,' she replied, 'and there's not a thing he could do if he were. Officer, if you don't need us any more, could we please get on with what we came to do?'

'I guess so.'

The police lieutenant gave Sarah a remarkably human smile which, for some reason, made her want to burst into tears. 'You folks go ahead with your funeral. We'll see that everything's in order for tomorrow. Right, Ralph?'

'Right,' sighed the foreman. 'Mind if I grab a bite to eat first?'

Adolphus Kelling brightened. 'Now, there's an excellent idea. Come on, Sarah, I'll buy you a drink.'

Though a bore and a bully, Dolph was no mingy host. Fortified with two cocktails and a great deal of excellent food, Sarah decided she didn't particularly mind going back with him to the cemetery.

Spectators were still clustered around the fence, but there wasn't much to see. The door of the vault was closed and one of Ralph's helpers was carrying away the last of the bricks in a wheelbarrow. The policeman on guard told Sarah and her cousin they couldn't go in.

'But I'm Adolphus Kelling, blast it! That's my vault.'

'Sorry, Mr Kelling.'

'Come on, Dolph,' Sarah coaxed. 'We have to see the minister anyway, and he'll probably let us go out through the church. Anyway, it looks as though they're doing what they said they would.'

'I'll believe that when I see it,' Dolph snorted. However, he had sense enough not to pick a fight with the law. There were still the minister and the organist to hector.

While her cousin spent upwards of an hour discussing a service that was going to take perhaps twelve minutes from start to finish, Sarah rested in the family pew, trying to draw strength from the lovely old sanctuary and wondering how she was going to cope with the multitudes tomorrow afternoon. She ought to be shopping or cleaning or at least letting her own family know about the bizarre discovery in the vault. Nevertheless, she stayed until Dolph had got things squared away to his and presumably Uncle Fred's satisfaction. By the time they went out it was almost dark.

'Dolph,' she said, 'I'll have to leave you now. Alexander must have got home ages ago. He'll be wondering where I am.'

'Alex? Forgot about him. Managed pretty well by myself after all, didn't I? Maybe we'd better just take one last look at that vault. Don't want any more chorus girls slipping in unbeknownst, eh? Come on back, we'll get the Rev to open the side door for us.'

Reluctantly, Sarah obeyed. The minister, kind as ever though no doubt wishing by now that he were burying the whole Kelling tribe, led them through the vestry and out to the ancient burying ground.

'I'm sure you'll find everything in order,' he said hopefully.

They did, except for one brick that had somehow got left behind. Dolph picked it up and began to fume.

'Oh, stop fussing and give it to me,' Sarah told him. 'I'll drop it in a trash basket on my way home.'

It was rather a nice little brick, actually, small enough to fit inside her leather shoulder bag. She dropped it in, thanked the minister, took grateful leave of Cousin Dolph, and started across the hill towards Tulip Street.

CHAPTER THREE

Alexander had the front door open before she was halfway up the steps. 'Sarah, I've been watching out of the window for you. Where have you been?'

'With Cousin Dolph. He called right after you left for the hospital.'

'In a flap about Uncle Fred's funeral, I suppose. Too bad he wasted your whole day. Harry's home, and they want us for dinner.'

'Oh, dear!' If there was anything Sarah didn't need at this point, it was one of the Lackridges' spur-of-the-moment dinner parties. 'Alexander, the most utterly incredible thing happened!'

'Tell me later. You've about five minutes to change.'

Furious, she rushed up the stairs to the third floor, the brick she'd forgotten to take out of her handbag thumping against her hip at every step. Trust Alexander to put Harry Lackridge before anyone else. He was wearing his dinner jacket, not because the occasion was going to be all that elegant, but because he'd been forced to buy one ages ago for some function or other and felt duty bound to get his money's worth out of the investment. It would hardly do for his wife to appear at his side in a ratty plaid skirt and stretched-out oatmeal-coloured pullover.

At least she'd be going fed this time, which was a blessing. She was going warm, too. Knowing Leila Lackridge's disdain for creature comforts, Sarah had devised herself a garment especially for these affairs, long-sleeved, long-skirted, cut simply as a paper doll's dress from thick, soft blanket material in a blue the exact shade of Alexander's eyes. She needed something more dramatic to set it off than her grandmother's amethyst brooch and the little string of pearls Alexander had given her when they were married, but those were all she had, so she put them on.

Some day, she'd possess more jewels than any one woman could possibly wear. It was ridiculous that she mightn't be allowed to enjoy a few of the pieces now. What a ghastly life, hanging around waiting for Aunt Caroline to die!

Was that what they were doing? Startled by a thought she had never allowed to enter her head before, Sarah stared, with no sense of identification, at the face reflected in the greenish, speckled mirror. It was only some young woman with light brown hair and grey-brown eyes, one set a tiny bit higher than the other in a pale, square face. She dabbed a little colour on the lips, grabbed up the amethyst eardrops that went with the brooch, and ran downstairs, fastening them in her ears as she went.

Alexander was still waiting. He had the shiny, balding muskrat cape that had been her mother's ready to throw over her shoulders.

'You mustn't hurry so in that long skirt,' he chided gently. 'You might trip and fall.'

'But you said to rush,' she snapped back. 'Where's Aunt Caroline?'

'Out on the front steps. Mother likes to take her time going down, you know.'

Of course Sarah knew. There was not one quirk or whim of her mother-in-law's that she hadn't had drilled into her during the past seven years. This was still Caroline Kelling's house, and around Caroline it still revolved. Who could object to that, when common sense dictated that everything be left where it always had been so that a blind woman could find her way about the rooms without having to be guided, and common decency decreed that somebody doubly afflicted be given every consideration? Could a wife begrudge her husband's spending most of his waking hours with his mother, when it was only through Alexander that Caroline was able to lead anything like a normal life?

Not even if helping Caroline live as she wished meant that Sarah and Alexander had no life at all? They hardly even talked to each other any more. They'd had a more satisfying relationship back when Sarah was six years old and Cousin Alexander a godlike young man in Brooks Brothers flannels who took her for walks in the Public Garden on Sunday afternoons while his mother played chess with Sarah's father. She'd adored him then. She supposed she still did. Anyway, there wasn't much she could do about it now.

Hugging the inadequate wrap around her shoulders, Sarah tagged after her husband and the white-haired woman who was almost as tall as he. Caroline Kelling kept one hand on her son's arm because the sidewalk had an almost precipitous pitch, but she held her back straight as the white cane she carried, and never once stumbled on the uneven bricks.

The Lackridges lived on the water side of Beacon Hill, in a smart town house converted from what had once been Leila's grandparents' carriage house. What was originally the family mansion now housed a prestigious but not always lucrative publishing business that Leila's family had established and Harry Lackridge had married his way into.

When Leila and Harry were married, they'd scouted their respective families' attics and storerooms for whatever oddments of furniture they could lay their hands on. Leila had then called in an interior decorator and bullied her into making visual sense of the hodgepodge. Now she had a cleaning service in once a week, and every six or eight years she had the place repainted and papered in much the same patterns and colours as before. Over the years, the rooms had taken on a curious quality of being embalmed. Leila never noticed. She had other things to do.

It was in good part because of Leila Lackridge that Caroline Kelling led such a busy life. The pair of them were among the movers and shakers in local civic affairs, Leila doing most of the moving and shaking, while Mrs Kelling gained sympathisers by her mere presence on any platform, her sightless eyes hidden by tinted glasses, her beautiful face attentive to the message that her friend or her son spelled out into the palm of her hand.

Not all people who lose both sight and hearing in adult life succeed in learning alternate methods of communication. Caroline had mastered Braille and also a shorthand system of hand signals that only Leila and Alexander could transcribe fast enough to keep up with her quick mind and sometimes biting tongue. Sarah had tried hand-talking, but the impatient crisping of Aunt Caroline's fingers discouraged her from plodding on. Now she poked out notes in Braille with a stencil and stylus, or let Alexander translate when she had anything special to say to her mother-in-law. She seldom did nowadays, since she'd taken over most of the housekeeping and no longer had to be coached about what to do.

These dinners of the Lackridges' were always last-minute affairs because both Harry and Leila were on the go so much that it was hard to schedule them in advance. As a rule, Sarah could have done nicely without them. The cocktail hour dragged on and on, with Leila and Aunt Caroline holding forth about their latest cause and the two men reminiscing about their days at prep school and college, years before Sarah was ever born. The house was always cold, even in summer, and the food was abominable.

Tonight perhaps it wouldn't be quite so bad. They might let her tell her amazing story. If not, she could curl up in her wool cocoon and sneak a nap. She was drowsy from hanging around in the cold air, and sated with her late, heavy lunch. At least being with Leila and Harry was better than having to spend the evening in an undertaker's rooms listening to Cousin Dolph pontificate. There were to be no visiting hours. Great-uncle Frederick's codicil had also been explicit about letting relatives gloat over his remains.

Sarah had always thought Leila and Harry rather resented her marriage to Alexander. The Lackridges had made such a cosy foursome with him and Caroline for so many years that they tended to shunt the young bride into the background whenever possible. Tonight, however, she was the guest of honour. To her astonishment, Harry swooped her into his arms even before he gave Caroline her ritual kiss.

'Here she is, in person! How's our little celebrity? Still speaking to us common folks?'

Sarah was too flustered to say anything. Alexander asked a mild question.

'Celebrity?'

'Didn't you see the news?' crowed Harry. 'Oh, I keep forgetting you intellectual snobs don't watch television.' His yellowed teeth flashed in the grin that looked so charming in photographs Alexander treasured from their school days. The years had not been kind to Harry.

'Sarah!' His wife was upon them now, swathed in an oriental caftan that didn't sit well on her angular form. Unlike her husband, Leila had never been even passably good looking. At forty-seven, she was ugly as one of the dragons printed on her robe, yet she made a more pleasing impression than he did because her face was always aglow with some new enthusiasm. This was the first time she'd ever shown any wild interest in Sarah.

Caroline, ignored for once, began to speak. Nobody paid her the slightest attention, not even Alexander.

'Sarah,' he demanded, 'have you the faintest idea what they're talking about?'

'I expect so. I tried to tell you, but you wouldn't listen.'

'Do you mean he hasn't heard?' Leila whooped.

'They say the husband's always the last to know,' Harry chimed in, 'but this is ridiculous!'

'It's his own fault,' said Sarah. 'I didn't get home till a little while ago. I wanted to tell him then, but he wouldn't listen. Then he rushed us over here at such a pace I could hardly pant, let alone talk. You know what a punctuality freak he is.'

'But, Sarah,' Alexander began,

'But her no buts, old buddy,' Lackridge interrupted. 'Come and have a drink. If anybody was ever about to need one, thou art the man.'

By now, Caroline Kelling was furious. They got her calmed down and into the living room amid a good deal of

confusion. Sarah headed for her usual corner by the
fireplace before she noticed that end of the sofa was already
pre-empted. A young man was standing there rather
awkwardly waiting to be introduced. Since the Lackridges
were both occupied with placating the elder Mrs Kelling,
Sarah went up to him and put out her hand.

'How do you do? I'm Sarah Kelling.'

'Yes, I know,' he replied with a diffident smile. 'I'm Bob
Dee, one of the elves from Harry's office. Was that your
first time on television? You carried it off like a pro.'

Sarah smiled back. 'Did I really? I have to confess I
hadn't the foggiest idea they were taking my picture until it
was done. Otherwise, I'd have been scared to death.'

It would have been pleasant to sit down for a quiet chat
with this personable chap, so much closer to her own age
than anybody else in the room, but that was not to happen.
As soon as Harry had supplied them all with drinks, he
commanded that she tell her story. Sarah started talking,
piling on the lurid details in response to Leila's urgings, and
had got almost to the end of her tale when she noticed that
Alexander's hands were absolutely still. Aunt Caroline
wasn't getting one word.

She was so surprised that she stopped in the midst of a
sentence. 'Alexander, aren't you going to tell your
mother?'

He looked at her blankly, as though he'd forgotten who
she was. Then he shook his head.

'No, I think not. It would—upset her dreadfully.'

He seemed to be having a hard time getting the words
out.

'I—she—never would—'

'Believe there was an honest-to-God skeleton in the
family closet, as one might say?' Harry pounded him on the
shoulder. 'Relax, old buddy. Bask in the reflected
limelight. Ready for a freshener?'

Alexander Kelling shook his handsome head. 'Not now,
thank you. I—I just can't—'

'Come on, Alex, you're overreacting. Lord a'mercy, if
old Fred ever knew the kind of company he's getting into!
Lots of fun and games next Hallowe'en night, eh?
Personally, I think you're a double-barrelled fink not to tell

Caro. Go on, Leila, you tell her.'

'No, please,' the son insisted. 'She's already disturbed about having to go to Uncle Fred's funeral tomorrow. You know how she is about changes. This—this would—'

Her husband's agitation went to Sarah's heart. She ought to have made him listen, back at the house. It was cruel to spring such a shocker in company, just because he'd pushed her to do something she didn't want to. At least she could support him now.

'Alexander's right, Harry. You people don't realise how moody Aunt Caroline can get. She locks herself in her boudoir and does embroidery on the curtains, which is heartbreaking because the stitches don't even show up against the pattern. We never know what's going to set her off, and sometimes she mopes for days. You won't, Leila, will you?'

Mrs Lackridge shrugged, causing the dragons printed on her caftan to crawl about in a most unsettling way. 'Not if Alex is going to have a snit about it. I must say it doesn't seem particularly important to me one way or the other. Harry, didn't you say somebody else was coming?'

'Yes, my pearl of the Orient. A bloke named Bittersohn, who's some kind of expert on rare jewels. He's doing a book for us, and I thought he'd get a charge out of meeting Caro.'

Alexander looked at the publisher sharply. 'I hope you haven't made him any promises. You know how Mother is.'

'I do, and I have not. Come to think of it, I'm not sure why I did invite him, except that he's getting a whooper of a subsidy out of some jewellers' guild to defray the costs of printing, which automatically makes him our Fair-haired Boy of the Month despite the fact that he's a trifle on the swart and Semitic side. Right, Bob?'

'Right, Chief,' the elf replied smartly, helping himself to a large handful of salted peanuts.

'Trust a Jew to know where to pick the lettuce.'

There were several things about Harry Lackridge that annoyed Sarah. This attitude of his towards all non-Wasps was one of them.

'I thought anti-Semitism was passé,' she snapped.

Her host raised a colourless eyebrow. 'Who's anti?

Business being what it is these days, we could hardly be more pro. Right, Bob?'

'Right, Chief.'

Young Dee took more peanuts. Probably he knew more or less what his chances were of getting an edible dinner. Most times it was Sarah who ate the peanuts. She felt a twinge of fellow-feeling for him, although she did wish he weren't quite so ready with his, 'Yes, Chief'. That was hardly fair, to fault Harry's employee for agreeing with a boss who could, she suspected, be something of a tyrant.

Apparently the jewellery expert was in no hurry to push his way into their group. He didn't show up until they were well along with their drinks, and he didn't look as if he'd made any special effort to impress them. In contrast to Alexander's sombre finery, Harry's purple velvet Edwardian smoking jacket, and Bob Dee's turtleneck jersey and dashing plaid blazer, Bittersohn had on a dark grey worsted suit, a plain white shirt, and an unassuming tie. His hair was brown, his eyes were either blue or grey, and his complexion was closer to fair than swarthy. Nevertheless, there was something about him that made the other men look washed-out by comparison.

'Hope I haven't held you up, Mrs Lackridge,' he apologised. 'I was watching the news and the time got away from me. Did you happen to see Channel Seven at six o'clock? They had a thing on about a family that wants to bury some old uncle in one of your historic tombs. When they opened the vault, they found the skeleton of a chorus girl who'd been missing for almost thirty years.'

'Yes, we saw it.'

'Quite a show, wasn't it? This pop-eyed Colonel Blimp character sounding off about outrage and desecration, and a skinny little kid with a red nose trying to shut him up and preserve the dignity of the family. Kelling, I believe the name was. You don't happen to know them?'

'As a matter of fact,' said Lackridge, 'yes. The gentleman with his foot in his mouth, people, is Max Bittersohn. And reading from left to right we have Caroline Kelling, Alexander Kelling, and in living colour up to and including the red nose, Sarah Kelling.'

'My God,' said Bittersohn.

He walked over to the older pair, hesitated for a second as people always did when struck for the first time by Alexander's incredible beauty, then shook the stiff hand that was automatically held out to him.

'How do you do, sir?'

As Caroline made no sign of acknowledging the introduction, he must have assumed he'd annoyed her by his tactlessness, for he added, 'Mrs Kelling, I hope I haven't offended you or your daughter.'

'My mother does not see or hear,' said Alexander in a dead flat voice. 'Sarah is my wife.'

'Flubbed it all around, Max,' said his host with no sign of concern. 'What are you drinking?'

'Got any strychnine?'

'Not till after you deliver your typescript. Settle for scotch?'

'Fine.'

The author took his drink and looked around, presumably for a hole to crawl into. Moved by compassion, Sarah beckoned him over.

'Sit here, Mr Bittersohn. You can admire my red nose and tell me about your book. Are you a jeweller yourself?'

'No, but I had an uncle who ran a hockshop.'

Bittersohn took the place beside her, squeezing Bob Dee over to the far end of the sofa and causing Sarah to regret her charitable impulse. She might have had brains enough to move to the centre so she could have one on either side. After having been mistaken for Alexander's daughter, though, it might be wiser to stay clear of the younger man. In any event, Leila soon sent Dee for more ice, leaving Sarah alone with the writer, which was probably just as well.

Bittersohn must be ten years or so younger than Alexander, which could still put him close to forty. His features were rugged but by no means coarse, and he did have a marvellous head of hair. He'd tried to slick it down, but it kept rising in exuberant waves as he sipped at what was no doubt a tumblerful of cheap straight scotch. Sarah had often said Harry's drinks were strong enough to curl one's hair, but she'd never actually seen it happening before.

She started to giggle, then realised what her own drink was doing on top of the two old-fashioneds Dolph had bought her. She felt as if the sofa were floating, and her eyelids had to be kept from snapping shut by a stern effort of will. For Alexander's sake, she must stay alert.

For once, Sarah was grateful to Leila for being an impossible hostess. It was a house rule at the Lackridges' that while Harry might invite his business acquaintances whenever he wished, Leila wasn't to put herself out for them. The publisher's wife had hardly bothered to greet Bittersohn, now she was ignoring him and holding forth to Caroline and Alexander about a hearing at the State House, talking with both voice and hands, her thin fingers writhing and twisting in the deaf woman's palm to keep up with the rapid-fire of her words.

Alexander appeared to be paying close attention. Sarah thought he was using Leila as an excuse to avoid chatting with the man who'd hurt his feelings. He always hated it when strangers mistook him for Sarah's father. Then she realised he wasn't doing anything at all but sitting. There was no more life to him than there was to that pile of bones in its rotted finery, waiting now at the city morgue for somebody to claim what was left of Ruby Redd and bury her in a grave of her own. What a ghastly comparison!

Bittersohn was watching Leila's incredibly swift fingers, fascinated as people always were. After a moment he asked Sarah, 'Has your—Mrs Kelling always been like that?'

'Oh, no,' Sarah told him. 'It didn't happen till about thirty years ago, when she was in her forties. She was in a boating accident. She went deaf right away, but the blindness came on gradually. I can remember when Aunt Caroline could still see.'

'How long have you known her?'

'Forever. Her husband was distantly related to both my parents, and we used to live practically around the corner from them. Alexander used to be my baby-sitter. Weren't you, darling?' she called across the room in a sudden panicky urge to get some kind of reaction out of him.

Perhaps he didn't hear, at least he didn't respond. Bittersohn might have noticed Sarah's hands clenching. He said quickly, 'How did the accident happen?'

'They were becalmed in a fog in their sloop, the *Caroline*, about a mile offshore. Actually the boat wasn't in any danger, but Uncle Gilbert, Alexander's father, found out he'd forgotten his heart medicine, which he needed very badly. They'd bashed up their dinghy so Aunt Caroline decided to swim in for help. She'd always been a marvellous distance swimmer—she even trained for the English Channel when she was a girl, but her parents wouldn't let her do it. Anyway, a squall came up and she lost her bearings. She finally made it to shore, but she'd taken a terrible beating. Both eardrums were broken and she developed an infection that left her totally deaf. Her eyes were also injured. They tried all sorts of treatments but nothing helped. The worst of it was that Uncle Gilbert died while she was in the water. Alexander was with him, and I don't think he's ever gotten over it.'

'Why did he let his mother make the swim instead of going himself?'

'Because she was the better swimmer and a complete dud at handling the boat. They made the sensible choice, even if things turned out wrong.'

'That's the trouble with being sensible,' said Bittersohn. 'How old was your husband when this happened?'

'Seventeen. He'd just finished prep school and was about to start college. He and Harry were roommates, as you may know.'

He shook his head. 'I don't know Lackridge at all, except as my so-called publisher.'

'Why so-called? I thought your book was all settled.'

'Hardly. I still have to write most of it.'

'Have you written before?'

'A few articles for trade publications. Nothing anybody's ever read.'

'Cheer up,' said Bob Dee, who had come back with a fresh lot of peanuts. 'By this time next year, you'll be a household word.'

'In how many households? Do you suppose we're going to eat soon?'

'One never knows,' said Sarah. 'If you want another drink, you may as well have it.'

'I don't, particularly.'

Nevertheless, since Leila showed no sign of budging, Bittersohn held out his glass and Bob Dee sped off to fill it.

'What does your husband do, Mrs Kelling?'

'Do?'

Sarah was surprised by the question. Bittersohn must assume her husband led the life of a normal man. She fumbled for an answer.

'Well, he does some editing for Harry,' footling assignments he performed with a conscientiousness far exceeding their importance and never got paid for, 'and—and manages our properties and so forth. And, of course, his mother takes up a lot of his time. Alexander is the only person other than Leila who can do that hand signing to her satisfaction.'

'But it's only tracing the letters of the alphabet, isn't it?'

'Essentially, yes, but they have a sort of shorthand. There's also an international symbol language, but she doesn't know that one.'

'What about Braille?'

'Oh, yes, she started learning that as soon as she realised she was going blind. Aunt Caroline is a very determined lady.'

Sarah essayed a light laugh to show she didn't consider her mother-in-law the least bit formidable, but Bittersohn probably wasn't fooled one iota. Mrs Kelling's voice, pitched too loud and edged with vexation over something that hadn't gone to her liking at the State House, told its own story.

CHAPTER FOUR

They went in to dinner at about half-past nine and it was every bit as awful as Sarah had anticipated. The look on Max Bittersohn's face as he sampled Leila's cuisine for the first and undoubtedly the last time was almost worth having to endure the experience, but not quite. Bob Dee was the only one who ate much, perhaps it was one of his duties.

Leila and Caroline, deep in plans for a political coup, didn't seem to notice what they were putting into their mouths. Harry, who was well over the border by now, doused everything with ketchup from a messy bottle he insisted on keeping by his place. Alexander hardly pretended to taste his dinner.

Sarah was getting worried about her husband. She wanted to ask if he felt sick, but didn't. Making a fuss in public would upset him even more, if that were possible. At last even Harry Lackridge noticed.

'What's wrong with you tonight, old buddy? Mourning your lost love?'

Leila paused in her diatribe against the senate majority leader and turned to her husband. 'What lost love? What are you talking about?'

'The late, shall we say, lamented. The girl with the sparkle in her smile. She whose bejewelled bicuspids brightened his salad days. Namely and to wit, Ruby Redd.'

'You're blotto. Alex, did you know that woman?'

'Oh, yes,' he replied in the same dead voice. 'I knew her. We all did. We used to go to the Old Howard on Saturday nights to watch her dance, then buy her drinks in a squalid little bar across the street.'

'Danny Rate's Pub,' said Sarah.

They all looked at her.

'The old man in the cemetery,' she explained, flustered, 'the one who told us it was Ruby Redd. He used to be the bartender there.'

'Amazing!' cried Harry. 'I've just thought of a profound philosophical observation. I haven't worked out the phraseology yet, but it will be something to the effect that this is a small world. Catchy, eh? What was his name?'

'I forgot to ask.'

'That's our Sarah,' Leila remarked.

Alexander snapped out of his lethargy. 'Why is everybody picking at Sarah?' he blazed. 'Don't you realise she's been through a—a hellish—'

He lost control of his voice, and drank some of the nasty white wine in his glass. 'I'm sorry, Leila. I only wish I could have spared you this experience, Sadiebelle.'

His use of the old pet name made Sarah's eyes fill with

unexpected tears. She smiled across the table at him, swallowing until she could get the lump in her throat to go down.

'I know, darling. You'd like to keep me in a little velvet box, along with the rest of the family treasures.'

'Speaking of family treasures,' Bob Dee broke in, evidently under the misapprehension that he was offering an agreeable change of subject, 'I understand the Kelling family has a pretty spectacular collection of heirloom jewellery. Any chance Mr Bittersohn could get a look at some of the pieces? It would be a great boost for the book if—' He saw the look on Alexander's face, and faltered.

'I'm afraid that's quite out of the question, Mr Dee. The jewels belong to my mother for her lifetime, and she doesn't care to have them shown.'

'What is everybody talking about?' Caroline broke in. 'I haven't had a word for the past ten minutes.'

That was gross exaggeration, of course, but to one sitting in silent darkness, time must sometimes seem very long. Harry, always more demonstrative with Caroline than with anybody else, put a comforting arm around her shoulders. Leila glanced at Alexander.

'Shall I ask her?'

He shrugged. 'If you like.'

The fingers began to fly, Leila explaining who Bittersohn was and what he was presumed to want, although the man himself had voiced no interest in the collection. Mrs Kelling reacted as they expected.

'Out of the question. As long as I'm alive, the jewellery will stay where I put it. After I'm gone, Sarah may do as she pleases.'

'What will you do, Sarah?' asked Bob Dee.

'I expect I'll know better when I've seen them,' she replied.

'Don't you even know what they look like?'

'Only from some of the family photographs and portraits. I don't even know what's in the collection. The inventory is along with the jewels, in the vault at the High Street Bank. At least I think it's the High Street Bank. Anyway, it's wherever Aunt Caroline says it is, and that's where it's going to stay, so I'm afraid Mr Bittersohn will have to leave us out of his book.'

'But why won't she let you see the jewellery,' Dee persisted, 'if it's coming to you anyway?'

'I don't know,' said Sarah, who was getting very tired. 'Perhaps you'd like to ask her yourself.'

A smile crooking her thin lips, Leila transmitted Dee's question. Again Mrs Kelling made the anticipated reply.

'I prefer not to discuss the matter any further.'

'I personally feel Mother's attitude is a trifle unfair to Sarah,' Alexander half-apologised, 'but since she can't see the pieces herself, she believes she would be shirking her duty as custodian if she were to expose them to any possibility of theft or substitution. She doesn't let me see them, either,' he added drily, 'though I suppose I must have when I was a youngster. I'm sorry for my wife's sake that I remember practically nothing about the collection, but boys just aren't much interested in that sort of thing. I am, of course, familiar with the paintings that show some of the jewels.'

'The ruby parure,' Dee put in eagerly, 'in the Sargent painting of Hermina Kelling at the museum. I stand in front of it and cry every time I go there.'

'I do remember that,' said Alexander. 'Mother wore it to the opera not long before—her accident.'

Bittersohn put down the fork he'd been pretending to eat with. 'Are you saying that Mrs Kelling still owns the complete parure?'

'Strictly speaking,' said Alexander, 'I do. According to family tradition the jewels are passed down from father to son. The wives get to wear them, or allow their daughters to if they feel so inclined, but they are merely custodians, as I mentioned. It would have been appropriate for Mother to turn them over to Sarah when we married, since my father was no longer living, but she chose not to, and considering the circumstances, Sarah has been kind enough not to press the issue. All this is boring for you, I'm sure.'

'Far from it,' said Bittersohn. 'So your mother has never worn any of the jewels since then?'

'I don't believe so. Those she has on now are her own, her engagement ring and some India pearls my father gave her outright as a wedding gift. They were brought back by one of the Kellings who was in the tea trade back around 1850.'

'Does she always wear the pearls?'

'Now that you mention it,' said Sarah, who could see Alexander was getting impatient with this persistent questioning, 'I can't recall ever having seen her without them. Can you, Leila?'

'I bet she even wears them with her nightie,' said Harry. 'Go ahead, Leila, ask her if she wears them to bed. Tell her Bittersohn wants to know.'

To their surprise, Caroline Kelling smiled at the question.

'I can't imagine what Mr Bittersohn thinks he's going to do with that piece of information. Alex, I think we should be going. We have Frederick's funeral tomorrow, in case you've forgotten. Leila, you'll forgive us if we don't stay for coffee.'

Without a word her son got up and helped her out of her chair. Sarah rose, too, with mixed feelings. She was always relieved to get away from the Lackridges' and she was bone-weary after this gruelling day. Still, she wouldn't have been averse to another few minutes' chat with Bob Dee, since she so seldom got to meet anyone of her own generation. Bittersohn, too, might be interesting to know better, although there was something oddly disturbing about the man.

'Are you going to be working on that jewellery book?' she asked her husband as they started up the hill.

'I don't know.'

His voice was so utterly devoid of life and hope that she stopped short. 'Alexander, are you ill?'

'I'm fine.'

'You certainly don't sound it, and you didn't eat one bite of dinner.'

'I detest Leila's dinners.'

'Then why do we accept every time they ask us?'

'Because we always have, I suppose.'

'I think it's time we stopped.'

'We can't.'

'Oh, yes, we can. Alexander, I'm getting awfully fed up with the way we live.'

'Don't you think I know that?'

At least his voice could still show pain. 'Sarah, what can I do? She won't be around forever.'

'She's seventy-three years old and strong as a bull. The way things are going, she'll probably outlast us both. Can't you realise she's eating you alive?'

'I realise.'

'Then why can't we do something about it? Get a companion for her.'

'We'd never find anybody qualified.'

'How do you know? We've never looked.'

'Anyway, we can't afford one.'

'Alexander, that's simply nonsense. It's my money we're living on, isn't it? Why can't I have some say as to what we can afford and what we can't?'

'Sarah, we've been through this before. My trusteeship ends on your twenty-seventh birthday. Until that time I am not going to spend one cent that I don't absolutely have to.'

'Then sell some of those stupid jewels. What good are they, gathering dust in a bank vault?'

'They belong to the family.'

'You said they belonged to you.'

'My dear, must we air our problems on the sidewalk?'

'It's time we aired them somewhere.'

He didn't reply. After a while, Sarah began to feel guilty for attacking her husband when he was so totally down. She felt for his hand in the dark.

'I'm sorry, Alexander.'

'You have a right to speak your mind.'

'Yes, but I could have picked a more suitable time and place.'

The sound he made wasn't really a word, so she didn't try to answer. Perhaps it was better not to. She'd never seen Alexander in such a state before, and she hoped she never would again. She'd fix him a bowl of soup or some milk toast as soon as they got inside the house, and make him eat every bite of it.

It was odd that he'd been so totally unstrung by hearing of that stray corpse in the family vault. No, perhaps that wasn't what ailed him. It might not be because it was the family's vault, but because the bones belonged to a dancer he'd known back when handsome young Alex Kelling was one of the crowd from Lowell House, free to hang around Scollay Square on Saturday night buying drinks for a girl with rubies in her teeth.

The boy from Lowell House had died a long time ago. Since then, there had been little joy for Alexander. How much had she herself done to make him happy? When they married she was still numb from her own tragedy, abruptly bereft of a father, who'd been a widower since Sarah was ten and had original notions about bringing up his lone chick.

Tutored at home, never visiting anywhere outside the Kelling clan, not having a particularly warm relationship with her father but accustomed to being guided by him in everything, she'd felt lost when he died, immensely relieved when soon afterwards the man she loved best in all the world offered himself as a father substitute. Hardly as a husband. As far as their conjugal relations went, she might still be the young cousin he took to ride on the swanboats. Sarah let go of the hand she was holding and Alexander didn't seem to notice.

She was glad when they got into the house. Caroline Kelling dropped her wrap and handbag for somebody else to put away and said, 'Edith, I'm going straight to bed.'

Edith wasn't there. If they'd returned at their usual time, the Kellings' only live-in servant would be doing her old retainer act in the front hall. Since they were fifteen minutes early, she must still be glued to the television set in her basement lair.

'I'll get her.'

Sarah hung up her own cape and pushed through the swinging door that led to the long, dark back hall and the basement steps. Sure enough, from below came screams and gunshots loud enough to blast the dust out of the cracks in the hundred-year-old panelling. Edith was not yet so deaf as her mistress, but she soon would be if she kept on assaulting her eardrums at that decibel rate.

Knowing she could never make herself heard over the bedlam, Sarah did not bother to call out but flicked the light switch on and off in the hope of attracting the maid's attention. That didn't work, either. Sighing, she picked her way down over the worn matting on the staircase. Edith was sprawled in an overstuffed chair with her feet up on a hassock, her mouth open and her eyes shut.

Sarah switched off the blaring television set. 'Edith! Edith, we're home. Mrs Kelling wants you right away.'

The maid leaped to her feet, smoothed her rumpled skirt, and glared as though it were Sarah's fault that she'd been caught in such an undignified posture.

'You're early.'

'I know. You'd better go on up to Mrs Kelling's room.'

Muttering something that was probably discourteous, the elderly woman made for the staircase. Sarah let her get a head start. She found Edith rude, lazy, inefficient, and deceitful, making capital of her alleged devotion to Caroline Kelling while dodging as much of the housework as she possibly could. What Edith thought of Sarah was expressed mainly in sniffs and sneers behind Alexander's back. As she'd been with the Kellings since heaven knew when, there'd be no getting rid of her barring an act of Providence. And Providence, as Sarah's father had been wont to say, was in Rhode Island.

Edith was also clumsy. As she lumbered through the back hall, she'd nudged ajar one of the framed photographs that lined the wall. It was still swinging on its wire and Sarah paused to straighten it. She liked these sensitive views her husband had taken of the family's place at Ireson's Landing up on the North Shore.

Alexander used a camera with far more than an amateur's skill, did his own processing, and had supplied many photographs for Harry's various literary projects with little or no recompense. Sarah had pilfered these prints from his files and framed them as a surprise. He'd been touched by the gesture even while he deplored the expense. She'd meant to hang them in the dining room, to replace some water colours that had been insipid to start with and were now faded to pale tan mush, but Aunt Caroline said she'd always been fond of those water colours, so the exquisite pictures wound up here, where Mrs Kelling seldom came.

This particular photograph was one of Sarah's favourites. It showed a single branch of a gnarled pear tree just coming into blossom against the wall of the Secret Garden. Alexander and his mother had laid the bricks to an intricate pattern of their own devising back when Aunt Caroline could still see well enough for such projects. They'd done a beautiful job, using some delightful, smallish bricks of an unusual orangey-red colour they'd unearthed in a deserted brickyard up along the Maine coast and carted back home to Massachusetts in a wood-panelled Ford beachwagon they used to have. Aunt Caroline had told the story many times. There couldn't be another wall exactly like this anywhere.

There had been one, though, this morning. Sarah tried to tell herself she was seeing things, but how could she be mistaken? She'd stared at that wall long enough. She still had that one leftover brick in her big shoulder bag upstairs, along with the sketch she'd made while they were waiting for the man to come back with the pickaxe to tear it down. She'd been so careful to draw in every single brick to exact proportion. Now what was she going to do?

Make Alexander his milk toast and keep her mouth shut. Nobody was ever going to know except herself. Cousin Dolph wasn't likely to notice. He'd been too resentful of the wall, too eager to get it down, to pay any attention to the way it was laid. Thank God there'd been nothing left but rubble when the photographers arrived.

But what if by some freak Dolph did remember? He'd be here tomorrow; what if he should come wandering out here, catch sight of the photograph and notice the similarity? Dolph was obtuse enough to go whooping back to the drawing room with his discovery, not stopping to think of the consequence.

Then Sarah would just have to lie and say he was wrong. If bad came to worse, she could fudge up a copy of the sketch with the details altered. As to the brick, she'd claim to have dropped it into somebody's trash can along the way. She wished to God she had!

She might take down the photograph and hide it, but Edith would notice the gap and raise a great hue and cry. The safest course was to leave it alone and pray. With her heart in her shoes, Sarah went to make milk toast.

CHAPTER
FIVE

'Alexander, I'm not going to the funeral.'

The way she felt this morning, it might have been her own funeral Sarah was talking about. What little sleep she'd got had been filled with nightmares, bones dancing in gowns of rotten satin, skulls that grinned and twinkled, Alexander doing things she'd rather not try to remember. He looked more dead than alive right now. She felt a qualm to be sending him off without her, but she couldn't cope, and that was that.

Her husband looked up from the boiled egg he was decapitating for his mother with the deftness that characterised all his hand movements. 'Are you sure you don't want to? Uncle Fred was always fond of you.'

'I don't believe he cared two hoots for me or anybody else, except perhaps you and Dolph, but that's beside the point. The thing is,' she stirred her coffee with one of the old coin-silver spoons, trying to choose the right words, 'Dolph says everybody will want to come here after the service. That means cleaning and food and sherry and so forth, and we've nothing ready.'

'Dolph is taking rather a lot on himself, isn't he?'

'Putting a lot on us, you mean. I know, but they'd come anyway because we're the nearest except for Uncle Jem, and you can imagine the sort of welcome they'd get from him. It's because of the last-minute change from Mount Auburn, otherwise Aunt Appie would get stuck as usual, I suppose. Last night I was so rattled that I never gave the funeral a thought, and of course we had to gallop off to the Lackridges'.'

There, she'd done it and she hadn't meant to. He thought she was holding a grudge.

'I know, Sarah. I was wrong, and I apologise.'

'What are you two talking about?' demanded his mother.

Alexander had to explain about the upcoming reception, and that led to a good deal of futile discussion.

'I don't see why Edith can't do it,' was Aunt Caroline's contribution.

'Neither do I,' Sarah replied crossly, 'but you know

perfectly well she won't raise a hand unless somebody stands over her with a blacksnake whip.'

'Sarah, that's hardly fair, is it?' said her husband.

'Not to me it isn't.'

She pushed back her chair and began gathering up the breakfast dishes. 'Why you've let her pull the wool over your eyes all these years is beyond me, and don't start about loyalty because I don't want to hear it. Make my apologies to anybody who asks for me at the church and tell them I'll see them here about half-past two. I'll need some money for shopping.'

Alexander looked up at her haggardly. 'How much?'

'Twenty dollars ought to do it. A gallon of sherry will be adequate, won't it?'

'I suppose so.'

He dragged out his wallet as though the effort were almost too much for him, and handed her two tens. 'Are you sure you can manage?'

'I always do, don't I?'

He looked so woebegone that she felt ashamed of herself for giving way to her feelings. She went around the table and dropped a kiss on the hair that was turning so quietly and unobtrusively to grey.

'Thank you, darling. We'll both feel better when this is over.'

'Oh, Sarah!'

Most uncharacteristically, her husband swung around in his chair, pulled her close, and buried his face in her cardigan. Edith, with perfect timing, poked her head through the swinging door and whined, 'Want me to clear now?'

'Yes,' snapped Sarah. 'Then get down every sherry glass in the house and rinse them out. Bring them into the drawing room after you've cleaned and dusted. Try to hit more than the high spots for a change.'

Alexander, now bolt upright and slightly pink in the face, found it necessary to add, 'There's been a last-minute change of plans. The family will be coming here for tea after the funeral.'

'Oh?' sniffed the old retainer. 'I was sort of hoping to go myself. I'd known him so long.'

'I'm sorry, Edith, but I'm afraid that won't be possible. Miss Sarah needs you to help get ready, so please do as she says.'

He stood up and held the chair for his mother. 'Does Dolph still expect Mother and me to go out to Chestnut Hill and be with the family this morning?'

'Yes, and the earlier you get started the better,' Sarah replied. 'Cousin Mabel and heaven knows who else will be there. If you're not around to keep them away from each other's throats, nobody will be speaking to anybody by the time they get here, and it will be plain, unmitigated hell. You know what Dolph's like when it comes to tact.'

'I do,' sighed her husband. 'Perhaps you're wise to keep out of it. I'll never forgive myself for letting you get stuck with him yesterday.'

'Darling, what is there to forgive? You couldn't know what was going to happen, and Dolph did make up for dragging me over there by standing me a marvellous lunch at the Copley afterwards, which I forgot to tell you about. Now get cracking before your mother throws a conniption. Can't you see she's champing at the bit for a good old family knock-down-and-drag-out? Have a lovely time.'

'The occasion is hardly conducive to revelry.'

'Bah, humbug. You adore being head of the clan.'

She gave him another kiss and pushed him lightly towards the door. Dear Alexander! Blessed were the peacemakers for they, God willing, would see peace somewhere this side of the grave. She wished she could get her mind off graves and off that wall so damnably identical to the wall that only Alexander would know how to build. She wished desperately that her husband had not been looking and acting so stricken ever since he heard about Ruby Redd. Was it possible, was it even thinkable that a man so gentle, a man so dedicated to keeping up the dignity of the Kellings could beat a striptease dancer's brains out, then wall up her body in his own family vault?

How did she know what was possible in this world? When had she ever been given a chance to find out? The irritation she'd been fighting down returned full force. Sarah grabbed up her coat, shouted to Edith that she was going down to Charles Street, and slammed the door.

Grocery shopping with Alexander was a process of deliberation, comparison, and anxious consideration as to whether Brand X was in truth a wiser choice than Brand Y. For Sarah it was a matter of finding what she wanted and getting out of the store. She'd make a lot of cheese puffs, she decided. They were cheap and filling and looked impressive. Also, they had to be served hot from the oven, which would give her an excuse to dodge the relatives and spend most of her time in the kitchen.

She bought a large sandwich loaf of the least squashy kind, a pound of cheese—half Swiss and half Cheddar—a quart of milk and a dozen eggs along with fresh vegetables and a few other oddments. By now, Sarah had catered enough committee meetings and political teas for Aunt Caroline and Leila to be clever about making a show of bounty at small expense. When she paid for her groceries, she had almost ten dollars left. She needn't buy the cheapest sherry after all. A gallon would have to suffice, it was all she could possibly carry.

Laden with her purchases, she climbed back up the hill and let herself in at the basement door. From above came the whine of a thirty-year-old Hoover. Edith was at least going through the motions.

They didn't use the huge old downstairs kitchen any more. Around the time it became impossible to get immigrant housemaids for five dollars a month and their keep, a small room at the back of the first floor had been fitted up with a gas stove, sink, and a few cupboards. Sarah took her bundles there, set the jug of wine on the counter and the perishables in the high-domed fridge, and stood hesitating.

What next? There really wasn't a great deal to do, except wash the breakfast dishes so she'd have the sink clear to prepare the vegetables. She dumped everything into the dishpan, squirted detergent, ran water. Five minutes later the sink was empty and the drainer full. Edith would have taken upwards of an hour, moaning the while about being overworked.

Sarah washed and separated a cauliflower with equal speed, got carrot and celery sticks ready, and set them to crisp in cold salt water. Then she pulled a sheet off the memo pad she always left notes on so that Edith couldn't claim nobody had told her to do whatever she'd left undone, and printed in large, clear capitals, 'Doing errands. Will be back in time to finish fixing refreshments. Edith, set out tea tray and all cups along with wine glasses.'

She didn't have to add, 'Make sure the silver is polished.' The old retainer could be counted on to do those things that would best impress the company. Edith adored having people gush, 'However do you keep everything shining and still do so much for our dear Callie?'—as if Sarah and Alexander sat around on their hands all day and didn't hire a kind lady to come in once a week and do all the chores Edith ought to but wouldn't do. Tomorrow was Mariposa's day, thank goodness. They'd leave the cleaning up to her. Sarah had more urgent business on hand.

The trouble was, she didn't know where to start, though she had to do something. It seemed rotten to go snooping behind her husband's back, yet one could hardly march up to him and ask point-blank, 'Did you murder Ruby Redd?'

What she'd do when she found out was another question, one that could be answered later. Not to know would be worse than anything else. While the life she now led with Alexander was one long frustration, at least she loved and trusted him as she always had. How could she go on trusting, with this hanging between them, and what would she do if she ever lost faith in Alexander Kelling?

Harry might know something, but it was useless to expect he'd betray his best friend to the young wife he didn't like much anyway. Her best and perhaps her only hope was that rather sweet old man who'd tended bar for the college boys and thought Ruby Redd was a mean woman.

How could she find him? Today was even more inclement than yesterday, so it wasn't likely he'd be hanging about the cemetery again. Nevertheless, she walked over. He wasn't there but a policeman was stationed at the locked gate to keep out spectators who were still coming to gawk at the place where the bizarre find had been made. Great-uncle Frederick's funeral would get on the news tonight, perhaps, and wouldn't the Kelling clan love that!

One of the sightseers evidently recognised Sarah from

the previous newscast, and started to say something to her. She turned up her collar and walked away, fuming. If that pest hadn't butted in, she might have described her old man to the policeman and found out if he'd been around again.

Now, there was a thought. Perhaps some of the older policemen who'd been stationed around Scollay Square when it still existed might remember who tended bar for Danny Rate. It wouldn't hurt to go and ask. Better still, why not try Uncle Jem? Jeremy Kelling had been haunting Boston's hot spots for upwards of seventy years, or claimed he had. If she went over to Pinckney Street right now, she'd catch the retired rake at breakfast, no doubt with his vintage wind-up gramophone blaring bawdy songs of the twenties.

She went, and she did. Jeremy Kelling was eating sausages and bellowing at his long-suffering houseman, Egbert. Egbert was delighted to see Miss Sarah, the elderly bachelor less so.

'Look here, young woman, if you've come trying to drag me to Fred's funeral—'

'I wouldn't dream of it, Uncle Jem. You two always did hate each other's guts.'

'Hunh. Nice talk from a young lady, I don't think.'

Sarah sat down at the table without being invited and helped herself to a piece of toast. Her own father was one of the few Kellings who'd been able to stay on speaking terms with Jeremy, and she'd been in and out of this flat all her life.

'At least he's going to be in lively company,' she remarked. 'What do you think of this Ruby Redd thing?'

Jeremy Kelling told her what he thought in sulphurous detail. Sarah sipped Egbert's coffee, which was pure nectar compared to Edith's, and waited until he'd run out of swear words. Then she said, 'Really? I took it for granted you'd put her there yourself, although of course I didn't say so to the police.'

Her uncle took the sally as a compliment, as she'd known he would, and regaled her with several too-familiar anecdotes. Finally, she managed to get in the question she'd come to ask.

'By the way, here's a little nugget the reporters didn't get hold of. There was an old man in the cemetery with me while I was waiting for Dolph. We got to talking—I get my bad habit of picking up odd characters from you, you know—and by the maddest coincidence he turned out to have been the bartender in a place Ruby Redd used to frequent, called Danny Rate's Pub. Would you happen to know him?'

'Ah, sweet memory! Many's the libation I've lifted to the buxom beauties of the burleycue over that sudsy oaken timber. Gad, the nights I spent in Danny Rate's Pub! I could tell you stories—'

Sarah knew better than to let him get started again. 'All I want is for you to tell me that bartender's name,' she interrupted firmly. 'He was actually the first one to identify the body, though Dolph hogged the credit, and he was such a dear to me, lending me money for the telephone which I forgot to give back. He simply faded out of the picture before I had a chance even to thank him. I thought I'd like to return his dime and write a little note of appreciation. He was so—oh, old and seedy-looking and probably living in some poky room—'

'At the taxpayers' expense,' snorted Uncle Jem, who had never done a tap of honest work in his life. 'What did he look like?'

'Short and thinnish, and I'd say he may have been fair-haired when he was younger. He had pale blue eyes, I know, unusually pale, with something odd about them.'

'One eyelid drooped, and the other didn't?'

'Yes, that was it!'

'Funny sort of crack in his voice?'

'Yes, I thought it was just old age.'

'No, he always talked that way. Well, well! Imagine his turning up like that. I remember one night—'

'Never mind,' Sarah broke in relentlessly. She couldn't spend the whole morning here. 'What's his name? You must remember that, you never forget anything.'

'Wait, don't rush me. Let me think. It was a funny sort of name. Not peculiar, amusing. We had a standing joke around the bar. "Oh, gee, Tim," we'd say. That was it, Tim O'Ghee, with a h. Some corruption of Magee, I daresay, unless his mother made it up, which is not without the realm of possibility. Speaking of names—'

'Edith will be calling me names,' said his niece, 'if I don't get back and do Edith's work for her. The hordes are descending on us after the funeral. Sorry you won't be among them, but I shouldn't be, either, if I didn't have to. It'll only be sherry and cheese, anyway. Thanks for the lovely coffee and the help. I'll drop over in a day or so and tell you all the nasty things Cousin Mabel says about you.'

She kissed him goodbye. She'd never minded kissing Uncle Jem because he was plump instead of craggy like the rest of the uncles, didn't have whiskers, and smelled pleasantly of Bay Rum. Besides, he'd given her what she came for.

Now that she knew Timothy O'Ghee's name, she must surely be able to track him down. Sarah hastened over to the pay phones on the Common, found a phone book that hadn't yet been vandalised, and hunted among the Os. No O'Ghee was listed, which didn't surprise her. That would be too easy.

The voting lists would be a likelier place to find him. Sarah knew all about voting lists, she'd ploughed through enough of them addressing postcards in the interests of one or another of Aunt Caroline's causes. She was at City Hall within five minutes.

Behind its ultra-modern façade, the new City Hall had taken on much the same homey atmosphere as the old. A friendly clerk, who must have been somebody's favourite aunt, was delighted to leave her typewriter and assist in the search. They found one lone O'Ghee on the list, at an address which was more or less where Sarah had thought it might be. She copied down the information, thanked the clerk profusely, and made a beeline for the subway.

CHAPTER SIX

Though Sarah had been born and reared in Boston, the regions out beyond Andrew Square might have been Timbuctoo, for all she knew of their geography. She and the lady at City Hall had picked out O'Ghee's address on a street map; nevertheless she had to search for the place, and when she did at last find it she could hardly believe she'd got it right. This wasn't even a street, merely a sort of cul-de-sac that appeared to be one solid block of disused-looking warehouses.

At last she noticed a few yards of chain-link fence spanning what she first thought must be a driveway. Behind it, cramped between the massive warehouses, stood a sliver of a house three storeys high but not more than fifteen feet wide, covered in green asphalt shingles that had begun to curl and break at the edges. The front yard was about five feet deep, grown up to crabgrass and ragweed, the door badly in need of paint. However, lace curtains at the one front window framed a card that read, 'Room for Rent,' and a wire shopping cart leaned against the railing of the minuscule porch. This had to be the place, after all.

It looked like, and probably was, the sole remaining unit of what was once a row of wooden town houses. Some die-hard householder must have fought to the end against creeping industrialism and won what was surely a hollow victory. The chain-link fence suggested a watch dog, so Sarah approached with caution. However, nothing happened when she opened the gate. She ventured up the two steps and knocked at the door.

The woman who answered was another surprise. These tacky surroundings would have prepared Sarah for birdsnest hair and a filthy apron, but Tim O'Ghee's landlady, if such she was, clearly spent a good deal more effort on herself than she did on her house. Her hair was an architectural marvel, her face a work of art. Her rigorously girdled form was encased in a tight nylon jersey dress of exuberant pattern and her nether extremities in imitation snakeskin boots with high heels and inch-thick soles.

'Yes?' she said doubtfully with an up-and-down glance at

Sarah's once-good tweed coat and sensible shoes.

'I'm looking for Mr Timothy O'Ghee,' Sarah stammered. 'Do I have the right address?'

'What do you want him for?'

'Well, I—I borrowed some money from him yesterday and wanted to pay it back.'

'That's a hot one. I never knew he had any to lend.'

'It's a very small amount, just change for the phone, actually, but he was so kind to offer it, and slipped away before I could even thank him properly. Later I described him to my uncle and he said it must have been Mr O'Ghee, so I thought I'd run over and see him. I live not too far from here.'

'Oh, yeah? Whereabouts?'

'Towards the West End,' Sarah hedged. 'Is Mr O'Ghee in now?'

'I dunno. I been over to the Avenue, grocery shopping. Tim don't generally come downstairs till late. I don't serve no meals, see, but I give him coffee and maybe a piece of toast or something. What the heck, he's an old man. It wouldn't seem right making him walk all the way to the Avenue for a cup of coffee.'

She turned her head and screamed, 'Tim! Tim, you up yet? Somebody's here to see you.'

She got no reply.

'He don't hear so good no more. Prob'ly laying in bed reading the racing forms. Why don't you go up? He won't mind.'

Sarah hesitated. 'Couldn't you?'

'I don't climb them stairs no more'n I have to. Doctor's orders.'

Sarah didn't believe that for a moment. Any woman who could tramp around the stores in those murderous boots must be rugged enough for anything. However, she wasn't about to start an argument.

'Where would I find him?'

'Straight upstairs and turn to your right. Tell him I got coffee on the stove.'

The woman stepped back and disappeared into the murky recesses of the house. The stairway was directly inside the front door, steep and dark and covered in a runner that ought to have been replaced ages ago. Praying she wouldn't catch her toe in a worn spot and break her neck, Sarah picked her way to the top.

The old man's door was shut. She knocked and called, 'Mr O'Ghee,' but he didn't answer. Perhaps he'd got up and left the house while his landlady was shopping. Now that she'd come this far, she might as well make sure.

Barging into strange people's bedrooms was not the sort of thing Sarah had been brought up to face with equanimity. She had to fight with herself to turn the knob and push the door open.

Tim O'Ghee was in. He lay sprawled half out of a narrow iron bed, his eyes and mouth half open, his face shrunken and still. He would not be wanting coffee, then or ever.

Sarah wasn't frightened, only sorry. She had seen plenty of dead old men, grandfathers, great-uncles, cousins twice and thrice removed. They had died in their own comfortable beds, most of them, or in hospitals with trained nurses in attendance and relatives around to make sure they got decently buried. Moved by pity, she reached out and touched one of the stiff, yellow hands. It felt like wax that had been kept in a refrigerator. The cold drove her back to the head of the stairs.

'Mrs—oh, what is your name? Please come up! Something's happened to Mr O'Ghee.'

'What's the matter?' The blonde wig gleamed in the dusk below. 'What happened?'

'I'm afraid he's dead.'

'What do you mean, you're afraid?' The strident voice grew harsher. 'Either he is or he ain't. You sure he ain't in a coma? Tim's a diabetic. You better stay with him while I get the doctor.'

Sarah knew the old man was beyond any earthly need of her company, yet common humanity demanded that she not run out at a time like this. She started to pull the spread over him, then decided she'd better not touch anything until somebody came.

At least she didn't have to stand right over him. She went to the one narrow window and stood looking out, but there was nothing to see except brick walls, and these were too unpleasant a reminder of that other brick wall which she and Tim O'Ghee had seen together.

A prickling began at the back of her neck and inched its way down her spine. Surely it could be no more than a tragic coincidence that this little man who'd appeared so chipper less than twenty-four hours ago, this man who'd known Ruby Redd and the men who bought her drinks, should so suddenly be lying here dead?

Sarah had surprisingly little time to wonder. Hardly five minutes later she heard voices on the stairs.

'Caught me on the bleeper,' the doctor was explaining. 'I was in the car on my way to the hospital. Checked back on the CB and my office told me to come here. Lucky you caught me when you did. Where is he?'

'Right in here.'

The landlady ushered a man with a leather satchel into the room, flipped her head at Sarah, then at the door. 'Okay, miss. Thanks for staying.'

It was a clear invitation to leave but Sarah didn't budge. The doctor, obviously in a rush to do what he must and get on, hardly seemed to notice she was there, although the room was so small they were almost on top of one another. He bent over the body, tried to lift an arm and found it stiff with rigor, made a perfunctory gesture at rolling back the eyelids, then straightened up.

'That's the story, Mrs Wandelowski. Too bad, but the poor old guy's been living on borrowed time as you know. At least it was quick and peaceful. You might as well go ahead and call the undertaker. Tell whoever you get to call my office, and I'll have my secretary send over the death certificate.'

'What are you going to put on it?' Sarah asked.

'Heart failure, what else?'

The doctor turned around and gaped as though he had, in fact, been unaware there was somebody behind him. 'Who are you?'

'A friend,' she snapped, 'and I must say I don't think much of your examination. Mr O'Ghee was perfectly hale and hearty yesterday afternoon.'

'If you're such a pal of his, miss, you ought to know better than that. Tim was in rough shape and had been for years.

Mrs Wandelowski, had he been taking his insulin on schedule?'

'How'm I supposed to know? I gave him the vials regular out of the icebox like you told me to. I didn't watch him take no shots. What do you think I am? Them needles turn my stomach.'

'Um.'

The doctor looked around the tiny, bare room. There was a waste basket beside the dresser. He looked into it, finding nothing but the front section of the previous night's newspaper. Sarah noticed with dismay that her own face appeared on the first page in a group shot with Dolph and some policemen. The caption read, 'Stripper's Body Found in Historic Tomb.'

He held up the paper. 'Anything in here to upset him, I wonder?'

'Oh, God, yes,' cried Mrs Wandelowski. 'I should have thought of that in the first place. Tim was right there watching when they dug her up, can you believe it? Came home white as a sheet, shaking so hard he could barely get his coat off. I sat him down in the kitchen and gave him hot coffee with a little whisky in it, not enough to hurt a fly. I know what he can have and what he can't. Couldn't, I mean. Poor old Tim, I'm going to miss him.'

She sniffled, not very convincingly, Sarah thought. 'He said he knew who it was the minute he laid eyes on her. Between you and me, I think they had something going for a while, 'way back when. Tim wasn't a bad-looking guy when he was young. I seen pictures. You know how old people are always dragging out snapshots they want you to look at. Same old lies over and over about how great they used to be.'

She touched her eyes very carefully with a tissue. 'So last night he sat there at the kitchen table talking my ear off about this broad with the rubies in her teeth till I couldn't take no more. Made me sick to think of her laying there all this time. Anyhow, I had a date with my friend from over the Avenue, so I made him a cup of soup and told him he better go to bed.'

'You never saw him after that?'

'Nope. I was kind of late getting in and I figured he must

be asleep. His door was shut.'

'Anybody else in the house?'

'Not last night. My husband's away. On business,' she added with a glare at Sarah.

'I see.'

The doctor put down the paper and knelt to peer under the bed. 'Ah, here we are.'

He reached in and scooped out a handful of dust fluffs and a stray sock. With the debris came two small plastic vials and some scraps of paper.

'Here's the insulin he didn't take, and here, I'd say, is what finished him off.' He spread out the scraps so the printing on them was visible. They were all alike.

'He's been into my candy! Tim knows better than that. It could kill him.' Mrs Wandelowski began to laugh hysterically. 'What a way to go.'

'But those are all Milky Way wrappers,' Sarah protested.

'So what? They been having a special.'

'I know, we bought some too. I offered one to Mr O'Ghee yesterday, and he refused. He said he couldn't eat them.'

'Look, Miss whoever-the-hell-you-are,' said the doctor wearily, 'if a despondent old man decides to kill himself, he'll take any means that comes handy. You ought to be able to figure out what happened as well as I can. It must have been one hell of a shock when they knocked down that wall and he saw his old girl friend lying there like something left over from a horror movie. Maybe he'd been day-dreaming all these years she'd come back to him some day. Maybe it just started him thinking about the past and what he had to look forward to, and he decided what was the sense in going on any longer?'

'But she wasn't his old sweetheart,' Sarah protested. 'He didn't even like her. He said Ruby Redd was the meanest woman he'd ever known. He was not upset, he was excited.'

'Look, sister, what a person says and what he feels can be two very different things. Who the hell knows why people kill themselves? It happens a damn sight oftener than you might think. Being a nice old guy, he fixes it up to look like a natural death instead of jumping in front of a subway train and messing up the tracks. And for your information, I'm still going to put heart failure on the death certificate. If you want to report me to the medical association, please feel free. Say, don't I know you from somewhere?'

As she had feared, his eye lit on the newspaper. 'So that's the little game, is it? You're the Kelling girl.'

Mrs Wandelowski snatched the paper away from him. 'You mean that's her, the one in the picture? Sure, look, she's even wearing the same clothes. What gall! Weaselling her way in here, making out she's a friend of Tim's. What's she after, anyways?'

'Good question.'

The doctor took a step that brought him nose to nose with Sarah. 'What's the big idea, kid? Figured you'd get O'Ghee to tell you which of your rich uncles was the stripper's boy friend so you could blackmail him into buying you a mink coat or a trip to Europe?'

'That's ridiculous,' cried Sarah. 'I—'

'Don't you believe one word she says,' Mrs Wandelowski broke in. 'After the way she lied to me, I wouldn't trust her one inch. Now you listen to me, toots. I don't care who you are or where you came from, you're nothing but a little tramp, and I won't have you in my house. Get out and don't never show your face around here again or you'll damn soon wish you hadn't.'

'Take it easy, Mrs Wandelowski,' said the doctor. 'Don't get your blood pressure up. Come on, Miss Kelling, whatever you're after, you came too late. Sorry I can't give you taxi service back to the family mansion, but you've wasted too much of my time already.'

He was herding Sarah down the stairs as he spoke, and out on the porch. Mrs Wandelowski slammed the door behind them. There was nothing Sarah could do except walk back to the subway station and catch a train to Park Street.

She was much later getting home than she'd meant to be. Edith was in a tizzy, messing around the kitchen, doing her best to ruin the refreshments.

'Leave that alone and go put on your afternoon uniform,' Sarah ordered. 'I told you I'd be here in time to do the food.'

'Don't see how,' the maid retorted. 'They'll be here in half an hour.'

Sarah wasted no breath arguing. She had more time than that, but she was going to need every minute of it. She welcomed the rush, it kept her from brooding on that neatly timed suicide of Tim O'Ghee. By the time she'd arranged her trays of savouries and crudités, and got sheets of cheese puffs chilling in the fridge, ready to pop into a hot oven at the first sound of the doorbell, she'd worked herself into a reasonable frame of mind. She even managed to change her dress and be downstairs pouring sherry when Edith, elegant in black sateen, white organdy apron, and perhaps the last frilled lace cap extant on the Hill, opened the door to the first lot of friends and relatives.

Fortunately, Alexander and Aunt Caroline were in the group. Sarah left them to do the honours, got Edith started passing drinks and food, and bolted for the kitchen. From then on it was back and forth, lugging trays and boiling kettles, gathering up used dishes and fetching clean ones, Edith having provided about half the required number.

The old retainer might have known there'd be a record turnout. The Kellings, one and all, adored a funeral, and with the disagreeable publicity this one had evoked they'd rallied in droves to prove they had nothing to hide. She caught a sputter here and there about not knowing better than to talk to reporters, but didn't stop to listen.

Thank goodness the Lackridges had come. Harry was making himself agreeable and Leila was interpreting for Aunt Caroline. That was a blessing, since Alexander would hardly have been up to it. He looked even greyer around the mouth than he had the night before. Some of the relatives were noticing.

'Alex is taking it hard. Didn't realise he was so fond of old Fred. Edith, these cheese puffs are marvellous. I cannot see how you do it all by yourself.'

At last the tea, the sherry, the food, and the family were gone. Only Harry and Leila stayed on, she still talking and he still drinking, though by now Harry had switched to scotch out of his friend's private stock. Sarah lit the library fire and shooed them toward it.

'Go warm yourselves while I straighten up the drawing room.'

Alexander roused himself to say, 'You've been working all afternoon, Sarah. Can't Edith do that?'

'She's washing dishes,' said Leila.

'She is not,' Sarah retorted. 'She's downstairs soaking her corns and watching television. She's furious with me because I wouldn't let her go to the funeral.'

'People were wondering why you both stayed away.'

'Pity the obvious answer never occurred to them. Harry, before you quite finish that bottle, why don't you fix my husband a drink of his own whisky? Perhaps Leila and Aunt Caroline would like one, too.'

'What about yourself?'

'Not if anybody expects supper. It won't be much, I warn you.'

In fact, Sarah hadn't the faintest idea what she was going to serve, but nobody seemed to care. She went back to picking up cups and glasses. As a rule, Alexander would have helped, but tonight he sat hunched in the vast leather armchair that was once Uncle Gilbert's special place, nursing his drink and letting the others talk around him. Sarah looked in once or twice to take them ice or a few leftover canapés, and it seemed to her that he hadn't moved a muscle during the intervals.

She opened a tin of pâté they'd got in a Christmas box and were saving for some grand occasion, and took a great deal of care making dainty sandwiches. Alexander had finicky tastes for a man. Those and a cup of soup, along with what had been served earlier, ought to suffice. They were none of them big eaters.

When the food was ready she went downstairs and told Edith, 'I've fixed us a tray so you can forget about supper. There's soup on the stove. If that's not enough, boil yourself a couple of eggs.'

'They had the funeral on the news,' said the maid without moving her eyes from the flickering screen. 'You wasn't in it. They said you was home, prostrated with shock.'

'I'll be prostrated all right, before this day is over.'

Sarah climbed the stairs one at a time with a rest in between, and picked up the last, heavy tray.

CHAPTER
SEVEN

'Alex! Alex, where are you? It's almost eight o'clock.'

Caroline Kelling's strident call woke Sarah from the soundest sleep she'd had in ages. Eight o'clock? They never slept that late. Could her husband—she froze, recalling old Tim O'Ghee sprawled half out of that sleazy boarding-house cot.

But no, Alexander was getting up. She could her a muffled groan, the squeak of bedsprings, then water running in the bathroom between their bedrooms. Sarah jumped out of bed, called down the stairs, 'Edith, tell her we'll be down in a minute,' and snatched her oldest slacks and a bedraggled jersey out of her closet.

Mariposa would be here on the dot of nine. Three minutes later, the cleaning woman would have tied up her elaborate hairdo in a flamboyant scarf, changed from street clothes to a cotton wrapper, put on a pair of holey sneakers in place of her chic high-heeled pumps, and be making the dust fly. They could afford this paragon only once a week, and nobody, not even Mariposa, could get through the whole house in a single day, so Sarah and Edith were supposed to help.

Sarah generally enjoyed tagging along with this human whirlwind, dusting and polishing and listening to a steady run of piquant gossip about life as it was lived at the other end of the city. Edith would spend the entire time puttering around Aunt Caroline's bedroom and bath, and the adjoining room that Mrs Kelling called her boudoir. Admittedly, this was no small responsibility since everything had to be kept in meticulous order, even the blind woman's embroidery silks laid out strand by strand. It was to Edith's credit that she never slacked her duties in this area.

By the time they got settled around the breakfast table, Aunt Caroline was in no sweet humour.

'I particularly wanted an early start this morning. You know it's a two-hour drive to Marguerite's, and she wants us there well in advance of the others so that you'll have time to read me her latest chapter. She's anxious to get my opinion before she goes any further.'

'Well, that's just too bad,' Sarah snapped. 'Alexander, why don't you tell your mother you're not going? You know you hate these ladies' luncheons, and that book of hers is a total farce. Why should you drive seventy-five miles and back again for the sake of hearing Aunt Marguerite spout drivel?'

'Why not?' he said wearily.

'Because you look like death warmed over, for one thing. Won't you please go back to bed and stay there till you've got rid of whatever is ailing you?'

His exquisite lips curved in a wry smile. 'That might be rather a long stay. Don't worry about me, Sadiebelle. Actually, I'll be glad to get out of Boston for a few hours. I only wish you were coming, too.'

'What I wish,' she sighed, 'is that the two of us could go off by ourselves for once in our lives. Can't your mother understand that you're a human being instead of a seeing-eye dog?'

'No, I don't think so.'

Alexander pushed back his chair and leaned down to kiss his wife. 'Don't work too hard. You look washed-out, yourself. I'm afraid you did too much yesterday.'

Sarah grabbed him by the necktie and pulled him closer. 'Nonsense, Edith managed everything singlehanded. Didn't you notice the becoming modesty with which she was accepting all those compliments?'

'You're a nasty little girl, Sadiebelle.'

He was going to kiss her again but his mother demanded, 'Aren't we ever going to get started?' and Edith came to announce that Mariposa was starting to wash dishes and weren't they finished yet?

'In a minute,' said Sarah. 'Alexander, don't let them wear you to shreds. Tell Aunt Marguerite your wife has turned into a shrew and will hit the ceiling if you're not back in time to rest before dinner. And don't think I'm joking, because I'm not. Edith, help Mrs Kelling on with her things and go get whatever she claims she doesn't intend to take with her because you know she'll change her mind at the last minute and want it, after all. I'll clear the table, unless you'd like me to get the car, Alexander?'

'No, my dear. I'm not that far gone.'

Parking around the Hill was impossible. They had to garage their 1950 Studebaker down on Charles Street at a rate that would have bought them a new car every few years, fees being what they were in the area. They'd have been better off not to keep a car at all and rent one when they needed to, but Aunt Caroline wouldn't hear of giving up the vehicle she'd once been able to drive herself.

Thanks to Alexander's skill as a mechanic, the Studebaker continued to run like a charm and was no doubt a fairly valuable antique by now. Some day, perhaps, they'd relegate it to the shed at Ireson's Landing with the Milburn, and get themselves something to ride in that wasn't a collector's item.

Some day, maybe, Sarah would pry Alexander loose from this ruinously expensive, hard-to-maintain town house and move into a place of her own. She was sick of Beacon Hill, sick of never being able to get her hands on a little spending money, sick to death of being married to Aunt Caroline. That day, the sofa cushions got the beating of their lives.

Work, as always, was therapy. It wasn't until Mariposa was gone, the mops and brooms put away for another week, and Sarah soaking off the dust in a hot tub, that she had time to start worrying again. Alexander and his mother ought to be back any minute now, provided he hadn't fallen into another of those frozen trances and cracked up the Studebaker. She ought to have left Mariposa to cope and gone with him. He wasn't fond of driving long distances at any time, and in his present state the trip must have been sheer murder.

She wished she hadn't thought of that word. Ruby Redd had almost certainly been murdered, according to a story in the morning paper which Sarah had been able to wrest away before Mariposa used it to protect the newly scrubbed kitchen linoleum. The skull had been caved in at the back by a blow that was unlikely to have been accidental, especially in view of the macabre entombment. An investigation would be made, but little hope was held out for a solution.

That meant a few perfunctory inquiries, no doubt, then one more file left to collect dust. Boston had too many fresh corpses turning up in vacant lots and alleyways for the police to spend much time on a crime that might or might not have occurred some thirty years ago.

Sarah was absolutely convinced that Tim O'Ghee had been murdered, too, but there wasn't even an outside chance the police would ever get to investigate that death, unless the undertaker found a bullet lodged in his heart. That wouldn't happen. Probably no undertaker would be called in. Thanks to modern technology, bodies were a lot easier to get rid of than they used to be. Anyway, why shoot him when it would be so easy to inject poison? Even if the body were examined, one more hypodermic puncture in the flesh of someone who took insulin regularly would never be noticed.

Again she felt a compulsion to ask herself if Alexander could have done such a thing? Physically, yes. There was an old hypodermic needle of Uncle Gilbert's still in the house and plenty of poisons available: things like bleach and lye in the kitchen, atropine in Aunt Caroline's eye drops, a croton growing in the drawing-room bay window and heaven knew what else, plus that bag of candy he himself had bought, ready to take along and set the scene.

Alexander had driven his mother out to Dolph's early yesterday morning, some time before Sarah left the house. Aunt Caroline wouldn't know if he swung around through South Boston and left her sitting in the car while he pretended to be doing some trivial errand. Finding Mrs Wandelowski out shopping might have been a lucky accident, or else he could have phoned first pretending to be the serviceman from the gas company or something, and learned that she was about to leave the house. The lock on that ramshackle door would present no difficulty to his talented fingers. He could have been in and out before anybody in that virtually deserted neighbourhood knew he was there.

Of course the whole notion was absurd. Alexander would have to know where the old barman lived, that Tim was diabetic, that he had a landlady who shopped over on the Avenue in the mornings.

Perhaps he did know. Tim might have been boarding in that same house for years and years, ever since Alexander's student days. He might have talked about his flashy landlady, might have refused to let the boys buy him drinks because of his ailment. Alexander remembered details like that.

As Uncle Jem would say, poppycock! Alexander wouldn't even set mousetraps. The hot water was soothing her nerves a little, even though the dumpy claw-footed tub was too short for a satisfactory loll. The one on the second floor was twice as big, but only Aunt Caroline got to use that.

Before they married, Alexander had papered and painted the third-floor suite, trying to make things attractive for his young bride. However, he hadn't been able to do much about the cracked and sagging plaster, so the paint had soon begun to flake and the paper to peel away from the walls. While she was soaking, a chip fell off the ceiling and plunked into the water beside her.

Everything was falling apart. Sarah crawled over the high side of the tub and rubbed furiously at her body with a towel that, like everything else in this house, had seen its best days. She put on her blue cocoon because she felt cold, and was on her way down the front staircase when her husband and his mother came in.

'Are we going out?'

Alexander's question was almost a groan. Sarah stood on tiptoe to give him a kiss.

'What kind of greeting is that? Can't I dress up for my husband if I want to? Did you have a good time at Aunt Marguerite's?'

'Mother enjoyed herself.'

Most uncharacteristically, he dropped his overcoat on a chair instead of bothering to hang it up. 'Have I time for a drink before dinner?'

'Of course. It's only half-past six.'

'It feels like midnight.'

'Go flop in the library. I'll do the drinks. Edith can look after your mother.'

Mrs Kelling always expected a good deal of attention after one of these all-day excursions, but her daughter-in-law was not about to give it this time. Aunt Caroline was perfectly capable of doing a great deal more for herself than she did, and it was high time they quit spoiling her rotten. Sarah hung up the overcoat, went to call the maid, then hurried back to her husband.

Alexander was in no mood for talk. He didn't even thank her for the stiff whisky she brought him, or for poking up the fire that he usually attended to. Sarah stood looking at him for a moment, and decided what he needed most was a hot meal and no fussing.

Cooking was supposed to be one of Edith's duties, but the maid had learned several years ago that by producing thoroughly uneatable meals, she could manipulate the younger Mrs Kelling into taking most of that work off her hands. Aunt Caroline required food that could be managed with a minimum of fuss and fumble, which meant a lot of chopping and puréeing. It was quite a while before Sarah got back to the library. Aunt Caroline was holding forth at length about her sister's book. Her son wasn't even pretending to pay attention. At last the blind woman became aware of his indifference.

'Alexander, are you there?'

Sarah picked up her mother-in-law's hand. 'Dinner in ten minutes,' she spelled out. 'More sherry first?'

'No,' snapped the older woman, trying to jerk her hand away as she always did when Sarah used hand signals to communicate with her. 'Why doesn't Alex answer me?'

'Tired,' Sarah spelled out.

'What of that? I'm tired, too. Those luncheons of Marguerite's are always exhausting, but if I can stand them, why can't he?'

Sarah caught her husband's eye. 'I suppose it wouldn't be kind of me to explain that it's because you have to stand her at the same time. Alexander, we simply must find some kind of nurse-companion for your mother, whether we can afford one or not.'

'Please, Sarah, not tonight.'

Alexander Kelling took his mother's hand and began making signals in the palm. His long, pale fingers seemed to be working automatically, with no direction from his conscious mind.

CHAPTER EIGHT

The trouble Sarah took over preparing dinner might as well
have been saved. Mrs Kelling declared that Marguerite had
served too much rich food as usual, and she'd just have a
bowl of corn flakes. Alexander didn't appear to notice
there was food in front of him. Sarah took away his
untasted plateful and fetched her Braille pad.

'I'm sending Alexander to bed,' she put down, poking
out the dots with fierce jabs of her stylus. 'He is not well.'

Mrs Kelling ran her fingers over the tiny bumps, then
passed the note over to her son. 'What's wrong with you? I
thought we'd play backgammon for a while. I need to
unwind after that long drive.'

'Sarah,' Alexander sighed, 'couldn't you play with her?'

'No, I could not! You know I detest backgammon. Your
mother was out to the Lackridges' night before last, she
went to Dolph's and the funeral yesterday and had the
whole family here afterwards. She's been away all day
today. She's got an armload of Braille books you lugged
home from the library that she hasn't even had time to
open. You're going to bed and she can entertain herself for
a change.'

She picked up the pad again and punched savagely,
'Suggest you read . . . A. going to bed now.'

Caroline flicked her fingers over the message, slapped
the paper down on the table, reached for her cane, and
stalked from the room. Alexander started to get up, but
Sarah grabbed his arm.

'Don't you dare! She's a lot better able to take care of
herself than you are. Give her a minute to settle, then you
march yourself upstairs.'

Her husband gave her a ghastly attempt at a smile, and
did as he was told. She tucked him up with a hot water
bottle and an extra blanket, dosed him with aspirin and
kissed him goodnight.

'Don't get up in the morning unless you truly feel better.'

She knew she was whistling in the dark. They were
committed to tea at the Protheroes', and feisty old Anora

was capable of coming to fetch them bodily if they didn't arrive on schedule. That should be no great strain on him, though. She could do the driving herself, and Leila would probably be there to handle Aunt Caroline.

After she'd got her husband settled, Sarah fiddled around downstairs for a while, putting away the uneaten food, doing the dishes while Edith loafed down in the basement before her everlasting television, and tidying the already neat kitchen. She went back to the drawing room and played softly on the rosewood Bechstein for a while, but the antique piano was out of tune and so was she. She didn't feel like drawing or reading or doing the crossword puzzle. She didn't feel like much of anything. At last, for want of a better idea, Sarah went up to her room although it was still far short of her normal bedtime.

Aspirin and exhaustion had done good work for Alexander. He was sound asleep, breathing deeply and regularly. In the exquisite boudoir below, his mother was no doubt embroidering French knots on the draperies. That did seem an odd way to relieve frustration, but perhaps Aunt Caroline enjoyed the nubbly texture that the heavy draperies had taken on as a result of her labours over the years. Anyway, she kept on working French knots and would do so, no doubt, until the curtains fell apart. What difference did it make, so long as the strange occupation kept her from pestering Alexander?

Sarah thought of washing her hair, but feared the running water might wake her husband. She fussed with her nails, straightened her dresser drawers, and finally started on her closet, which was a mistake. Stuck away on the shelf, where she'd thrust it while she was rushing to get ready for the Lackridges' dinner, was the brick she'd lugged home from the cemetery. Dolph thought she'd got rid of it. Why in heaven's name had she not done so?

She turned the small, heavy block over in her hands. Was it really identical with those in the wall at Ireson's Landing? How could she be so positive on the strength of memory and a black-and-white photograph? She might be giving herself nightmares over nothing. Mightn't she?

The little sketch was still in her bag, she got it out and studied it. She ought to go down and compare her drawing to the photograph in the hall, but somehow she didn't dare. What if Edith caught her?

Well, what if she did? Could nobody else ever hit by coincidence on the same pattern Aunt Caroline and Alexander had worked out? There couldn't be all that many different ways to lay bricks. Could there?

What was the sense of standing here asking herself questions? There was one way to find out, and she'd never find a better opportunity than now, with her husband asleep, Aunt Caroline sulking, and Edith thinking the household was bedded down for the night. Sarah packed the brick and the sketch back into her shoulder bag, tiptoed into Alexander's room and took the car keys that were lying on his dresser, and picked her way down the back stairs. A hooded storm coat she'd had since she was fifteen hung on a hook in the entryway. She bundled herself into it and let herself out into the alley.

This was no night to be going anywhere. The rain that had begun to spit about the time Alexander and his mother got home was turning into a steady downpour. The Studebaker's tyres had barely squeaked through the state inspection in October, the gas tank might be close to empty, and she had three dollars and twenty-seven cents in her pocket-book. What difference did that make? This was something that had to be done. She pulled her hood over her forehead and slogged down the hill.

The attendant, who knew the Kellings well, was surprised to see her. 'Not taking the old girl out in this weather, are you? Sure she can stand the strain?'

'I'm more concerned about the young one,' Sarah tried to joke back. 'A little family emergency has come up, and Mr Kelling isn't feeling well.'

'I thought he looked kind of down in the mouth when he brought the car in just after I came on duty. You don't suppose it's flu?'

'I hope not. I chased him off to bed, and don't you dare tell him I took the car out by myself tonight. He'd have fits if he knew, but somebody has to go. Must I give you another coupon?'

'Ah, forget it. Going to be out long?'

'It's hard to say. Probably two or three hours.'

'Well, take it easy.'

The attendant went back to reading his Mickey Spillane paperback. Sarah eased the Studebaker out into Cambridge Street Circle and headed for the bridge over the Mystic River. She was relieved to see the gas gauge registered almost full. Alexander must have stopped to top it up on the way back. He was good about things like that.

He was good about everything, too good. Sarah felt her eyes smarting and angrily blinked them dry. This was no time to get emotional. Traffic was a mess for no particular reason except that Boston drivers always go into syncope at the slightest hint of rain.

Sarah didn't mind, she'd driven in worse jams than this. In fact, the sheer awfulness of the situation began to cheer her up. By the time she'd got herself untangled and out on Route One, she was feeling some of her usual pleasure in handling the willing little double-ended car.

However, Ireson's Landing was a long way up the pike, and by the time she reached their familiar turnoff, her heart was in her soggy boots. She'd forgotten to bring the keys to the house, which meant she would not be able to go in and throw the switch that controlled the outside lights. That didn't matter a great deal. Thanks to Alexander's forethought, there was a good flashlight in the glove compartment. It would be a bit spooky with that one little light, but she was a big girl now.

She was almost to the drive entrance, it was time to blink her direction signal. She hoped to goodness that clown who'd been tailgating ever since she left the highway would see it in time to keep from ploughing into her when she slowed down. It was probably some kid who'd never seen a Studebaker before, trying to figure out why the car was being driven in reverse.

Whoever it was got the message and swerved out around her as she shifted into low gear and started the long, treacherous climb to the house. Uncle Gilbert had kept the drive tarred over while he was alive. She and Alexander were always going to have it repaved, but there was never enough money. By now it was a mine field of potholes and boulders that got heaved up by winter frosts. They spent a good part of every summer trying to smooth it out, but each spring revealed fresh disaster areas.

Sarah could feel the car slipping and slewing as she hit slick mud or loose gravel. Going down should be an interesting experience, assuming she ever succeeded in getting up. She'd have been wiser to leave the car at the bottom and make the climb on foot, but even the illusion of security it gave her was preferable to being out there alone with the rain and the dark.

Knowing the terrain and the vehicle as she did, she made the ascent with a few bad scares but no serious mishap, and pulled up against one of the railroad ties that had been laid down to mark the parking area. The moment of truth was at hand.

She could feel the weight of the brick in her shoulder bag, nevertheless she reached in and touched it to make doubly sure it was there. The chalky hardness was at least something tangible in this streaming nightmare.

Because Alexander kept the glove compartment so fully stocked with maps, first-aid kit, emergency flares and other things they might conceivably need at some time or other, the flashlight did not come readily to hand. Sarah could have found it easily by turning on the dome light instead of fumbling around in the dark, but the thought of exposing herself inside a lighted coach paralysed her, which was stupid. Nobody could possibly see up here from the road, and any animal that might be braving the storm nearby would only run away.

Nevertheless she continued to fumble until the grooved bakelite cylinder snugged itself into her hand. Now she had no further excuse to procrastinate. Sarah zipped up her storm coat as tight as it would go, eased herself out of the car, and started walking towards the Secret Garden.

She was still chary of showing a light, until wet leaves and sprawling roots made the path so treacherous that she absolutely had to. This was no time or place to sprain an ankle.

Alexander had been trying for years to get his mother to let him sell off some of the land and ease their financial pressures, but so far the deeds were still in Aunt Caroline's keeping. The Kelling estate remained one of the largest in the area, with the Secret Garden fully a quarter of a mile from the house. Sarah had never thought it much of a walk before, but tonight the path seemed to have no end.

In the summertime she'd have all sorts of familiar night noises for company. Now, with her head muffled in the pile-lined hood, all she could hear was rain drumming on poplin that was supposed to be water repellent but was acting more like blotting paper. She could feel wetness soaking through, spreading across her shoulders and down her back. Her feet skidded. She sat down hard, got up and slogged on.

After a while, Sarah began to giggle. This was such an utterly harebrained thing to be doing, the sort of scrape she and her cousin Beth used to get into when they were youngsters. Beth was out in California now twiddling switches in some television studio, or had been at last report. When she'd got the announcement of Sarah's wedding to Alexander, she'd sribbled across it, 'Best wishes for a speedy annulment' and sent it back. Since then they hadn't corresponded much.

Thinking about Beth and summers long ago, Sarah didn't realise at first that she was walking alongside the wall she'd come to see. Involuntarily, she switched off the flashlight, blasted herself for a coward, turned it on again and got out the brick and her sketch. The match was perfect.

Now there was no more room for hoping. Sarah let the brick fall among the dead leaves that had drifted against the wall, tore up her sketch and gave the shreds to the wind and the rain. She might as well go home.

That was when she realised she was not alone. Sarah didn't know who or what was in the woods with her, she wasn't sure she'd seen or heard anything, she simply knew. It might be a tramp or a deer or some neighbour's dog or an old male raccoon, but it was big and it was not far away and she didn't want to stay here any longer.

Hampered by bad going, poor visibility, and clingy wet garments, Sarah began to run. She ought to have known better. She hadn't gone a hundred feet before she tripped and skinned her knee on a rock. Worse than that, she broke the flashlight.

There was nothing she could do but get up and keep going, relying on instinct and memory to keep her on the path, praying she'd get to the car before anybody or anything got to her. The knee hurt a great deal and she could feel a warm stickiness trickling down into her boot, but she couldn't bother about that now. Once something grabbed her and she thought her heart was going to stop, but it was only a squirrel briar. She tore herself loose and fought her way on.

After an eternity, she could make out the great bulk of the house against the grey-black sky. Then the car wasn't too hard to find. She got in, locked the door, and began to shake. Then she began to scold. A grown-up, married woman going into a blind panic, thinking the bogeyman was after her simply because she got upset at having proved what she'd known all along. That brick meant no more now than it had before she came.

And no less. Sarah started the car with a jerk. The sore knee was making it hard for her to work the clutch and brake. She ought to fix it up from Alexander's first-aid kit before she tried to drive.

Later. Somewhere down the road, where there were lights and people. Fool or not, she wasn't going to sit here one more second. She began to swing out of the parking area before she realised the headlights weren't on. That was an easy way to commit suicide. Sarah flipped the switch, lighting the path from which she'd just emerged, catching a glint from something metallic, something tiny and square, with a tall, dark shape around it.

Something like the belt buckle on a man's raincoat. Perhaps she was not a total fool, after all.

CHAPTER
NINE

Sarah was fairly brave as a rule, and she'd dealt with trespassers before. She knew she ought to swing around and try to get a proper look at the man, but she just couldn't. Her only impulse was to get down that precipitous drive without cracking up the Studebaker.

She was probably alarmed over nothing. The man might

be an owl watcher out for a stroll. She and Alexander often went tramping in the rain, and these big estates were always declared open country once the summer people cleared out. He'd have to be an awfully dedicated outdoorsman to enjoy walking in this weather, though, and he must have come from some little distance.

To get this far, he'd have to come up the drive. For almost a century, the Kellings had been letting the underbrush grow up around the perimeter of their extensive property for the express purpose of discouraging sightseers and picnickers. By now, anybody would need a machete to hack a path through. The only alternative was to climb the long wooden ladder that came straight up the cliff face from the rocky beach some thirty feet below, and who'd attempt that in a citified raincoat on a night like this?

Sarah began to wonder about the car that had tagged her so persistently. Might it not be parked just up the road? The driver, knowing where she'd turned off, could easily have walked back and followed her slow progress up the bad path on foot, then tracked her to the Secret Garden by the light from her flashlight, though why he'd want to was a puzzle.

He might be one of those nuts who followed women, in which case she'd been fortunate to get away with nothing worse than a skinned knee, or a tramp looking for a place to sleep, or a burglar. If that was all, good hunting to him. There was nothing in the house worth stealing. With luck, he might set it afire and they'd be able to collect the insurance.

Whatever he was, she was not about to notify the police there was a man on the place. They'd know who she was, and they might report back to Alexander in Boston about the complaint his wife had lodged, which was the last thing she wanted. Her wisest course was to keep going.

That in itself was almost more than she could manage. Her knee was hurting worse every time she moved her leg. Her flesh was trying to crawl away from her sodden clothes. If only the heater didn't take so long to warm up! A wet oakleaf got stuck under the windshield wiper and was blocking her view at every sweep. She absolutely had to stop and get herself straightened out, but where? Not on this lonely road, not in the village where she and the Kellings' ridiculously out-of-date car were too well-known and too easily noticed now that the season was over. She'd have to stick it out till she got back on the highway.

Hating the honky-tonks that had encroached on the historic Newburyport Turnpike was part of the Kelling creed, but tonight Sarah would have given her back teeth for a neon sign with a cup of hot coffee under it. The rain was blotting out landmarks, making the familiar route a no-man's-land. The ride took on that eerie quality of timelessness she'd felt on the path. When the longed-for sign did appear, she was so disoriented she forgot to brake before she turned in. Fortunately the parking lot was almost empty. She managed to get the car under control by swinging around to the rear of the building before she went through the plate-glass windows.

Sweating and panting, Sarah switched on the overhead light, pulled up her skirt, and examined her damages. The flesh on her knee was puffed, already purple, crisscrossed with deep scratches that were still oozing blood. Dark red rivulets had dried on her skin. Her panty hose were in tatters and she decided bare legs would be less noticeable. She switched off the light and wiggled out of the clinging shreds of nylon. Even her underpants were damp, so she took them off, too, and held them out in the rain to get thoroughly wet so she could use them as a washcloth to swab off the blood.

The first-aid kit was a great help. Once she'd mopped up the mud and gore, she swabbed out her wounds with merthiolate, put on a large gauze pad to stop the bleeding, and strapped it in place with adhesive. Alexander had even included a little pair of blunt-nosed scissors to cut the tape. She'd never tease him about being the eternal Boy Scout again.

Putting on wet boots with no stockings was like stepping into a bucket of shucked clams, but that was the least of her problems. She combed her short hair, looked in the rear-view mirror to apply some lipstick and saw that her face was filthy, found a few clean inches of underpants and wiped it as best she could. She was not aiming to make herself attractive, just to avoid looking as if she'd lost a wrestling match with a gorilla. When she thought she'd got to a point where she was unlikely to attract particular notice, Sarah picked up the bag which felt oddly light now that she'd jettisoned the brick, and went into the restaurant.

She was lucky enough to find an empty booth well away from the windows, since the place was all but empty. A tired waitress in a bedraggled uniform slouched over to her table.

'What'll it be?'

'Black coffee, please, and a chicken sandwich.'

'No chicken. Tuna.'

Sarah and Alexander were boycotting tunafish on account of the porpoises, but she was too tired to stand on principle.

'Fine.'

'White bread?'

'I don't care.'

She did care. Sarah abominated that squishy, pallid travesty of honest food. It was just that she couldn't make the effort of saying so. She folded her hands on the clean paper place mat the waitress put in front of her, and sat looking at them, wondering why they were so dirty and whether she ought to go and wash them before she ate. She didn't notice the man who came in until he slid into the bench across from her.

'Hello, Mrs Kelling. Mind if I join you?'

He might as well have hit her over the head. Sarah was so stunned her mind went blank. He noticed.

'I'm Max Bittersohn. We met at the Lackridges'.'

'Yes, I—I know. I was just so surprised—'

'So was I. What brings you so far from home on a lousy night?'

She tried to force a laugh. It was a pitiable failure. 'Oh, I'm not far from home at all. We have a place at Ireson's Landing, and we're always running back and forth. I just had to—attend to something.'

'Where's your husband?'

Why did he sound so—was it angry? Scornful? Was he wondering what she'd been up to? Did he already know? Could Bittersohn possibly have been the man on the path?

He was wearing another plain dark suit tonight. It was perfectly dry, so he must have a better raincoat than she. There was a rack near the door with several wet garments on it, all looking about the same. Some had belts, some didn't. Why hadn't she been watching when he came in?

'Aren't you afraid someone will take your raincoat if you leave it over there?' she ventured.

The man shrugged. 'That's how I get all my raincoats.'

He had a smile that was surprisingly gentle and appealing in that rugged face, yet even while he smiled, his eyes stayed fixed on hers with a sad, thoughtful gaze, as though he somehow felt sorry for her. She must present a woebegone spectacle.

The waitress came back with Sarah's order and didn't seem at all surprised to find a man in the booth. 'Want something, mister?'

'Tea with lemon, if you have any.'

'Beverage without food is forty cents.'

'The hell it is. Okay, bring me a muffin or something.'

'Toasted English is all we got.'

'Great. Drink your coffee while it's hot, Mrs Kelling. You look as though you could use it.'

'Couldn't you pretend not to notice?'

She took a sip to steady herself. 'This was housecleaning day, and I am a bit frazzled around the edges. How is your book coming? You never did tell me how you happened to become involved with jewellery.'

'Oh, it's a long story,' he replied vaguely. 'This errand of yours must have been pretty urgent.'

'Not particularly.' Sarah had to set down the cup because her hands were shaking. 'My husband managed to pick up a bug of some kind, so I sent him to bed early. Then I got fidgety hanging around by myself, so I decided I might as well come along and get it over with. Alexander doesn't even know I'm out.'

She took a bite of her sandwich so that she wouldn't have to say any more. It was awfully difficult trying to act nonchalant with those oddly compassionate eyes fixed on her. Were they grey or blue?

Perhaps Bittersohn was feeling sorry for having frightened her and made her fall. If he had, he jolly well ought to be. With some food and a hot drink inside her, Sarah began to get her courage back.

'And what brings you to these parts, may I ask? It's an incredible coincidence, our bumping into one another like this, don't you think?'

'Not specially.'

The waitress came back with muffins and tea, and he busied himself fishing the teabag out of the sloppy mug. 'Once you've met a person, you seem to run into him every time you turn around. Lackridge tells me you're going to do some drawings for my book.'

'Does he? He hasn't told me yet. What is it I'm supposed to draw?'

'Details of settings, things like that.'

'It sounds rather dull.'

Sarah rubbed at her hands and lips with a paper napkin, and started to struggle back into her wet coat. 'Harry manages to get a good deal of unpaid labour out of the Kellings, one way and another.'

She was savagely pleased to see him flush.

'I don't intend to let any work you do for me go unpaid for. Look, Mrs Kelling, I'm on my way back to Boston and I assume you are, too. If you'll tell me where you park your car, I'll meet you there and walk you home.'

'That won't be necessary, thank you,' she said as airily as she could manage. 'My husband will meet me.'

'You just told me he's in bed with the flu and doesn't know you're out.'

'Did I? No, please.'

She snatched back the check he'd tried to pick up. 'Then I'll no doubt be seeing you again soon in some—unexpected place. Goodnight, Mr Bittersohn.'

It wasn't a bad exit line, but she realised at once that she was foolish to go so soon. She ought to have waited to see what style of raincoat the man was wearing, and she certainly should have visited the convenience before committing herself to another half-hour's driving. Getting back to Boston before he did wasn't going to accomplish anything.

If Bittersohn's meeting her like this was no more than a wild coincidence, he'd be likely to mention the fact to

Harry Lackridge, who'd tell Leila, who'd pass it on to Caroline and Alexander, who would insist on knowing what she'd been up to and why. God alone knew what might happen then.

If Bittersohn didn't say anything, she'd be forever wondering if he had some special reason to keep quiet, which would be lovely since there was absolutely no way she could get out of working with him. Now that Harry had decreed Sarah was to do those drawings, Sarah would deliver, or she'd never hear the end of it.

How could this meeting have been a coincidence? The most reasonable assumption was that Bittersohn had happened to notice Sarah heading for the garage, which wasn't far from the publishing house, and decided to find out where she was going by herself in such a downpour—but why? She'd met a number of men who assumed the young wife of an elderly husband must be looking for something she wasn't getting, but if he thought that, why follow her all the way to Ireson's Landing and back? Why not simply stop her and ask if she'd like to have a drink or go to a coffee house with him, right there on Charles Street? He could always use the excuse of wanting to discuss the artwork for his book.

For some reason, Mrs Wandelowski popped into Sarah's head. What was it the landlady's doctor had accused her of, wanting to get the dirt on some male relative so she could blackmail him into buying her a mink, which was the last thing on earth she'd ever want? Was the idea of being followed so ridiculous, after all?

Suppose, for instance, Max Bittersohn had seen Alexander Kelling's wife sneaking down the Hill alone. Wouldn't it be natural for him to think she might be slipping out to meet a lover? Might he not wonder who the man was, and think it might be to his advantage to find out? There again, why? Not to pressure Sarah into doing his piddling drawings for nothing, certainly, he'd been genuinely embarrassed about that. It would have to be something big.

The Kelling jewels were big. If Bittersohn was the expert he claimed to be, he must have a far better idea than the family did about what such a collection might be valued at in today's market. That ruby parure alone must be worth a small fortune. Whatever was she going to do with it when she got it? The mere thought of rubies gave her the horrors.

Maybe Bittersohn had some ideas about that. If he'd had any notion of coercing Caroline Kelling into letting him into that bank vault, he'd wasted an evening. Even if he'd caught Sarah in the midst of an orgy, Aunt Caroline would only laugh in his face and tell him to go peddle his findings wherever he liked. What did she care if people sneered and gossiped when she could neither see nor hear them? Should scandal cause a divorce, she'd get back her son's undivided attention, and that wouldn't break her heart.

The only way anyone could threaten Caroline Kelling would be through Alexander. If Bittersohn was the one who'd followed Sarah down the path this evening, he was now in a position to do that. He knew from the talk at the Lackridges' that Alexander had known Ruby Redd. He knew the vault had been bricked up. If he saw her take that brick from her handbag and compare it to the ones in the wall, he'd have to be an awful idiot not to draw the obvious inference, and he looked to be anything but that. He could have gone down to the wall after she left, found the brick where she'd dropped it, and made his own comparison. Perhaps he'd kept the brick.

What if he did? How could he prove she'd brought it from the vault? No picture was made of the barrier it was part of except her own sketch, and she'd destroyed that.

No, she hadn't. She'd torn it up and thrown away the pieces, which wasn't the same thing at all. What if he'd picked them up and pieced them together? Oh, why in God's name hadn't she buried them or rubbed them to pulp in the mud?

A car honked frantically. Sarah flinched and pulled back into her own lane. She'd better forget about Max Bittersohn for now and concentrate on getting home alive.

CHAPTER
TEN

She made it back to Charles Street more by luck than by skill. To her astonishment, the clock in the garage said it was only a little after ten. Around here, that was barely the shank of the evening. Her chance of meeting somebody else she knew was all too good. Sarah ducked into the corner grocery that never seemed to close, and spent her last dollar on a quart of milk and a loaf of bread.

That was an intelligent move. She'd hardly got out the door with her bundle, when she heard somebody calling her name.

'Mrs Kelling? Hi, Sarah, I thought that looked like you. I'm Bob Dee from Harry's office, in case you don't remember.'

'Of course I do,' said Sarah with what little cordiality she could muster. 'Isn't this a wretched night?'

'You can say that again. What brings you out?'

'I happened to remember we've run out of some things we'll need for breakfast, and my husband has a bug. Otherwise he'd be here getting soaked instead of me. Are you a Hillite, too?'

'Isn't everybody? I share a squalid pad with a couple of guys on Anderson Street. Any chance of luring you up for a drink?'

'Not tonight, I'm afraid. I must get home in case my husband wakes up. He'd have fits if he knew I'm out alone at this hour.'

'Then I'll walk you back.'

Dee took the wet paper bag from her and fell into step. 'This saves me a phone call. We were wondering if you'd be willing to do some artwork for us. Harry says you're quite an artist.'

'How kind of him,' Sarah replied guardedly. 'What's your project?'

'Remember that author who was with us Monday night, the guy who mistook you for your husband's daughter, as who wouldn't?'

'The near-sighted Mr Bittersohn.' Did Dee think he was paying her a compliment? 'What about him?'

'This book of his is giving us a few problems. He's got a lot of photographs showing clasps and settings and stuff in close-up that he wants to use. We think some of your nice little line sketches would be more appealing.'

'Also cheaper to reproduce,' Sarah replied. 'Harry's idea is to make him pay for extra artwork while reducing your own production costs, is that it?'

Dee thought that was pretty funny. 'Right on! Why not? Bittersohn's loaded and God knows we're not. We honestly do think, though, that drawings would add visual interest, and it's a chance for you to pick up some extra cash. I don't know if that's any consideration for you, living on the opposite side of the Hill from us peasants.'

'Anybody who lives around here needs all the spare cash he can get, I assure you.'

Sarah was by no means averse to making money, but she did wonder how valuable her contribution would be in proportion to what Bittersohn might hope to realise out of his book. This sort of thing seldom made the best-seller list, it was more apt to wind up on the remaindered tables at bookstores.

Whose side was she on, anyway? A little while ago, she'd been thinking Bittersohn might be a blackmailer, now she was seeing him as the innocent pawn in one Harry Lackridge's well-known Yankee horse trades. She was not going to turn the job down flat. This would be a welcome task to keep her occupied over the winter while Alexander was squiring his mother to teas and committee meetings. Still, she didn't like being used, and it was high time Harry found that out.

'I think what we'd better do,' she said, 'is sit down with Mr Bittersohn and make a list of everything I'm suppposed to do and how much it would cost. Then he can make up his own mind whether or not he wants to spend that much extra money.'

'Harry usually prefers to make his own arrangements,' the young assistant demurred.

'I know he does.'

Sarah had a shrewd suspicion that what Harry preferred was to charge the author about three times what he paid the artist. 'However, I'd rather handle it my way. If you care to work on that basis, let me know and I'll meet with you and Mr Bittersohn whenever it's convenient. Thanks for seeing me home. I shan't ask you in now, but perhaps you'd like to come another time?'

'That would be great.' Dee didn't sound altogether sure it would. 'Then I'll tell Harry what you said, and get back to you later.'

'Do that. Goodnight.'

Sarah took back her soggy bundle and let herself into the house. She kicked off her boots, tiptoed out to the kitchen in her bare feet, got rid of her wet coat and the groceries. Then she sneaked up the back stairs and put the keys back on Alexander's dresser. He was still sleeping, fortunately.

At last she was free to shut herself in the bathroom and take stock of her damages. It was a good thing she hadn't been insane enough to visit Bob Dee's pad. What would he have thought if he'd seen her under a light, barelegged, battered, looking like a corpse washed up by the tide? Maybe that offer of Bittersohn's to see her home had been prompted simply by the visual evidence that she wasn't safe to be out alone.

She wondered what the author would say when next they met, assuming they ever did. Harry might not give her the chance of doing Bittersohn's drawings when he found out she wasn't going to let him manage the business to suit his own notions. Harry could be awfully petty sometimes. No matter, she had graver things to worry about.

However, she'd done all the worrying she was going to do tonight. Sarah got herself washed and into bed, read two pages of that never-failing soporific, *The Philosophy of William James*, and knew no more until she heard her husband in the bathroom at seven o'clock the next morning.

'Alexander, how do you feel?' she called out.

When he didn't answer, she got up and barged into the room. He was standing in front of the open medicine cabinet, staring blankly at the crowded shelves.

'What are you looking for?' she asked, more sharply than she'd meant to.

He turned his head in her direction, but she was not at all sure he saw her.

'What is it, Alexander? Can I get you something?'

He only shook his head. She took him by the arm.

'You're going straight back to bed, and stay there.'

That roused him a little. 'But Mother will be—'

'No, she won't. This is her morning for the hairdresser, and Edith will go with her as she always does.'

'Oh, yes. I forgot.' He managed something like a smile. 'You're getting very bossy, Sadiebelle.'

'You haven't seen anything yet. Here, put your feet up.'

She got him back into bed and settled among the pillows. 'Now lie still and behave yourself. I'm going to fix you an eggnog.'

When she brought back the egg drink, he was asleep again. Sarah left the glass on his night stand and went to give Aunt Caroline a note explaining that Alexander wouldn't be down.

Mrs Kelling flicked her fingertips over the Braille message, said, 'Humph,' and ate her breakfast without saying a word to her daughter-in-law. After that, she and Edith set out for the beauty shop she'd patronised ever since she came to the Hill as a bride. She was due for a permanent luckily, so they'd be gone for hours. Edith was carrying a Braille book for her mistress and no doubt looking forward to catching up on the movie magazines herself. The proprietress, who thought Mrs Kelling was wonderful, would fetch coffee and sandwiches and a good time would be had by all.

After last night's soaking, Sarah's own hair was in desperate need of attention. The budget wouldn't run to two hairdressing appointments, so she gave herself a shampoo. While she was drying, she busied herself making some minor alterations to a thin silk dress she intended to wear to the tea, because Anora was sure to have the fireplace roaring and the thermostat set at eighty-five.

The dress was one she could dimly recall her own mother wearing when Sarah was a little girl. No doubt some of the other guests would remember it, too, but she didn't care. Nobody in that crowd was going to fault a woman for wearing what she had instead of squandering money on the paltry excuse of being in style.

Nevertheless, as soon as she could get her hands on some

ready cash, this and all the other relics were going straight to the Bargain Box and she to Hurwich Brothers for a sumptuous wardrobe that had never known a mothball. How easy it was to beguile one's mind with trifles. Sarah bit off her thread and went to check on Alexander once more.

He must have waked long enough to drink his eggnog, since the tumbler was empty and she could not believe he'd pour good food down the bathroom sink. This frugality of his had alternately amused and exasperated her, now she was beginning to wonder if there could be something pathological about it.

His father, Uncle Gilbert, had been as rich as any of the Kellings, and that was saying a good deal. To be sure, Aunt Caroline's medical bills must have been enormous, money wasn't worth what it used to be, and keeping up the two places was getting more expensive every year, even though they ran them both on cheeseparings. Nevertheless, there ought to be a good deal left of Uncle Gilbert's fortune besides the real estate and the jewellery.

In spite of that, ever since they had been married, Sarah, her husband, and his mother had all been living on the interest from Sarah's own inheritance which was a relative pittance by family standards. Sarah knew they had, because Alexander insisted on presenting her annually with an itemised account showing what she'd earned in interest, what they'd spent, and precisely how much was left in the trust fund.

She'd never fully understood why they lived on her money instead of his. She'd assumed it was proper because Alexander was her legal guardian under the terms of her father's will, and he wouldn't do this if it were not in her interest. Besides, they were man and wife, so it was only right to share. But was it right? Ought she to have recognised this miserly streak as a sympton of some deep disturbance? Ought she to be realising this minute that her husband was having some kind of mental breakdown? Was it possible he'd had one before, and that Ruby Redd was what happened the other time?

No, it was not possible. Sarah went down to the kitchen and boiled herself an egg for lunch, put on her coat and walked twice around the Public Garden at a furious pace, came back and found Alexander up and dressed, looking like a marble effigy but clearly intending to go to Anora's tea.

'Mother's back,' he said. 'She's upstairs resting.'

'Why aren't you?' Sarah retorted.

'My dear, I slept all morning. I must go and bring the car around.'

'No, you mustn't. I'll do it as soon as I change. I have to run down to Clough and Shackley's, anyway. By the way,' Sarah added, trying to sound casual, 'could you give me a couple of dollars? I have to get some things.'

This was the family euphemism for articles of feminine hygiene and the one request Alexander was sure to meet without question. He handed over five dollars, as she'd known he would. Now she could put gas in the car before he had a chance to observe that the gauge was down. Goody for her. She'd rather have a flaming row than this grey-faced apathy any day.

'I'll fix you a bite before I go upstairs,' she said.

'Please don't bother.' He sat back in his father's chair and closed his eyes.

Sarah didn't press the issue. There would be plenty to eat at Anora's, and he'd hear nagging enough from his mother on the way. She got herself ready and went on her errand. When she got back with the Studebaker, Alexander and his mother were waiting in the library.

Caroline could have passed today for the younger of the two. Her hair was magnificently coiffed, she had on a lovely violet-coloured frock her sister, Marguerite, had picked out for her birthday. Her face had been delicately made up by the hairdresser, her lips touched with the pale rose lipstick she always favoured. She looked exactly like a beautiful lady going to a party with every intention of enjoying herself, probably because she knew Edgar Merton would be there, too.

Edgar Merton was what Alexander would turn into if he lived another twenty years: a gentleman of the old school, handsome, quietly distinguished, exquisitely courteous, always impeccably dressed in a style that had never varied during the past fifty years. It was generally supposed that he cherished a lifetime's adoration of Caroline Kelling, although he had never told anybody so and never would so long as his wife was alive.

Alice Merton was in a rest home now, practically a vegetable according to last report, and Edgar had a little freedom at last. It was hardly thinkable that he'd care to saddle himself with another such responsibility as Caroline after having had to cater to Alice all these years. Still, he played backgammon with her three or four times a week, and when he tried to converse with her in sign language, Caroline did not pull her hand away and demand that Leila or Alexander do the translating.

The Kellings were putting their coats on when Leila called in a fury to say that Harry had taken her car and gone off God knew where till God knew when without saying a word as usual, and could they give her a lift to Anora's?

'Of course,' Sarah told her. 'We'll pick you up in about three minutes.'

That was a stroke of luck. Leila could keep Caroline amused and let Alexander rest. Sarah didn't ask if he'd prefer to drive now that his mother had someone to talk with, and he didn't offer. It seemed about all he could manage to get out and open the door for Leila, who piled in beside Caroline and went on airing her grievance.

'I ought to be used to it by now, I suppose. I've put up with him for twenty-three years, don't ask me why. Just picks up his heels and goes, comes back when he feels like it. Probably got a woman somewhere. What do you think, Caro?'

Caroline thought the idea was uproarious. She was in tearing spirits this afternoon. Could there be a little more going on between her and Edgar than she was letting anybody know? What absolute heaven it would be if Edgar should inherit Alice's fortune and take Aunt Caroline off their hands! Even now they'd make a handsome couple, although he was almost a full head shorter than she.

Sarah murmured something to that effect to her husband, but he didn't seem to take it in. He was so remarkably silent the whole way that at last even Leila noticed.

'What's eating you, Alex? I've never seen you so mopey.'

'He has a bug,' said Sarah. 'I tried to make him stay in

bed, but he came along to infect everybody, thus proving
that he's the noblest Roman of them all. Aren't you,
darling?'

'No, my dear. Where did you say Harry went, Leila?'

'Alex, you're getting deafer than your mother. I've been
telling you for the past fifteen minutes that I haven't the
foggiest idea. Harry goes where he pleases. At least I
assume he pleases, because he keeps going. Which
reminded me, Caroline. I've decided I'd better ride along
with the delegation to Washington next week. Somebody's
got to be around to light a fire under those halfwits or we'll
never get anywhere.'

'Better tie a note to Harry's toothbrush this time,' Sarah
put in slyly. 'Speaking of not knowing who's where, it
seems to me we've heard a good deal from him on that
score. Remember the time you forgot to tell him you'd be in
California for three weeks, and he took it into his head
you'd been kidnapped?'

'Oh, that.' Leila shrugged and kept on talking. Sarah
couldn't get another word in, and Alexander didn't even
try. Once they got to Anora's, he made a beeline for the
inglenook.

Sarah could hardly believe what she was seeing. Nobody
ever went to the inglenook of his own free will. For one
thing, it was blistering hot next to the open fire. For
another, that was where old George Protheroe sat like a
bloated spider, never moving from his place but always
alert to net any victim who ventured too near, and tell him
the story about the bear.

Nobody had ever heard the end of George's bear story.
He never got that far. He rambled, lost track, went back
and repeated, lapsed into boozy mumblings but would
magically revive and bellow, 'Wait, I'm not done yet,' if his
exasperated prey tried to tiptoe away. Those who felt
duty-bound to pay their respects to their host were wont to
go in groups so that George couldn't fasten on a particular
target. Even Alexander, long-suffering slave to duty that
he was, never went to the inglenook as a rule without
arranging with Sarah to call him away on urgent business
after a decent interval.

From force of habit, Sarah went once or twice to see if

her husband wanted rescuing, but he appeared content to sit baking by the red-hot logs, letting the old man's ramblings wash over him unheard. She brought him a large whisky and a plate of sandwiches, and left him to the bear.

Caroline was having a gorgeous time with Edgar at the backgammon table. Leila was holding forth about the perfidy of some elected official, always a popular topic with this group. Sarah ducked out of the party and went to visit the cook, who'd been her special friend since milk-and-cookie days and had once owned an obese tortoiseshell cat named Percival. She'd much rather reminisce about Percival than have to describe Ruby Redd's teeth one more time.

She stayed with Cook as long as she dared. When she went back to the drawing room, Alexander and George were both asleep in the inglenook, Leila still pontificating, and Aunt Caroline beating the pants off Edgar Merton, who seemed content to have it so. He showed signs of wanting Sarah's attention, so she walked over to the game table.

'I was wondering,' he said, 'if I might ask Caroline to dine with me at the Harvard Club after we leave here. You and Alex, too, of course.'

'Edgar, how sweet,' she replied. 'I'm sure Aunt Caroline would adore to. I'm afraid Alexander and I couldn't. He's not feeling well, and I was just thinking I must chase him home to bed. Why don't you take Leila Lackridge if you're nervous about managing by yourself? She's at loose ends tonight because Harry had to go off on business, and you know how good she is with Aunt Caroline.'

'Yes, I know.'

Edgar eyed the chattering Leila with no particular favour, but must have decided he wasn't up to coping with the blind woman's needs alone. 'I'll do that, then. Too bad about Alex. I'd been thinking he wasn't quite himself today. Perhaps you and he might come another time?'

'That would be lovely. Shall I tell Leila while you finish your game?'

'Would you?'

Sarah got the dinner party organised, then went to the inglenook and unobtrusively shook her husband awake.

'Alexander, we've got to go.'

He looked up at her, still in a daze. 'Is Mother ready?'

'She's not going home with us. Edgar Merton's inviting her and Leila to the Harvard Club for dinner.'

'Oh.'

He didn't look surprised or pleased, or anything but exhausted. Sarah steered him across the room to take leave of his mother and his hostess, got him his coat, and led him out to the car. On the way home he spoke not one word.

She drove up to the house, had to double-park in the narrow street, drawing outraged yells and horn blasts, long enough to get him into the front hall. When she came back from taking the car to the garage, he was still slumped in one of the carved rosewood chairs that flanked the doorway. He hadn't even unbuttoned his overcoat.

CHAPTER
ELEVEN

'I'm going to call the doctor,' said Sarah.

'No, don't.'

Alexander struggled to his feet. 'I'm feeling much better. Truly.'

'I don't believe you,' she sighed, 'but I don't suppose he'd come anyway. Give me that coat, and go into the library. You look totally worn out.'

'Perhaps I wasn't quite up to George's bear story,' he admitted with a ghastly attempt at a smile. 'Where's Mother?'

'I told you she'd gone to dinner with Edgar and Leila. Don't you remember?'

She wasn't sure he understood even now. He stumbled into the next room and collapsed into his father's armchair as he'd done the night before. Sarah went after him and made up the fire. It occurred to her that he'd left the sandwiches untouched at Anora's, which meant he'd had nothing in his stomach all day but an eggnog and two stiff whiskies. Perhaps he was simply a little bit drunk. It would be a comfort to think so. She poked a few more bits of kindling into the fire and went to fix him a snack.

She found Edith in the kitchen, doing nothing in particular.

'I was wondering what you expect me to do about dinner,' the old retainer said with an air of being greatly put-upon.

'Nothing,' Sarah replied. 'Mrs Kelling has gone out with friends. Mr Alexander and I will have something on a tray. You fix what you want for yourself.'

'What, for instance?'

'I don't care. If you can't find anything in the fridge that suits you, go out to a restaurant.'

'Costs a fortune.'

Sarah didn't bother to reply. Edith went on grumbling.

'Seems to me there's been mighty few decent meals cooked in this house lately.'

'If the cooking were left to you, I daresay there would be even fewer,' Sarah replied. 'Would you mind standing away from the stove so I can get at it?'

'I'm not putting up with insults! I'm going straight in there and talk to Mr Alex.'

'You're doing nothing of the kind. He's not well, and I won't have him bothered with your nonsense. I mean it, Edith.'

Edith looked into Sarah's face and must have decided she did mean it. She flounced off down the basement stairs. Sarah filled the teapot, heated soup, made toast with melted cheese on it, and carried the tray into the library.

'I want you to eat every bite of this.'

Her husband didn't move, so she filled the soup spoon and held it to his lips. Automatically he swallowed a mouthful or two, then began to feed himself. By the time he'd emptied the cup, he did look a trifle more alive.

'Feeling better?' Sarah asked.

'Yes, my dear. You're being very patient with the old man.'

'Why shouldn't I? You've always been an angel to me.'

'I wish that were true. Though God knows I've tried!'

The sudden agony in his voice was like a blow in her face. Sarah sat on the arm of his chair and took his head in her arms.

'Has it been that desperate a struggle?'

Alexander set down his teacup with fumbling care, and closed his eyes. 'Sarah, I'm afraid I can't keep it up any longer.'

'What do you mean? Do you want a divorce?'

'A divorce?' Her question jerked him out of his lethargy. 'Good God, no! Whatever put that into your head?'

'What you just said.'

'I don't know what I said. I only know that I've reached the end of my tether. One does, sooner or later, I suppose.'

'But why now? It's something to do with—what we found in the vault, isn't it?'

His hands came up to close over her arms in a spasmodic grip but he made no answer. She had to keep on talking.

'Alexander, I know about the wall. I made a sketch of it while they were off getting tools to tear it down. I thought you'd be interested to see what it looked like.'

He began to shudder and so did she, but she couldn't stop now.

'When they carted away the bricks, one got left behind. Dolph started waving it around and fussing, so I said I'd get rid of it. I stuck it into that big shoulder bag of mine, meaning to dump it somewhere on the way, but forgot. I was in a rush because I was so late getting home. Do you remember that?'

'Yes. I was annoyed. It seems so foolish now.'

'You may also recall that after we got home from the Lackridges', I went to make you some milk toast because you hadn't eaten and looked so ill. I know now that I gave you a dreadful shock by not telling you about the vault before we went. I truly didn't mean—'

'I know, Sarah. How did you—find out?'

'Well, as I started to say, I went out to the kitchen and that photograph you took of the Secret Garden happened to catch my eye. Your mother's often told how she and you worked out the pattern yourselves, and the bricks are an unusual size and colour. It seemed too much of a coincidence. Last night, after you went to bed, I drove out to Ireson's Landing with my sketch and the brick, and compared them. I know it was a dreadful thing to do, but I had to know. You can understand that, surely?'

'Yes, my dear, I understand. Is there any more tea?'

She filled his cup, and he drank.

'In a way, I'm relieved that you found out for yourself. I've been wondering how I could ever tell you. I thought it would be the end of everything, but you're still here. Why, Sarah?'

'Because I love you, silly! I won't say I'm exactly happy about—'

'Sarah, you can't think I had anything to do with Ruby's being killed? I was crazy about her!'

The corners of Alexander Kelling's exquisite mouth curved in a sweet, tragic half smile. 'Does it disgust you to learn that your stuffy old crock of a husband once made a fool of himself over a striptease dancer?'

'No, I think it's rather—touching. You must have been awfully young.'

'Young and brainless. If I'd had sense enough to keep away from things I didn't know how to handle, Ruby might still be alive. Do you suppose I could have a little whisky?'

'Of course, darling.'

Sarah took her time getting the drink, aware of his need to be alone for a few minutes with whatever he was seeing in the firelight. She went out to the kitchen to fetch ice and make sure Edith wasn't within listening distance. The maid had evidently fixed herself a strange supper of leftovers, baked beans, and poached eggs, leaving the tin, the shells, and several dirty pans in the sink as a gesture of defiance. They needn't worry about her coming up again before Aunt Caroline was due home. It was an oddly peaceful moment.

Alexander would tell her when he was ready. She was in no special hurry to hear the story, she thought she could almost tell it herself. Another lover, jealous of Alexander's incredible beauty as all men must be, threatening the dancer, 'If you don't stay away from that college boy, I'll kill you.' The kind of woman who'd get her teeth set with rubies wouldn't care much for being bossed around.

Tim O'Ghee had called Ruby Redd the meanest woman he ever knew. Mean enough to play off one lover against another, no doubt, not believing the jealous one had nerve enough to carry out his threat until it happened. Alexander would have helped to hide the body not out of fear but because he'd feel responsible for having been the cause of the fatal quarrel.

Poor Alexander! No wonder he'd shied away from women for so many years before marrying his eighteen-year-old cousin. No wonder he was still not able to function as a normal husband. Coming, as this must have done, so soon after his father's death and his mother's tragedy, it was a wonder Ruby's murder hadn't sent him straight over the edge. Then to keep it bottled up inside him all these years—she added an extra dollop to the drink and carried it back to the library.

'I made sure Edith hasn't got her ear glued to the keyhole,' she explained. 'She's downstairs listening to some idiotic programme, so we're safe for a while. Now would you like to tell me? You'll feel better once it's out of your system.'

'Are you sure you want to know, my dear?'

'Yes, I'm perfectly sure. You have to remember, Alexander, that this is a lot easier for me than it is for you because it happened years before I was born. I'm not personally involved, you see.'

'I wish that were true.'

'What do you mean?'

'I—I'm finding this extremely hard, Sarah.'

'I know you are, darling. Why don't you simply begin talking? Start with something easy. How did you happen to meet Ruby Redd?'

'Oh, a bunch of us from Lowell House got into the habit of catching the show at the Old Howard on Saturday nights, then doing the Scollay Square bars. We thought we were seeing life. God!'

'Go on,' Sarah prodded.

'Well, needless to say, those teeth of Ruby's captured our puerile fancies, and we started a sort of fan club. Rubies—crimson for Harvard—that sort of nonsense. There was a certain—carnivorous fascination about them. And, of course, Ruby was a striking creature altogether; vibrant, flamboyant, totally different from anyone I'd ever known. I grew up in a somewhat bloodless atmosphere, as I daresay you realise. Father was an austere sort of man. I suppose he'd learned to keep his emotions under control because of his heart trouble. Mother was never demonstrative, either.'

'That's true enough.'

In all the years she'd known Aunt Caroline, Sarah could not recall her making one spontaneous gesture of affection towards the son who'd sacrificed his life to her needs. It wasn't hard to see why a naturally loving youngster like Alexander would be drawn towards any woman who promised even a spurious warmth.

'We were all climbing the walls one night with excitement when Ruby came into Danny Rate's Pub after the show. We found that was her regular hangout, so it became ours, too. As I recall, it was Harry who first got up nerve enough to approach her, but she soon took a fancy to me, for some reason. Needless to say, I was pretty cocky at that. I haunted Danny Rate's until Ruby invited me to her dressing room. After that, one thing led to another. I shan't bore you with the details. It didn't last long, in any event.'

He shook his head and gulped down about a third of his drink. 'I came home one night and found her dead in the front hall.'

'Home? You don't mean here?'

'Yes, my dear. On the floor in front of that marble-topped console, with her red satin skirt spread out around her like a great pool of blood, and the back of her head—'

He got his voice under control after a while, and struggled on. 'I don't know how long she'd been there. She was cold when I touched her. I don't know why I touched her. I suppose I thought there might be something I could do.'

'But how did she get here?'

'I have no idea. I wouldn't have thought she'd even know where I lived. I stayed in the dorms, you know, my freshman and sophomore years. Mother still had her vision then, and we were trying to live normal lives. I did come home a good deal more than I might have if Father was still alive, but I wasn't quite besotted enough to think Ruby was the sort of girl one brings home to Mother. All I can tell you is that she was lying there, and it was clear that she'd been murdered.'

'Are you sure? Couldn't she have slipped and cracked her head against the edge of the console?'

'I don't see how. She was lying on her face, and it was obvious she'd been struck from behind.'

'By whom?'

He shrugged. 'Mother, of course.'

'Alexander, you can't be serious! Aunt Caroline wouldn't kill anybody.'

'She killed Father.'

'But that's crazy! Uncle Gilbert died of heart failure because he forgot his medicine. Your mother almost lost her own life trying to save him.'

'Father didn't forget his medicine. Mother emptied the bottle overboard.'

'How can you know?'

'I saw her. She thought she was alone on deck. We were becalmed in a fog, as you've heard. That part of the story is true enough. Father was resting in the saloon, and I was supposed to be in the galley fixing lunch. I couldn't find something or other, so I poked my head up through the hatch to ask Mother where she'd stowed it. When I saw what she was doing, I pulled back fast.'

'You actually saw her do that?'

'Oh, yes. She was only a couple of feet away from me. I couldn't believe it at first, I tried to tell myself it was some trick of the fog. But then she came below and a bit later she started fussing at Father for having been so careless as to bring an almost empty bottle instead of a full one. He said it was full, so then she said he mustn't have got the cap on tight. They had quite a row over it, which of course wasn't supposed to happen. Father started getting short of breath and having chest pains. It was obvious we'd have to put in to shore, which we couldn't do because there was no wind.

'I said I'd row ashore, but Mother was already in her bathing suit insiting she could swim in faster than I could row, and get the harbour master to bring out the medicine in his motorboat. She'd happened to bash in the bow of our dinghy that same morning on a rock, which struck me at the time as a strange thing for Mother to do. She was never careless as a rule. We'd left the dinghy to be mended and were making do with a war surplus flotation raft that was designed for survival rather than easy handling.

'We argued a bit, but it was obvious she could do the swim in much less time than I could paddle that cranky raft to shore. It was also true that I could handle the *Caroline* better than she if the wind came up. A squall was unlikely under those conditions, and I fully expected Mother'd be able to swim the distance easily in a dead calm. She really was a marvellous distance swimmer—I'd raced her in the dinghy and lost more than once. You see, it made beautiful sense at the time, and there was no use arguing with Mother anyway.

'But she hadn't been gone long when a squall did come up. I had all I could do to keep the *Caroline* afloat. Father tried to help, but collapsed almost at once. By the time I'd got the boat under control, there wasn't much I could do but heave to and watch him die. I don't know whether he realised what she'd done. He never said anything, just—suffered.

'Once I knew he was dead, I thought I'd better try to find Mother. I circled for a while, but we'd been blown off course and I couldn't pick up a landfall. I hadn't the faintest idea where I was, much less where she might be. As it turned out, she'd got to shore some time before I did. They had her in the hospital. She'd taken such a beating from the squall that I—I couldn't say anything.'

'And you've never told her that you know?'

'No, never. What was the use? She's been punished enough.'

'And you've been punished a great deal more than enough.'

There was another long silence, that Sarah finally broke.

'Alexander, are you absolutely certain it was your mother who killed Ruby Redd?'

'Who else could have done it?'

'Mightn't she have been followed here by a jealous boy friend? Ruby seems to have been a type who'd attract violence. But Aunt Caroline is not a violent woman, she's a conniver. I can see her doing what she did to your father after she'd checked out the tides and weather, cracked up the dinghy on purpose, and goaded your father into an argument so that he'd need his medication even more urgently than usual. That's how she operates. All right, she miscalculated, got caught in a squall and suffered terrible consequences, but she did achieve what she'd set out to do. She got rid of Uncle Gilbert, and she came out of it a heroine. If by any chance your father had survived, she'd still be a heroine, and she'd be in a perfect position to try again because nobody would believe she'd want to kill the man she fought so hard to save. You yourself might have wound up thinking you didn't really see her dump out the medicine, mightn't you?'

'Perhaps. Who knows?'

'Well, one thing I know is that whacking somebody over the head on a sudden impulse in her own front hall is just not something Aunt Caroline would be apt to do. Can't you see my point?'

'Yes, my dear. You want to convince me that some outsider came here with Ruby, fractured her skull in a quarrel and ran off leaving her dead, perhaps in the hope I'd be blamed for her death because I'd been seeing her.'

'Why is that so impossible?'

'For one thing, if he was jealous of my going around with Ruby, why didn't he attack me instead of her? He could have found me easily enough at Danny's or the theatre. For another, if he was in this house, how did he get out? The night latch was on when I came. I distinctly recall having to use both my keys. As you know, that extra lock has to be worked with a key both inside and out. When he had it put on, Father got three keys cut, one for himself, one for Mother, and one for me. His is the one you're using now.'

'What about Edith?'

'Servants didn't use the front door in Father's day. They came and went by the basement, not without permission. That was another point, you see. We still had a cook then. She and Edith were off on some overnight excursion, for which Mother had given them the tickets as a surprise. She'd never done such a thing before or since.'

'Oh.'

'Lastly, Mother had a plan to dispose of the body all figured out before I got there. I can see her now. I was kneeling on the floor beside Ruby's body, trying to find a pulse although I knew she must be dead, when Mother came in from the back hall. She had on her black coat and hat. She said to me, "Alex, I know what's happened and I don't care to discuss it. Do exactly as I say. Don't stop to argue because I can't hear you anyway."'

'Was she implying that you'd killed Ruby? How could she have the nerve?'

'She accused Father of forgetting his own medicine, didn't she? In any event, I was too shocked to do anything but obey. I'm not trying to excuse myself, Sarah. I acted like a fool and a coward. I had just enough wits about me to realise what a spot I was in. All my friends knew about my affair with Ruby. So did the crowd at Danny's and the girls Ruby worked with and God knows who else. Don't ask me how Mother found out.'

'Maybe Uncle Jem told her,' Sarah suggested, 'not to be malicious but because he'd think it amusing that you were turning into a stagedoor Johnny.'

'No doubt a lot of people thought it was funny, and there's always someone ready to spread gossip. Mother could lip read after a fashion then, and people used to write her notes on a pad she always carried. Anyway, there it was. I suppose Ruby might have dropped in for a friendly chat about being bought off, and Mother lost her temper, but considering Mother's general *modus operandi*, as you so wisely pointed out, and the fact that she'd got the servants out of the house, I'm inclined to believe she'd planned everything in advance.

'She knew her eyesight was going. Once she was blind as well as deaf, she'd need me to take care of her. I don't suppose you or I could possibly begin to comprehend the anger and frustration she must have been suffering then. Finding out that I was being lured away from her by the kind of woman she'd consider hardly fit to live in any case might have been just one blow too many.'

'I can understand that,' said Sarah. 'It would be hard to judge her actions by rational standards.'

'Oh, she was rational enough, though she might not have been altogether sane. She'd got hold of the key to that old family vault and informed me that was where we'd hide the body. I tried to tell her we could never do it without being seen, but she wouldn't pay any attention, and I realised she meant exactly what she said about not arguing. I had my choice of calling the police and perhaps landing us both on Death Row, or taking the desperate chance that her scheme might work.'

'But how could it? How did you ever manage without being caught?'

'The reason I went home in the first place was that I'd been to a party here on the Hill and it was too late to go back to the dorm. It was about two o'clock Sunday morning. The weather was nasty, pitch-dark with a cold drizzle. Nobody was on the street downtown. We were both wearing black clothes. We pulled our collars up around our faces and carried Ruby wrapped in an old black tarpaulin that used to be kept in the cellar for hauling coal. When we got to the cemetery, we hung the tarpaulin over a low branch that used to grow right over the vault, making a sort of tent that we could work inside of. From even a few feet away, the black canvas simply melted into the shadows.'

'That's incredible!'

'I know, but it worked. We had one of those little pencil flashlights with us. Mother shielded the lock with her coat and I got the vault open. Then we shoved Ruby in as best we could—she'd begun to stiffen by then—and walled up the vault. Mother had that all reasoned out. It was just after the family had been through that historical site business, and she was afraid some city official would take a notion to inspect the vault. She claimed that if a wall was there, they wouldn't have the right to tear it down without permission, which we'd refuse to give. I don't know if we'd have got away with it.'

'But you did, for thirty years.'

'Yes, Sarah. Sometimes I even managed not to think about it for weeks on end. Then something would bring it to mind and it would be every bit as ghastly as before.'

'Poor darling! You must have been terrified while you were in that tent.'

'I was, but Mother was perfectly cool. She stayed there most of the time by herself, laying the wall by touch while I ran back and forth through the alleyways fetching armloads of bricks under my coat. We'd brought the leftovers up from Ireson's, thinking we'd do something or other with them here, I forget what. As to why she laid such a fancy pattern, we'd been working on the Secret Garden wall for so long that I suppose she instinctively followed the method she knew best. The opening isn't very large, as you know, and the whole job took only an hour or so, but I think I must have aged ten years before we got that tarpaulin back in the cellar.'

'Did you ever talk about it at all?'

'Not one word. The closest we ever came was some years later when Mother said something about building another wall at the summer place, and I said I'd rather not. Naturally I had to endure a good deal of needling from the crowd about being ditched by my flashy girl friend. When Ruby disappeared so abruptly, the general assumption was that she'd run off with some more interesting man. I think the worst of all was having to show my face at Danny Rate's the following night and act surprised that Ruby wasn't around.'

'Oh, Alexander!' Sarah rubbed her cheek against his hand. 'It's a wonder you didn't go clean out of your mind.'

'Perhaps I did. I don't know, Sarah. I don't think I've ever felt quite real since then. I realised at the time we were married how bitterly unfair it was to saddle you with half a husband, but what else could I do?'

'What do you mean?' she cried. 'Alexander, why did you marry me?'

He sighed, like an embarrassed parent faced with having to explain the facts of life. 'I've always known you'd ask me that some day. If you want the unvarnished truth, I married you because Mother forced me to.'

'No! You couldn't!'

'My darling, please don't look at me like that. Let me at least tell you how it happened.'

Sarah wet her stiff lips. 'Go ahead.'

'It was the money,' he began. 'Father had left Mother as executor of the estate, which was a very large one. She should have more than plenty to last her lifetime, but she has nothing. Don't ask me what she did with it. I haven't the faintest idea. All I know is that within ten years' time after she took over the handling of the estate, we began to be hard up. I tried to get her to explain why, but she wouldn't. I begged her to unload this white elephant of a house and some of the land at Ireson's Landing. She refused. I offered to sell some of the family jewels. She said they were hers for her lifetime and wouldn't let me so much as look at them. The box was and still is in her name, and I'd have to get a court order to open it, which I've never been able to bring myself to do. Instead, I've been trying for twenty years to make her see reason, and you know how far I've got.'

He wiped his forehead. 'Then Walter made that appalling will appointing me your trustee and, like a fool, I told her. You know the terms. I'm to give you whatever allowance I see fit out of the interest until your twenty-seventh birthday, when the principal reverts to you. If you should die before assuming control of your estate, everything comes to me. It was a hideous position to be put in. I begged Walter to choose somebody else, but he said I cared more about you than any of the others, and God knows that's true enough. At least having to look after you gave me an incentive to stay alive a while longer. I'd been about ready to call it quits.'

'You mustn't say that!'

'Sarah, please grant me the luxury of being totally honest for once in my life.'

'I'm sorry, Alexander. Go on.'

'Well, as soon as she heard what Walter had done, Mother decided you and I should marry so that we could all three live off your income. I wouldn't hear of it, not because I didn't want you, but because I felt you deserved a better fate than a man twice your age, saddled with a hideous burden of guilt and responsibility, who couldn't even support you. Furthermore, Walter was still hale and hearty and not all that much older than I. I told Mother her plan was out of the question, there wasn't going to be any income in the first place because Walter would no doubt outlive me. With that, she said I'd better marry you anyway and make your father give us an allowance, or something would happen to Walter.'

He took out his handkerchief and wiped his forehead. 'Mother was completely blind by that time, quite helpless to plan any more murders, or so I thought. One month to the day after that conversation, you asked me to be one of your father's pallbearers.'

'But his death was an accident! He ate a bad mushroom that he'd gathered himself by mistake.'

'Sarah, darling, Walter Kelling was a past president of the Mycological Society. He'd been gathering and eating wild mushrooms since he was a boy. His eyesight and his judgment were as sound as they'd ever been. I don't know where the amanita came from, but I'll never believe he picked it himself.'

'That was the weekend you drove Beth and me up to Maine,' Sarah said slowly. 'Aunt Marguerite was supposed to come and stay with Aunt Caroline, but she came down with hives and Father said he'd go in her place.'

'That's the story Mother told, at any rate. I shouldn't be surprised if Aunt Marguerite was never invited. She also told the doctor Walter had picked the mushrooms and cooked them himself. Of course she was believed because everyone knew Walter did that sort of thing, and it was so obvious that a woman in Mother's condition couldn't have had anything to do with them. Don't ask me how she managed to get a bad one and slip it past him. I began to wonder if she might be possessed of some uncanny power. I knew she ought to be locked up, but there wasn't a shred of evidence against her. I couldn't tell the police she'd already done two other murders because they'd arrest me as an accessory, and you'd be left with nobody to look after you.'

'It never occurred to you that I might be able to look after myself?'

'No, never. I had to believe that you needed me. Oh, my darling, I had to have something!'

CHAPTER
TWELVE

Alexander wiped his eyes and blew his nose. 'Sorry I made a fool of myself, breaking down like that.'

'It's a pity you didn't do it sooner,' Sarah mumbled into his hair. She had his head in her arms, cradled against her breast. 'So you only married me to keep me from getting killed.'

'I married you because I adore you, Sadiebelle, and always did and always will. It's only that I wouldn't have forced myself on you—'

'Forced yourself on me? You idiotic man! I suppose you tied me hand and foot, and dragged me screaming to the altar?'

That got a smile out of him. 'No, I will say you came willingly enough, but you were so young and you'd lost your father so recently. I thought it was because you felt you were—'

'Getting another one? I did welcome the prospect of having somebody to rely on, but I'd never have married you for that. Has it never occurred to you that I might be even goofier about you than you are about me?'

'How could you be? My darling girl, you are my whole life.'

'Then it's high time you started living with me instead of your nightmares,' she told him. 'From now on, you're to stop treating me as if I were nine years old and young for my age. I'm your wife. Whatever happens, we'll share it equally. I don't believe your mother has any secret powers. I don't think she's that much smarter than we are, and I think it's high time we stopped letting her rule the roost. What we ought to do is go to court and have you appointed her legal guardian or whatever it was that Dolph did when Great-uncle Frederick got so batty. Between her double handicap and the fact that she's thrown away a fortune without being able to say where it went, you wouldn't have a speck of trouble convincing a judge that she's not fit to handle large responsibilities.'

'Sarah, can you imagine how she'd react?'

'Who says we have to tell her, and how's she going to find out if we don't? If she ever did find out, what could she do about it?'

'She'd think of something. It's a terrible risk, Sarah.'

'From what you've been telling me, it's a risk being anywhere near her. She hasn't tried anything on either one of us yet, and she's had every opportunity.'

'That's only because we've let her have her own way in

everything. Why do you think I let her lead me around by the nose as I do? It's so that she'll leave you alone.'

'She'll leave me alone,' said Sarah grimly. 'Alexander, I am simply not afraid of Aunt Caroline.'

'I'd feel safer if you were.'

'No you wouldn't. You'd sink right back into the same old rut. I'm not going to stand for that, my love. We have plenty of good years ahead of us, and it's high time we quit dragging on from one day to the next as we've been doing. Promise me you'll at least give some thought to that guardianship.'

'Yes, darling. I'll talk to the lawyers about it next week.'

'Good. Now, my next bright idea is, how would you feel about getting out of this house for a few days and having a chance to pull yourself together?'

'Where should we go?'

'I suppose the sensible place would be Ireson's Landing. We could walk the land and make up our minds about what part we want to sell off so that you'd have some capital of your own and wouldn't have a fit of the guilties every time you spent a nickel of mine.'

'You're not wasting any time, are you, Sadiebelle?'

'Not if I can help it. Please understand me, Alexander, I'm not criticising anything you've done. I'm sure I shouldn't have handled things as well as you did, and I'd certainly never have had the fortitude to stick it out all these years. I don't care why you married me, I think you're the most wonderful husband a woman could have. Now come up to bed and start acting like one for a change.'

CHAPTER
THIRTEEN

It felt strange to wake up and feel her husband's body beside hers. Sarah opened her eyes and met his. She and Alexander exchanged delighted smiles.

'How do you feel this morning, dearest?'

'Much better, thank you, Sadiebelle. I was just thinking I ought to get up and phone Lomax about turning on the water and starting a couple of fires. It's going to be cold out there, you know.'

She snuggled closer. 'We'll manage to keep each other warm somehow.'

He laughed, a merry chuckle she hadn't heard in years. 'I shouldn't be surprised, Sadiebelle.'

'Stop calling me baby names. I'm a big girl now.'

'You're a wanton hussy, and we'll never get anywhere if you keep trying to seduce me.'

'Trying? I thought I was succeeding.'

'Baggage!'

Alexander was behaving in a thoroughly husbandly manner when Caroline Kelling came stamping up the stairs.

'Alexander, where are you? Didn't you hear me calling?'

'The voice of the turtle is heard in the land,' Sarah murmured. 'Let's hide under the covers.'

Sighing, her husband sat up and swung his long legs out of the bed. 'No, I'd better go. Nothing's been changed simply by our talking about it. You will remember that, my dearest?'

'We are going to change it.'

'Yes, we are, but there's no sense in asking for trouble.'

Looking worried again, Alexander put on his sensible grey Jaeger bathrobe and went to calm his mother. Sarah could hear her saying, 'I hope you've got over whatever was ailing you yesterday. Leila's out of town, so you'll have to take me to the protest meeting at Faneuil Hall.'

'If you do, I'll hold my own protest meeting,' Sarah called out.

'Yes, darling. I'm explaining about the change in plans. I didn't realise Leila would be out of town. I'm afraid that means we'll have to take Mother with us.'

'Of course, I'd assumed we would. It's better to have her where we can keep an eye on her.'

Sarah put on her own robe and went to brush her teeth. She could hear that Aunt Caroline was not taking kindly to the idea of spending the weekend at Ireson's Landing. Good. Maybe she'd stay home with Edith and sulk, and they could have the place to themselves.

However, by the time they were settled around the

breakfast table, Mrs Kelling had changed her tune and begun organising the expedition to suit herself. She was giving orders about one thing and another when the telephone rang. Edith must have picked it up on the kitchen extension, for she came into the dining room looking puzzled.

'It's some man wanting Mrs Kelling. I told him she don't talk on the telephone, but he says she'll talk to him. Name's Dee.'

'Edith,' said Alexander gravely, 'there are two Mrs Kellings in this house. Isn't that the chap from Harry's office, Sarah?'

'Yes, I expect it must be about the illustrations for that jewellery book. He said something the other night. Tell him I'll be right there, Edith. What time are we leaving?'

'Mother says after lunch. Would that suit you?'

'Let me see what this man has to say. I told him I'd be willing to meet with him and Mr Bittersohn, and he may have something already arranged.'

Dee, it appeared, had done exactly that. 'I've got it lined up for half-past ten this morning, Sarah, here at the office. Can you make it?'

'Yes, if we can be through before noon. My husband and I have plans for later.'

She went back and told Alexander about the appointment. 'Is it all right with you if I go?'

'Fine. That will give me a chance to get squared away with Lomax and do these multitudinous errands Mother is thinking up.'

'Forget them. None of them matters a rap. We can stop for groceries somewhere along the way, and since I'm going to do the cooking, I get to plan the menus.'

'We're not taking Edith?'

'No!' The negative came out more sharply than she'd intended. 'You know what a hothouse flower she is, she'd be complaining every minute. Let her stay and mind the house. She can have some of her cronies or that nephew from Malden in to visit.'

Sarah would much rather not have kept thinking about what Alexander had told her the night before, but how could she forget? As for her own father, if he had been deliberately poisoned, she could see only one way it might have been managed. She'd often wondered why, when Aunt Caroline had to let the rest of the servants go, she'd kept the one who was least competent. Now she could think of a possible reason.

Edith was a dreadful servant, but she might make a pretty good accomplice. If the woman had any loyalty at all, it was to Caroline Kelling. She had enough brains to carry out an order when she had to, and she was probably also shrewd enough to have figured out that her best hope of keeping a job was to have some hold over her employer. Until they could get Caroline Kelling under safe control, they'd be wise to keep her separated from the older retainer as much as possible.

Sarah did her customary morning chores, packed the few things she meant to take with her for the weekend, and told Alexander, 'I might as well pick up the car after I leave Harry's office, since I'll be so close to the garage. Let's take off as soon as I get back here and not bother with lunch. We can stop for a hamburger if we get hungry on the way.'

'Whatever you say, my love.'

He kissed her and went back to his own concerns. Sarah walked down to Charles Street thinking what a relief it was she didn't have to worry any more about what Bittersohn or Dee might tell Harry Lackridge. She would give Alexander the full particulars of her visit to Ireson's Landing in due time. Perhaps they might look for a clue as to who the trespasser was, although it wasn't likely they'd find anything after such a downpour.

The publishing house had the same mummified atmosphere that the Lackridges' apartment did. Everything was still pretty much where Leila's grandfather had put it. Even the titles in the bookcases didn't include many fresh jackets. It was surprising that Bittersohn hadn't taken his lavish grant to some more up-and-coming firm.

Meagre as his output was, Harry managed to keep going while larger houses foundered. He was his own sales manager, constantly searching out new markets, talking to book sellers, attending library conventions and book fairs wherever they could be found. Neither he nor Leila ever seemed to lack the price of a plane ticket.

Of course, they might be dipping into capital, and why not? They had no children to provide for, and it was stupid to go without the things one wanted in order to save for a future that might never arrive. Sarah thought of her own father and his scrupulous economies. He'd been so worried about not having enough for his old age. What an irony!

Nobody was sitting at the reception desk. Harry was between secretaries again, or perhaps the girl was just out for coffee. Sarah was wondering whether to venture past the switchboard when Bittersohn breezed in from the street and Bob Dee emerged almost simultaneously from some inner office.

'Good show! Both of you right on the button. Why don't we sit right down here at the conference table and lay it all right out? I'll get us some coffee. How do you take yours, Sarah?'

'I won't have any, thanks. If you don't mind, I'd rather get on with whatever we have to do.'

'Oh, yeah, that's right. You said you and your husband were going out to your other place for the weekend. Taking Mrs Kelling with you?'

'We always do. Mr Bittersohn, I believe you have some photographs to show me?'

Bob Dee wasn't that easily discouraged. 'Sure you won't have anything? Maybe a Danish? Wouldn't take a second. Bittersohn, what about you? Cream and sugar?'

'No, I just had breakfast.'

The author opened a large manila envelope he'd brought with him and spread some black-and-white glossies on the table. 'Got the outline, Dee? Mrs Kelling might like to know what we're talking about.'

Bob Dee hustled off with a great air of efficiency and was gone rather a long time. Bittersohn waited for him about thirty seconds, shrugged, and began explaining his project to Sarah. They worked through the pile, she taking notes and asking an occasional question, and had the business fairly well settled between them by the time the young assistant came back.

'Sorry to take so long, folks. I got stuck on an out-of-town phone call, then had a heck of a time tracking down your stuff. Harry's desk is something else.'

'I should think his secretary would keep track of things,' said Bittersohn.

'You would, wouldn't you? Okay, Max, old buddy, let's roll it.'

'We've already rolled, thanks. I think Mrs Kelling is pretty clear on what we want.'

'Oh. Well, look, could we take another quick run-through just to make sure we've touched all the bases?'

'I hardly think it's necessary,' Sarah told him.

Dee paid no attention. He began thumbing through the photographs, mixing up her notes, raising irrelevant points of dispute, all with a running patter of wisecracks which nobody else thought were funny. Sarah endured the performance for about ten minutes, then stood up.

'I honestly don't think we have to discuss this any more. Mr Bittersohn obviously knows exactly how the work should be done, and I'm sure he'll put me straight if I get into any difficulties. As for the technique, Harry knows the way I draw, and I can't imagine he'd have recommended me if he didn't think I could do an adequate job. Why don't I simply try one or two and let Mr Bittersohn have a look at them? If he feels they won't do, I shan't charge him anything, and you can find another artist.'

'Yeah, but we don't want to waste a lot of time,' said Dee.

'My feeling exactly.'

Sarah started to put on her gloves. 'I'll take along whatever photographs you want to give me, and have something ready for you by Wednesday at the latest, Mr Bittersohn. Where can I get in touch with you?'

She knew she was being rude to this young fellow, who was trying so hard to impress them and making such a hash of it, and was ashamed when he took the snub so cheerily.

'Great, then we'll leave it like that. Why don't you give me a buzz when you're ready, Sarah, and I'll set up a meeting? That okay with you, Max?'

'How much is this going to cost me?'

'Hey, what do you know? We never did get around to talking price, did we? What do you say, Sarah, thirty bucks apiece? Got to watch the budget, you know.'

'Thirty would be lovely,' Sarah replied. 'Harry generally gives me ten. I really don't see, though, why Mr Bittersohn should get stuck just because it's coming out of his pocket this time and not the firm's. Perhaps we'd better split the difference and say fifteen.'

'I can't let you do that, Mrs Kelling. Thirty's fine with me. You'll still be working cheap, considering the detail involved.'

The author was clearly amused by this turn of affairs. Dee's sense of humour, on the other hand, seemed finally to have deserted him. It really was not kind of her to have said what she did. He'd probably thought he was doing her a big favour, giving her the chance of making extra money off a novice who didn't know he was being skinned. If that was the sort of thing Bob Dee was picking up from Harry Lackridge, he might as well also learn that a sharp deal could cut more ways than one.

Bittersohn started to put his photographs back in the envelope. The publisher's assistant made one last attempt.

'Don't you think I should make some Xeroxes, in case these get lost or anything? It wouldn't take long.'

'I don't see why,' said the author. 'Xeroxes would come out looking like mud, and I can always get duplicate prints if we need them.'

'Please don't worry, Bob,' said Sarah, trying to make amends for her curtness now that the end of this unexpectedly trying interview was in sight. 'I shan't lose them. We'll see you next week, then, and perhaps we'll have time for that coffee you promised.'

'Sure, great. Any time you say. I'll look forward to hearing from you.'

He walked them to the door and still showed an inclination to stand and chat, but Sarah bade a firm goodbye and went to get the car. It would have been a wise move to telephone from the publishing house and tell Alexander she was on her way, but Bob Dee would probably have torn the switchboard apart in his eagerness to oblige.

If that young man thought he had a future in publishing, he'd better think again. He'd be more at home as master of ceremonies on one of those frenetic game shows Edith was always watching. There was a pay station in the garage, and she used that. Alexander said they'd be waiting on the sidewalk when she came up, and they were.

'Shall I drive, Sadiebelle? Oh, I forgot, you're a big girl now.'

'Yes I am, and just for that I shan't let you.'

Sarah smiled up at her tall husband, thinking he still looked a bit wan around the mouth, and wishing to spare him as much as she could. 'Do you prefer to sit in back with your mother or in front with your wife?'

'Need you ask?'

He helped his mother into the back seat and settled her with the Braille book and note pad she always took along to relieve the tedium of having nobody to hand signal for her, since Alexander would as a rule be driving the car. Mrs Kelling could write in longhand with a wire grid to mark off the lines, but she had become so proficient in Braille that she often preferred to punch out the dots with a stencil and stylus and have Sarah transcribe them later on the typewriter.

Sarah had gladly learned Braille and took pleasure in performing this service. She had never ceased to wonder at how lucidly the blind and deaf woman could express herself. Aunt Caroline's style was chilly and sometimes abrupt, but always to the point. She never rambled or repeated, she always knew precisely what she was going to say next and put it down in a way that left no conceivable doubt as to what she meant. She didn't misspell words or leave out letters, except when she abbreviated to save time. It was hard to believe there was much wrong with Caroline Kelling's mind.

Nevertheless, Sarah had said to her husband that it would be hard to judge Aunt Caroline by normal standards, and she still thought there was truth in that statement. One could not condone what she'd done to Uncle Gilbert, but one could make a fair guess at how she'd been driven to think of murder.

Caroline Kelling was still a beautiful woman; in her heyday she must have been stunning. She'd been a New York debutante, used to a lively social life, opera all winter long, theatre, parties, travel, contacts with fascinating people and places. Gilbert Kelling, with his handsome appearance, family connections, and great wealth, must have seemed like the catch of the decade, but Caroline would soon have learned he wasn't much fun to be married to. She'd also have found that Boston ladies of her circle were more involved with good works than good times. Life on the Hill had probably not been much duller for her than it was for some of her neighbours, but to a beautiful woman with a fabulous collection of jewellery to show off and no place to wear it, the marriage must have been one long frustration. Travel abroad was out of the question. Uncle Gilbert wasn't up to it, and he wouldn't have gone anyway. All he cared about was sailing in the *Caroline*, and since he refused to have an engine in the craft even that must have been a poky business at times.

Alexander described his father as austere. Uncle Jem always referred to him as the dead fish. Sarah's own mother had wondered how Caroline ever endured living with a human iceberg. That Gilbert's wife had tried to save his life instead of shoving him overboard was a source of general wonderment and, everybody thought, a tribute to her nobility of spirit. If Gilbert Kelling had been better liked, Caroline might have become less of a heroine. Had she taken that factor into account when she chose such a subtle and dramatic way to get rid of him?

Having married Gilbert Kelling for his wealth, Caroline naturally wouldn't want to give it up. He'd be impossible to divorce because he never did anything wrong, and if she herself gave grounds, she'd lose any hope of a settlement. She'd no doubt expected that his heart ailment would carry him off early, but he took excellent care of himself, and she wasn't getting any younger. Maybe getting rid of his medicine and letting nature take its course hadn't really seemed like murder.

But it was, and if she killed him for money, then where did the money go? Had she started gambling, piling up huge debts she had no other way to pay off? That didn't sound like Aunt Caroline.

Oh, what was the use of brooding on questions for which she had no answers? Why not concentrate on helping Alexander to enjoy his weekend? Resolutely, Sarah began

chatting to him about trivia such as whether to stop at the
Mall for groceries or wait till they got to Eddie's. Eddie's
prices were somewhat higher, but the Kellings had always
gone to Eddie's. They went to Eddie's.

Once there, it was easy to slip into a familiar comfortable
pattern, inquiring after Mrs Eddie and all the little Eddies,
debating between homemade walnut muffins and banana
loaf, since the cranberry bread was sold out, as it always
was. There was the stowing of bundles with much concern
over whether the milk would spill into the muffins if they hit
the big bump in the driveway. There was the thrill of
navigating the drive without hitting the bump, the business
of finding the right key, of opening the creaky side door and
being greeted by smells of damp and wood smoke, of
poking up fires and adjusting dampers, of lugging in parcels
and suitcases and getting Aunt Caroline oriented.

At last the three of them got settled with extra sweaters,
glasses of sherry, hunks of Eddie's rat-trap cheese and pilot
biscuits in front of the immense fieldstone fireplace that was
far and away the pleasantest thing about the barny old
house. Nobody felt much like talking by then. They were
content to bask like cats in the warmth of burning,
salt-soaked driftwood that spurted flames of blue and green
and red-orange and brilliant yellow; rolling tiny sips of wine
around their tongues, nibbling at the good, simple food.
Even Caroline Kelling was not demanding attention. She
said once, 'This cheese is excellent,' but nobody responded
and she seemed content to let it lie.

'She's getting old,' Sarah thought. 'Old and worn out.
Whatever she may have done in the past, she's no threat to
us now.'

It was strange to think of Aunt Caroline in the
background, not calling the shots any more; almost
terrible, in a way. Sarah roused herself enough to say,
'Darling, ask your mother if she'd like an early supper.'

Alexander reached out a hand to hold her back. 'Don't
go yet, Sadiebelle. I want to look at you.'

She picked up the long, elegant fingers and held them to
her cheek, not able to speak for the lump in her throat. Why
couldn't it have been like this always? Sarah didn't move
again until her foot most unromantically went to sleep.

Then she gave the hand a gentle squeeze and laid it back on the faded denim slip cover.

'I shan't be long. We're just going to picnic here by the fire. You might fix your mother's drink and do something about that front log which is about to burn through and spray live coals all over the hearthrug.'

'Yes, my darling. More sherry for you?'

'Not yet, thanks.'

Sarah went out, shutting the door behind her to keep the heat in the living room. It was almost completely dark by now. She flipped a light switch, but nothing happened. Lomax must have expected Alexander would turn on the electricity when he got here, and Alexander supposed Lomax had done it. No matter, they always kept oil lamps filled and ready in the kitchen. She got one off the shelf and reached towards the painted tin match safe that hung beside the window over the sink.

As she moved, something that was not her reflection moved along the glass. Her hand froze in mid-air.

Somebody was out there spying on them. She knew, as she had known Wednesday night about the man on the path, although nothing was to be seen now except forsythia branches black against a dark blue sky, whippy lines punctuated by sharp, pointed buds. The leafless shrubs could offer no cover. He must have ducked down beside the house, only a few feet away from her.

Ought she to call for help? What would that accomplish? If Alexander rushed out to confront the intruder, he might get hurt, even killed. If he stayed inside, he'd feel like a coward and the good work of last night and today would be undone. If it was the same person who'd been with her on the path and made no move to hurt her, there was probably nothing to be afraid of, anyway.

Sarah nerved herself to move forward and flick the damp-stained calico curtains across the windowpane, like any cosy housewife settling in for the night. She took the match, touched it to a couple of the lamp wicks, and turned them down so they'd give a soft glow without sooting the chimneys. Then she started heating soup and cutting sandwiches.

Years ago, as a lonesome little girl afraid to be upstairs in the dark by herself, she'd got into the habit of singing in bed. It always gave her courage to fall asleep then. She tried it now.

'Oh, where have you been, Billy boy, Billy boy? Oh, where have you been, charming Billy?'

'I've been to seek a wife, she's the joy of my life.'

She aged ten years before she realised the voice blending with hers was her husband's. He put his arms around her from behind, and nuzzled her hair.

'I missed you, Sadiebelle. Shall I help with the sandwiches?'

'No, they're done.'

Poor angel, if he ever knew what a fright he'd given her! 'I'm just waiting for the soup to heat. You could reach us down some plates and mugs if you like.'

'The nice blue ones or the awful old greenery-yalleries?'

'The blue, of course. Alexander, I have a charming thought.'

She pitched her voice a shade on the loud side, to let the lurker by the wall know she was not alone. 'Why don't we take the old uglies out on the back terrace, and smash them one by one?'

'I have an even brighter idea,' he said. 'Let's wait till Leila tries to rope us into joining another committee, and throw them at her.'

Laughing together, they set out the trays, and carried them back to the fireplace. Sarah had splurged on a can of crabmeat because it was something Alexander adored but seldom got. He was touched, and let her know with a warmth that brought another lump to her throat. How little it took to make him happy, and how seldom had she tried during these past difficult years. From now on, things would be different.

But in what way would they be different? Much as she'd rather forget it, Sarah couldn't help remembering that dark shape outside the kitchen window. There were too many dark shapes in her life lately. Ever since that day in the graveyard, they kept popping up everywhere she looked.

This one was nothing but nerves. The vast, neglected estate had always been a magnet for trespassers. She'd never been afraid of them before because Alexander was with her. He was here now, wasn't he? Whatever happened, they'd be together. What was the sense in worrying?

CHAPTER
FOURTEEN

Sarah woke up smiling and reached out to touch her husband. Alexander was no longer beside her, though. He must have gone down to light the fire, which meant he was over his awful lethargy, and thank God for that. She lay a few minutes listening to the seagulls' usual morning quarrel down on the rocks and making plans for the day. After breakfast they might run over to the fish shack and pick up a bucket of clams. She'd make a big pot of chowder. Alexander would eat great bowls of it and say, 'Thank you, Sadiebelle,' and give her a smile that now had nothing but love and joy in it.

She jumped out of bed, put on heavy corduroy pants and her old green Shetland sweater, and went to start a pot of coffee. The fire, she noticed, was new-laid but not yet alight. Alexander would be out at the woodpile, cutting neat splinters for kindling.

In the cold foggy air the smell of last night's smoke hung heavy and acrid. Faded walls and battered furniture didn't look homey now, only depressing. The bogles came creeping back.

Had she or had she not seen somebody prowling last night? Why hadn't she been brave enough to stick her head out the window and make sure? Sarah opened the back door and scanned the fog-beaded grass for signs of footprints, but couldn't see any. Then a tall form loomed out of the grey. That startled her again, until Alexander spoke.

'I'm sorry I couldn't arrange a sunny morning for you, Sadiebelle, but the radio says it's supposed to burn off by noon. Shall I do something about breakfast?'

'No, my love. Were you planning to light the fire?'

'Yes, my darling.'

He tilted her chin up so he could kiss her on the lips. 'Is that coffee I smell, or the allegorical nectar of the pagan deities?'

She kissed him back. 'You're in a bouncy mood today.'

'I am as merry as a schoolboy,' he informed her gravely. 'Are we having Eddie's muffins, I hope?'

'Name it and you shall have it, my love. Want me to barbecue a steer, or will you settle for scrambled eggs and sausages?'

'Whichever is faster. I seem to be getting my appetite back.'

'Good,' said Sarah. 'Shall we go ahead without your mother, or do you think she'll be down soon?'

Alexander looked startled. 'Good Lord! I'd completely forgotten we brought her with us.'

Sarah burst out laughing. 'To think I should live to see the day! Here, have some coffee and a muffin to stay your stomach while I find out if she needs help.'

However, Caroline Kelling had managed for herself, having her own precisely ordered suite here as she did in Boston. They heard her tapping her way downstairs, calling out for her son as always. He went to meet her, and Sarah started breaking eggs into a bowl, putting in an extra one for Alexander.

After breakfast, she and he did a few chores while Aunt Caroline sat with her book by the fire. Then all three rode to the fish shack for clams. It was too early to think of chowder after such a large breakfast, so Mrs Kelling decided everybody should go back to sit by the fire while she worked on a report she'd promised to have ready when Leila came back from Washington.

Alexander replied calmly that he'd made up the fire with oak logs so she'd be perfectly comfortable by herself for an hour or so while he and Sarah went for a walk along the beach.

'I'm surprised Sarah will let you go,' was the amiable reply. 'She goes into a swivet about your not feeling well when there's anything I want you to do for me.'

He didn't reply. Mrs Kelling shrugged and turned to her report. They left her punching Braille and went out into the fog. It had begun to thin a bit up along the road, but down under the cliff they could hardly distinguish between beach and sea.

'I hope you're not too disappointed,' Alexander apologised as if he ought to have managed better weather for their outing. 'I do so want you to be happy.'

'I am happy.'

That was true, although Sarah would have been happier if they could see more than three feet around them. She was getting prickles again, wondering if it was just her imagination working overtime or if there actually was somebody nearby. The pounding of the surf and the rattle of loose stones being pulled out by the undertow made racket enough to drown out any footsteps. So long as this fog held, they could be moving in the midst of a crowd and not know it.

Still she felt safe enough with Alexander. He'd been roaming this stretch of coast all his life. If any trouble threatened, he'd know how to get them away fast enough. She had only to stay close, clinging to his hand as she'd done before her head reached up to his coat pocket and heaven was a stroll with Cousin Alexander.

'Am I going too fast for you, Sadiebelle?'

How many times during the past twenty-five years had he asked her that same question? Sarah began to laugh.

'My legs aren't quite so short as they used to be. Look, there's my old wishing rock poking up out of the fog. Remember how we used to sit there looking out to sea while you told me stories about the mermaids?'

He chuckled. 'And you insisted you could see them riding the waves. Can you still, darling?'

'I'm not sure. I haven't seen a mermaid in ages.'

'Perhaps they're out there today. Come on, let's sit down.'

They crowded together on the narrow ledge that had been their special place for as long as she could remember. Alexander put his arm around her to keep her from slipping off the edge.

'Now, Sadiebelle, I wish you'd tell me what's bothering you. You've been edgy ever since we started out. Is it something in particular or—things in general?'

Sarah laughed uncomfortably. 'You're very perspicacious, my dear sir. I wasn't going to tell you.'

'If we're going to treat each other as equals, it has to work both ways, you know. What's the matter?'

'It's only that I keep having this absurd feeling we're being followed.'

'But why?'

'I suppose because somebody was around here the other night when I came to look at the wall, and I'm quite sure I caught a glimpse of him again last night when I went out to the kitchen to start supper.'

'Him? Are you sure it was a man?'

'No, but that was my impression. Someone fairly big, but not so tall as you.' She filled in the details as best she could. 'It doesn't sound like much, does it?'

'It's enough to make me wonder if somebody's camping out on the grounds somewhere. We've had that problem before, you know.'

'That was my own first thought, but I can't help wondering if there could be more to it then trespassing. For one thing, it seemed a fantastic coincidence that I ran into that Mr Bittersohn on my way home that night.'

'Where was this?'

'In a coffee shop up along the pike. I was in such a state that I was afraid to drive any farther without a hot drink to pull me together. I hadn't been there two minutes when he came in and sat down at my table. He's about the right size, and it popped into my head that he might have followed me out from Boston to see what I was up to.'

'Sarah, why would the man do a thing like that?'

'Because of the jewellery, was all I could think of. I thought he might have got it into his head I was sneaking off to meet a—a boy friend, and that he could blackmail me into letting him get at the collection.'

'How could you? The box is in Mother's name. You wouldn't be allowed to open it without her authorisation.'

'He wouldn't necessarily be aware of that, would he? I know we told him I'd never seen the things, but that was in deference to Aunt Caroline's wishes. He may think I could if I chose to. You must admit it's unusual for a person in her condition to have had complete control over such a valuable family property all these years. Now that I've met him again, though, I honestly don't think he's that sort of man.'

Alexander shook his head. 'We mustn't be too sure of anything. It does seem too much of a coincidence, his coming upon you like that, and the Studebaker would certainly be an easy car to follow anywhere. What did he say when he came to the table?'

'The sort of thing one might expect. Acted surprised to see me so far from Boston and asked what I was doing out by myself on such a miserable night. I told you weren't feeling well and I had to attend to something out here. I mentioned our having two places, and said we were always tootling back and forth. Then I asked him the same question, and he didn't really answer, but started talking about my doing the drawings for his book.'

'How did he know you can draw?'

'He said Harry told him. I'm afraid he, or whoever it was on the path, may also have got hold of a sample. Like a fool, I tore up that sketch I'd made of the wall, and simply threw the pieces away. He could have picked them up and stuck them back together.'

Alexander was looking grey again. 'I've landed you in a fine kettle of fish, haven't I?'

'No, I don't think you're responsible, Alexander,' Sarah replied, 'and I'm not saying this simply to make you feel better. I'm beginning to suspect there's something that's been going on for a long time without your knowing anything about it.'

'What makes you say that?'

'For one thing, this business of Ruby Redd. I cannot believe your mother killed her.'

'But she must have!'

'She never said so, did she?'

'Of course she didn't. Would you?'

'Probably, if I was asking my own son to help me get rid of the body. I'd feel I owed you some kind of explanation.'

'Sarah, she was trying to pretend I'd done it. I told you what she said.'

'Yes, and it seems to me that those words were carefully chosen for their ambiguity. They might also be interpreted to mean she knew who'd done it but didn't dare say. That would explain why she's never been willing to talk about it. There's no earthly reason why you and she should never have discussed the matter, unless she was shielding somebody. Then I keep getting back to the method of killing. Can you honestly see Aunt Caroline sneaking up behind another woman and bashing her over the head?'

'How can one say what another person will do in time of stress?'

'You know what she did to your father, and you have a pretty shrewd idea of what she did to mine. I can believe the poisoned mushroom theory because it's basically the same as the first murder—setting up a situation that's going to result in death without arousing suspicion. I've been thinking she might have got Edith to pick the mushrooms for her, but she mightn't even have had to do that. Couldn't she just have dumped her eyedrops or something into the pan?'

Her husband thought a moment, then nodded. 'Yes, that's entirely possible. Atropine is a vegetable alkaloid, too, if I'm not mistaken, and the symptoms might not be dissimilar. The doctor would be apt not to doubt the mushroom story because people who gather wild mushrooms so often do poison themselves by accident, and those who don't sometimes have an almost superstitious dread of the things—like thinking all snakes are dangerous.'

'And Aunt Caroline would be ready with a plausible story about how Daddy was always so cocksure of what was edible and what wasn't that he never bothered to check them against the reference books. She'd claim that was why she never dared eat what he picked, which would explain why she didn't get poisoned, too. You see, we can both accept that idea because it's so typical of the way she operates. Ruby Redd's murder was entirely different. Your theory is that your mother killed your girl friend because she didn't want to lose you, but I can't buy that. You were still under age and Aunt Caroline had control of the finances. All she had to do was cut off your allowance and ship you off with her on a trip somewhere. She'd be taking a fairly safe gamble that Ruby wouldn't be the sort of girl to sit chewing her fingernails till you got back, wouldn't she?'

'I suppose so,' Alexander admitted, 'but if she didn't kill Ruby, who did?'

'I'd say, offhand, it was most likely the person to whom she gave the money.'

'Gave the money? You mean Father's money? Good God, Sarah, why would Mother do a thing like that?'

'How should I know?' said his wife. 'But if she didn't give it away, what did she spend it on? A person couldn't fling huge sums about and have nothing left to show for it unless she bought phoney stocks or bet on horse races—'

'Not Mother.'

'—Or had to pay blackmail to somebody who knew she'd killed your father.'

Alexander licked salt off his lips. 'How could anybody know?'

'What if she confessed? She was in a really bad way when they found her, wasn't she? Maybe she thought she was going to die. To ease her conscience, she told a minister or someone at the hospital. Then when she got better and turned out to be a wealthy woman, that person threatened to expose her.'

'That doesn't hold water, Sarah. Mother could say she'd been raving, delirious, that it simply wasn't true. She'd count on my backing her up because she never did know I'd seen her get rid of the medicine. I suppose there's always the chance that some fisherman or someone happened to come alongside the *Caroline* in the fog at the precise moment she emptied the bottle over the rail, but if he was close enough to see her, then she'd also have seen him. Anyway, why should a blackmailer find it necessary to kill Ruby? They'd have no possible connection with one another.'

'Are we safe in assuming that? I don't want to undermine your ego, darling, but you did say that you were one of a crowd of fans and couldn't think why Ruby singled you out as her favourite. I'm sure you were the best-looking of the lot, but you probably weren't the richest or the most sophisticated.'

'Sarah, are you implying that her getting friendly with me was part of a scheme to fleece Mother? What could she get out of me?'

'The jewels, silly. Aunt Caroline would have had to tell whoever was getting the money that she couldn't give them up because they didn't belong to her, so they intended to use Ruby to wheedle them out of you. Then Ruby heard about that ruby parure and decided to double cross them because it would go so nicely with her teeth.'

'Darling, you're seeing mermaids again.'

'All right, I'm only guessing about that, but I do have one solid piece of information. Do you remember Tim O'Ghee?'

'The bartender from Danny Rate's? How could I forget? His being there when you opened the vault was like a judgment. Frankly, I've been wondering why he hasn't come around trying to blackmail me.'

'Because he's dead,' said Sarah.

'How do you know?'

'I found him.'

'Sarah!'

'Darling, don't look so aghast. Let me tell you how it happened. First, you must realise that by Tuesday morning, I was in what you might call a state.'

'You had every reason to be.'

'At any rate, I felt I simply couldn't endure sitting around waiting for the next awful thing to happen. It occurred to me that if I could find that old bartender, he might be able to answer some of my questions.'

She explained how she'd tracked O'Ghee to his rooming house, and how the landlady had sent her upstairs alone to discover his body.

'Oh, my God!' Alexander gasped. 'How did he die?'

'Some kind of poison injected by the needle he took his insulin with, I should think. It had been faked up to look like suicide by Milky Ways.'

He stared at her. 'Sarah, whatever are you talking about?'

'Milky Ways,' she repeated. 'You know, those candy bars I used to be so crazy about.'

'I thought you still were.'

'I'm afraid I've rather lost my taste for them.'

She told him why. 'You see, I was supposed to believe he'd stopped his medication and stuffed himself with candy so that he'd go into a coma and die.'

'And mightn't he have done just that? It doesn't seem such a bad way for an old man to go, my dear.'

'Of course he didn't. Why should he? He was chipper as a bee the day before. That landlady of his tried to pretend Mr O'Ghee was shattered by finding Ruby Redd's body in the vault because they'd been sweethearts, which was utter nonsense. You should have heard the earful he gave us about what an awful person she was! He wasn't the least bit sorry, only excited at being on the spot when she turned up and pleased with himself for being able to tell us who she was. Anyway, he couldn't eat Milky Ways because his teeth were no good. He told me so himself.'

Alexander pondered, his magnificent head bowed into the upturned collar of his threadbare pea jacket. 'Then you honestly believe that the landlady staged this whole performance?'

'She and that so-called doctor together, I should say. They were feeding each other lines like a couple of professional actors. Oh, and as a grand finale, they reached into the wastebasket and pulled out a copy of Monday night's paper that had the story about Ruby Redd and that awful picture of me and Dolph right on the front page. They recognised me from the photograph, accused me of coming there to—to make trouble for my family, and practically threw me out by the scruff of the neck.'

'Sarah, this is unbelievable!'

'I know. It was as though they knew I was coming and set the stage in advance. I suppose what actually happened was that they saw me dithering around outside, wondering if I'd got the right house, and recognised me from the news broadcast Harry and Leila saw. I was wearing the same old brown coat and no doubt looking just as idiotic. The man must have rushed upstairs and planted the things under the bed, then sneaked around back and waited till the landlady signalled for him to make his appearance as the doctor.'

'Would they have time for all that?'

'Easily. The woman kept me talking at the door for a few minutes before she let me in, and then after I found Mr O'Ghee dead, I stayed upstairs with the body while she telephoned—or pretended to. The man did drive up in a car, but he might have had it parked just around the corner somewhere.'

'Didn't he have a stethoscope or anything?'

'I don't know. He never opened that little bag he was carrying, and he kept his overcoat on so I've no idea what he was wearing underneath. We were only in the room together for a few minutes before they raised that big hullabaloo and forced me to leave, with dire threats of what they'd do if I ever came back.'

'What puzzles me is why the woman ever let you see the body in the first place,' said Alexander. 'Why didn't she simply tell you Mr O'Ghee wasn't around?'

'I suppose because they were afraid I'd keep coming and pestering them if they didn't scare me off good and proper. Or they may have wondered if Mr O'Ghee told me something they didn't want me to know, and thought they'd better take the chance to sound me out.'

'My God, Sarah! What if he had, and you'd let them know?'

'Obviously he didn't since I got out alive,' she replied with a shiver. She hadn't thought of that before. 'Anyway, don't you think this opens up some new possibilities?'

'Yes, I expect it does.'

There was a curious hesitation in his voice. Sarah caught the nuance.

'Alexander, don't you want it to be somebody else?'

'Darling, how can you ask that? Of course I'd rather not have to think of my own mother as a red-handed murderess, but what a terrible injustice I've done her all these years if she isn't guilty.'

'She is guilty of your father's death, you're positive of that.'

'Yes, but that's—not quite the same. The plain fact is that Father could be absolute hell to live with. There were times when I felt like doing something drastic, myself.'

'Not murder!'

'No, I don't think my destructive fantasies got any further than a punch in the mouth. What I actually planned to do was clear out of Boston as soon as I got my degree and find a job somewhere. I think Mother knew what I had in mind, although we never talked about it.'

'Leaving the family nest would be the normal and reasonable thing for any young man to do.'

'I've never been much good at doing the normal and reasonable thing, have I?'

Alexander slid off the wishing rock. 'Shall we walk on a bit? I'm getting stiff with sitting, and it looks as if the fog's beginning to lift.'

'Don't you think we ought to start back?' said Sarah. 'Aunt Caroline's fire must be almost out by now, and I should get going on that chowder if we're to have it for supper. It's always better if it stands a while.'

'You'll need me to open the clams, I suppose?'

'No, I bought them already shucked. And frozen, unfortunately, since those were all they had.'

'They'll taste just as good. You make a marvellous chowder, Sadiebelle.'

'Are you trying to butter me up?'

He smiled a little. 'Well, I was rather thinking that if you don't want my help, I might nip down and have a look at the Milburn.'

'I thought you'd got the old girl all tucked up in her winter nightie.'

'I have,' he answered eagerly, 'but it wouldn't take me ten minutes to untuck her if you'd care for a little spin.'

'Why don't you take your mother while I'm chopping the onions?' Sarah suggested instead. Jogging along at ten miles an hour in an antique electric car was not her favourite pastime, but Aunt Caroline loved the Milburn almost as much as her son did. 'Give her a nice ride, and then she won't feel quite so abused and neglected if we go off again by ourselves this afternoon. I do believe you're right about the weather. Look, there's the patch of blue big enough to make a Dutchman's breeches.'

'And the sun's trying to break through,' said Alexander. 'Perhaps it's an omen, Sadiebelle.'

CHAPTER
FIFTEEN

They were surprised to realise how long they'd been out. By the time Sarah and her husband got back to the house, Aunt Caroline was wondering in aggrieved tones if they were ever to get any lunch.

Alexander pacified his mother with the promise of a ride in the Milburn, then went to get the electric out of its winter wraps while Sarah broiled a fresh halibut steak she'd found, by a miracle, at the fish shack. They had it with grilled tomatoes and hot corn bread, and were thoroughly enjoying the meal when Alexander suddenly exclaimed, 'Sarah, I can't leave you here alone. What if that trespasser's still around?'

'Peeping Tom?' She shrugged. 'We didn't see anybody on the beach, and your mother stayed here alone all morning without being bothered. I'll lock the doors and windows, but I'm honestly not a bit frightened to be by myself for half an hour or so. You don't intend to be gone long, do you?'

'No, darling, just down the road and back. You're quite sure you don't want to come?'

'You know Aunt Caroline hates it if we all squeeze in together. Alexander, we mustn't let this situation get to us. I may simply have imagined that man last night. Go ahead and play with your precious toy. I'll be fine.'

'Then lock the door behind us, and if you get the urge to do some more investigating, wait till I get back. Promise?'

'I promise. Have fun.'

She kissed him goodbye and watched him help Aunt Caroline down the drive. They kept the Milburn in a shed not far up from the road, to spare her aged axles the torture of the climb. Sarah waited at the door until the dip of the grade hid them from sight, then she dutifully turned the key in the lock and went to peel onions and chop salt pork.

Preparing a genuine New England clam chowder is not a task to be taken lightly. Intent on what she was doing, Sarah again lost track of the time. It wasn't until she was adding the milk to the cooked onions and potatoes that it occurred to her Alexander and his mother ought to have returned some time ago. Even if temptation to go a bit farther than he'd planned got the better of him, he wouldn't dare keep the Milburn out very long for fear its batteries would run down.

Maybe they had. It might not be a bad idea to take the Studebaker and go out looking for the Milburn. Sarah knew the route they'd be most apt to take. Aunt Caroline always liked to be driven up along the cliff road, although she could no longer admire the view of the ocean.

That wasn't far, though, and there were a couple of year-round houses along the way. Alexander couldn't call his wife if they got stuck because the telephone had been shut off for the winter, but he'd surely be able to find somebody willing to bring Aunt Caroline back and explain about the delay. Everybody knew the Kellings and their crazy old cars.

The early dusk began to gather. Now Sarah was really scared. She was putting on her coat when she heard a car churning up the drive. That wasn't the Milburn; the little electric was virtually noiseless. They must have had to be towed. Alexander would be heartbroken. She went to offer condolences, and was confronted by a policeman in uniform.

'Mrs—er—Miss Kelling?'

'Mrs Kelling, yes. What is it, officer? Something's happened to the Milburn, hasn't it? Is my husband all right?'

'Your husband? I'd have thought—no, Mrs Kelling, I'm afraid he's not. He and his—the lady that was with him—'

'His mother. Where are they?'

'They went over the cliff,' the policeman said doggedly. 'A young fellow happened to be down on the rocks and saw the car go over the seawall into the water. He tried to reach them, but there was nothing anybody could have done. You know what it's like, a thirty-foot drop and all those big jagged rocks standing up out of the water.'

'Like teeth. When I was little, Alexander used to tell me they were giants' teeth.'

Automatically, Sarah stepped back from the door to let him in. She didn't seem to be very steady on her feet.

'Hey, you're not going to faint on me?' The policeman

caught her by the arm and steered her over to the sofa. 'Is anybody else in the house?'

'I—no, just myself.'

'Okay, Mrs Kelling, take it easy. Anything to drink around the place? Brandy? Whisky?'

'There's some sherry in the pantry. On a tray with three glasses. I was going to—I thought they'd like—'

Sarah twisted both fists into the ribbing around the bottom of her baggy green sweater. 'Are you sure it was Alexander?'

'Mrs Kelling, do you think I'd be here if I weren't?'

What a kind face the policeman had, she thought, kind and tired, as though he'd had to do this sort of thing too many times.

'The kid called us,' he explained. 'Jed Lomax is a volunteer fireman. He heard the sirens and came to see what was up. Soon as he found out what had happened, he knew who it was. He says he's worked for your folks a long time.'

'That's right. Ever since—I don't know when. Since Alexander was a little boy. I'll get my coat.'

The policeman said something, but Sarah didn't hear what it was. She put on the scruffy old storm coat, not noticing when her sweater sleeves got wadded up halfway to her elbows inside the coat sleeves, and let him lead her out to the patrol cruiser.

She didn't know where he took her. She was in a thick grey fog, like the one she and Alexander had gone walking through that morning. She was taken into a room where there were two high, rolling hospital beds with long bumpy ridges on them covered with white sheets. The sheets were damp in spots, and stained watery red-brown. Before anybody could stop her, she went over to the bed that had the longer ridge and pulled away the cover. Half of Alexander's face was handsome as ever. The other half wasn't there any more.

A hand put back the sheet. A voice said, 'He didn't have time to suffer, if that's any consolation?'

Sarah shook her head. How could there be any consolation? 'Is—is Aunt Caroline—'

'Jeez, I wouldn't look if I were you. For the record,

maybe you could tell us what she was wearing? It's a formality we have to go through.'

Sarah wet her lips. 'I can't seem to remember. Her blue tweed suit, I suppose, and a matching cape. And a blue-and-green-print scarf around her head, and her pearls. She always wore her pearls.'

'No other jewellery?'

'Little gold earrings and a plain gold wedding band. On her right hand, not her left, because she was a widow. Is—is that all right?'

'Fine. Thanks for coming. You'd better go on home and try to get some rest. Walt, you want to take her? Maybe those pearls had better go, too. Are they valuable?'

'Yes.'

Sarah didn't realise she was supposed to take the envelope that was being held out to her. The kind policeman slipped it into her coat pocket and took her by the arm. She pulled the fog back around her and was not aware of anything else until she smelled wood smoke and mildew and knew she was back in the living room of the summer house.

'How about drinking a little more of this wine?' he asked.

Sarah tried to sip at the sherry he was holding to her lips, ashamed that she was making things so difficult for him. 'Please have some yourself,' she urged. 'I'm sure you need it.'

'Thanks, but I'm on duty. I sure could use a cup of coffee, though. Sit still. I can make it, if you don't mind.'

'No, let me. I'd rather be doing something. Or perhaps I could give you a bowl of chowder. I was making it for my husband.'

That was when she went to pieces. The policeman found a clean tea towel and stood clumsily patting her shoulder while she mopped at her face with it and got the sobbing under some kind of control. At last she was able to talk.

'I do beg your pardon. You're being so sweet to me, and I'm acting like a fool. It's just that—I've loved him all my life!'

'Sure, sure. I know how it is. Say, isn't there somebody I can get hold of to come and stay with you? Your mother or your sister?'

'My mother's dead and I have no sister. I'll be all right. I need a little time to get used to it, that's all.'

'But you've got somebody,' he persisted. 'Friends? Relatives?'

'Oh, yes, scads of relatives.'

Poor man, what a pickle for him to be in, alone in a house with a weepy widow.

'Do let me get you a bowl of chowder,' she sniffled. 'Perhaps we'd both feel better if we had some hot food inside us.'

'Sounds great to me, Mrs Kelling.'

She put on the coffeepot and reheated the chowder, got out bowls and pilot biscuit, relieved to be doing something for somebody. The two of them sat down at the kitchen table and spooned up the hot, savoury stuff, not trying to make conversation. Sometimes the food got stuck in Sarah's throat, but she forced herself to swallow and the effort did her good. The policeman's bowl was empty, though, before she was halfway through.

'Please let me get you some more. And what is your name? You're being such a friend in need, I can't simply go on calling you Officer.'

'It's Jofferty,' he told her, 'Sergeant Walter Jofferty.'

'How do you do,' said Sarah mechanically. 'My father's name was Walter. I should have said that I'm Sarah Kelling. My husband is—was—Alexander, and his mother was Caroline. I expect Mr Lomax told you that.'

'Yes, he did. I guess that car was a real old-timer.'

'A nineteen-twenty Milburn. Alexander's grandmother used to drive it.'

'How come you—'

'Didn't get killed with the others?' Sarah made a poor job of smiling at her attempted joke. 'I stayed home to make the chowder. The Milburn wasn't really comfortable for us all to fit in together, and Aunt Caroline enjoyed riding in it much more than I did. She was blind and deaf, you see, so—'

'Oh, sure. You liked to give her what pleasures you could. Pretty helpless, was she?'

'Oh, no, far from that. She was perfectly able to get about and take care of herself so long as she knew where things were. She could read and write Braille and converse if people spelled out words into the palm of her hand. She's been very active in civic affairs with her friend Mrs Lackridge, whom you may have heard of. They work as a team. Aunt Caroline writes reports and so on, and Leila does the contact part. Leila's very good at hand signalling, she and my husband. I'm not fast enough, myself. Aunt Caroline gets impatient. I keep forgetting she's—'

'That's only natural, Mrs Kelling. These things take a while to get used to. How about some more coffee?'

'Not for me, thank you. I seem to have this permanent lump in my throat, as though I'd swallowed an orange whole.'

Sarah pushed away her still-unfinished chowder. 'What I don't understand, Sergeant Jofferty, is how the car went out of control. What was it that child said?'

'It wasn't a child. It was a young guy maybe twenty-two or three, who seemed to be a credible witness. He told us the car came over the crest of the hill fast, zoomed down the hill like a rocket, failed to make the turn at the bottom and sailed right up over the seawall, flipping upside down when it struck the top of the wall. Both passengers were thrown out on to the rocks.'

'But Alexander would never take that hill fast! He'd have to gun the motor to get up, but the brakes would be on all the way down.'

'We can only assume the brakes failed.'

'They couldn't have. My husband was an expert mechanic.'

'It was a very old car,' said Jofferty.

'I know. Perhaps the only Milburn in the world still being driven by the family that bought it. He loved the Milburn.'

Sarah was afraid she was going to cry again. She got up and started to clear the table. 'I suppose I'll have to start thinking about—arrangements.'

'If you'll let them know down at the station who your undertaker is, we'll handle it with him. You won't have to worry about a thing.'

That sounded pretty inane. Jofferty went on hastily, 'As for the car, I don't know if there's enough to salvage, but we can try if you want.'

'No, let the ocean take it. I could never—' Sarah started to tremble again.

'Mrs Kelling,' said the policeman, 'Jed tells me you folks live in Boston and were just here for the weekend. If you'll take my advice, you'll get some of your relatives to drive you back there and spend the night with you.'

'I can drive myself. I have another car here. A nineteen-fifty Studebaker Starlite coupé.'

Sarah began to laugh too shrilly, caught Jofferty's worried look, and sobered down. 'Please don't worry about me. I'll be able to manage now. I know this has been terrible for you, and I've behaved dreadfully, but I do want to thank you for your great kindness.'

'That's okay. You take care of yourself. Give us a call if there's anything else we can do. Thanks for the chowder.'

He unfolded his length from the kitchen chair and reached for the uniform cap he'd tossed on the counter by the sink.

'By the way, your husband didn't happen to be upset? About your mother-in-law's condition, or anything?'

'Upset enough to make him commit murder and suicide, you mean? Why didn't you ask me that in the first place?'

'Now, Mrs Kelling, don't get excited.'

'I'm not excited.'

Sarah was shaking so she could hardly get the words out. 'If you think my husband would do a thing like that, you'd better think again. His mother's condition was no worse than it had been for the past twenty years and he—he loved me very much.'

She had to blow her nose in a hurry. 'He'd never do a thing like this to me, never! And he wouldn't have let any harm come to the Milburn. He was going to leave it to the Larz Anderson Museum. It's right in his will.'

She blew her nose again. 'I suppose you're thinking any wife would say the same, but it happens to be true. I've known Alexander Kelling ever since I was born, and you never knew him at all.'

'We have to ask these things,' sighed Jofferty. 'I'm sorry.'

'I hope you are! Furthermore, I don't believe those brakes failed. Alexander could take the Milburn apart and put it together again in his sleep. He'd know in two minutes if the car wasn't running quite right. And he'd have come straight home to fix it, not try to tackle that ghastly cliff road.'

'Okay, Mrs Kelling, so he didn't do it on purpose and there was nothing wrong with the car. What's the alternative? Did your husband have any history of heart trouble, high blood pressure, dizzy spells, anything of that sort? He wasn't exactly a youngster, was he?'

'Not exactly,' Sarah had to admit. 'He hadn't been feeling awfully well these past few days. I wanted him to see the doctor, but then we—we thought everything was going to be all right. He acted so much better, we thought a—a quiet weekend by the ocean—it was my idea!'

'Sure, sure. Look, it happens to everybody sooner or later. At least we know he didn't have time to suffer.'

Sarah didn't even try to answer. She managed to hold herself in check until Sergeant Jofferty was out of the house. Then she threw herself into one of the broken-down armchairs—the one she'd sat in last night when Alexander told her not to go away because he wanted to look at her. He wouldn't have wanted to see her bawling like this, but what else was there to do?

CHAPTER
SIXTEEN

After a long time, Sarah sat up straight and wiped her eyes on the tea towel Sergeant Jofferty had put into her hand. Sitting here wailing her heart out wasn't going to bring Alexander back. She must get to a telephone and let Edith know what happened before the old retainer heard the news on television. She must hurry back to Boston and begin the dreary work of contacting the undertaker, calling Aunt Marguerite and Cousin Dolph and the rest of the clan, cancelling Aunt Caroline's appointments, getting food in the house, doing all the futile tasks the living have to perform for the dead.

Leila and Harry would be desolated. She ought to get in

touch with them, but how could she when she didn't know where they were? Sarah was trying to force herself to abandon the spurious haven of the armchair when Lomax knocked at the side door and let himself in without waiting for her.

'Miz Alex, I expect you must o' heard—'

'Yes, I know, Mr Lomax. Sergeant Jofferty from the police came and told me. He said you were the one who—'

'Shucks, I done what I could. 'Twasn't much.'

Lomax had paid her the courtesy of taking off the filthy swordfisherman's cap he generally kept on to show his customers they were no better than he for all their money. He was running his hands around and around the edge of the stiff peak; long, knowledgeable hands, like Alexander's.

'The police think the brakes failed on the Milburn,' she told him. 'Can you imagine Mr Alex taking the cliff road if he weren't absolutely certain they'd hold?'

The handy man shifted from one worn-out sneaker to the other, reluctant as always to commit himself. 'He sure was partic'lar about that old electric,' he conceded at last.

'Then could you please tell me what went wrong?'

'I dunno, Miz Alex, but somethin' sure as hell did. I never seen such a Godawful mess in all my born days.'

His lips drew back from his teeth and he began to sweat. Sarah could understand why.

'Oh, Mr Lomax, what a ghastly experience for you! Sit down and let me get you something to drink.'

The man shied off as though she'd made an indecent suggestion. 'Naow, Miz Alex, don't you fret yourself over me. I just come by to see if I could give you a hand shuttin' up the house or anythin'. Don't s'pose you intend to stay the night here, though I daresay I could find somebody to keep you comp'ny if you was o' mind to. Miz Lomax ain't feelin' too peart these days, but I don't doubt but what I could get sister Beetrice over from Gloucester. You know Beetrice, she's been here time an' again to help with parties an' such.'

'Yes, I remember her very well. That's awfully kind of you, but I must get moving as soon as I can pull myself together. There's so much to do, and it looks as though you and I are the only ones left to do it. Please turn off the water and do whatever else you think needs to be taken care of. Oh, and there's a fresh pot of chowder on the stove that I wish you'd take home. Since your wife isn't well, it will save her having to cook. I—I made it for my—'

'That's right nice of you, Miz Alex,' Lomax broke in hastily. 'Miz Kelling, I s'pose I ought to say now. Cripes a'mighty it don't feel right, does it? I 'member Alex a little boy in short pants helpin' me draw the lobster pots.'

He cleared his throat. 'I'll bring back the pot in the mornin'.'

'Don't bother,' Sarah told him. 'I don't expect I'll ever use it again.'

'Means you're plannin' to sell?'

There was alarm behind the question, and Sarah knew why. Estates like this one didn't get sold to private families any more, only to developers who tore down the barny old mansions and put up golf courses or supermarkets or rows of cracker-box houses whose owners weren't likely to hire an ageing caretaker with a sick wife. Sarah shook her head.

'I don't know what I'm going to do, Mr Lomax. Until you asked, it hadn't occurred to me that the place would be mine to sell. You'd better plan to carry on as usual for the time being. I might decide to get rid of the Boston house instead, and perhaps have that old coachman's flat over the carriage house fixed up so I can stay here year round. If I do, you'll have to supervise the work, which would mean giving me quite a lot of extra time for a while. Could you?'

She made the suggestion mainly because she couldn't endure that stricken look on Lomax's face, but it might not be such a bad idea, at that. She'd rather be out here with the bluejays and the woodchucks than have to go on living in Aunt Caroline's house surrounded by relatives and elderly acquaintances who'd all be trying to manage her life for her. Being free to go where she pleased, spend as she pleased would be a new experience. She must not make snap decisions she'd live to regret. Alexander wouldn't want that. Dear God, if he were only coming back!

At least she'd got Lomax looking a shade less grim. 'Sure thing, Miz Alex,' he was saying, 'I'd be glad to handle the whole shebang for you 'cept the plumbin' and wirin'. Got to have a licence for that. But I know a couple o' good men, an' I'd see you didn't get skinned. Just you think it over an' call me any time, day or night.'

He crab-walked himself to the kitchen. A moment later, she saw him through the window, carrying the chowder pot by its wire bail to his rusted-out station wagon. That was one thing taken care of, at any rate. Sarah went to the kitchen, washed up the few dishes she and Sergeant Jofferty had used, and left them to drip on the drainboard. That small sign of human occupancy made the place look one degree less forsaken.

Now that she was on her feet again, it became possible to start getting ready for the drive to Boston. She supposed she ought to change. The news must have come over the radio or television by now and the clans might already have started to gather by the time she got to Beacon Hill. Sooner or later, she'd have to do something about the luggage Alexander and his mother had brought with them. Not now. There were limits to what a person could stand.

Sarah hardly recognised her own face in the mirror. Her skin was puffy and blubbered from so much crying, greenish purple around the eyes, patched with red at the cheekbones. Wisps of hair stuck to her forehead. She looked like something washed up by the tide.

The shivering began again. What if that young man hadn't happened to be watching when the Milburn went over the seawall? They might still be down there, or carried away on the outgoing current with no sign left to show what became of them. That would be worst of all, never to know.

But she still didn't know what had actually occurred, only what little she'd been told. It didn't seem possible Alexander had suffered a sudden collapse. He was always punctilious about medical checkups, kept himself in trim, didn't smoke, and was practically a teetotaller compared to some of her male relatives and acquaintances.

Maybe she shouldn't have let him take that long walk on the beach, or told him about Tim O'Ghee and the rest of it. His nerves might have started playing up again. No, she didn't think so. He'd been fine at lunch, and if he had started to feel tired or tense he'd have brought the Milburn back at once rather than take any risk with the vehicle.

Nevertheless, it had happened. Took off like a rocket, the witness said. How could that be possible? Sarah sat down on the edge of the bed she had shared last night with Alexander, and tried to recall various things he'd told her about the Milburn.

Like other electric cars, it ran on batteries. Could someone have taken out the regular batteries and put in stronger ones? The Milburn's easy-change system took only a few minutes, according to a yellowed advertisement Alexander had kept hanging in the shed, but wouldn't a surge of extra power blow out the wiring and make the car stop short instead of going faster?

Once, ages ago, when Alexander took her for one of their trolley-car rides, he'd shown her how the motorman kept pressing the switch to get up speed, then letting the car coast for a while. He'd explained that the trolley worked on the same principle as the Milburn.

'What would happen if he didn't stop pressing the switch?' she'd asked.

'Plenty,' her cousin had replied with a laugh. 'This isn't like your father's gasoline-powered car, that will keep going at the same rate so long as he keeps feeding it the same amount of gas. This is a direct-current series motor. As long as the current stays on, it keeps accelerating at a faster and faster rate. If the motorman didn't let up on that switch as he's doing, either the motor would fly apart from the strain or else this trolley car would zoom off the tracks and go straight into orbit.'

Sarah had thought that sounded like great fun and tried to coax the motorman into keeping the power on, but he wouldn't. Alexander wouldn't, either. She knew exactly how her husband would take that hill, she'd seen him do it enough times. He'd start feeding current as the grade began to rise, keep the switch on until they were about halfway to the top, then ease off and let momentum carry the car over the crest. To pick up just enough speed and slack off at precisely the right moment required artful handling, but Alexander had been practising ever since he was a boy. He wouldn't make a mistake.

What if he'd tried to ease off the power and couldn't? Sarah had been driving the Studebaker once when its gas pedal stuck. That was scary enough, but at least the engine hadn't kept accelerating while she struggled to work her toe under the pedal and hook it back up.

No, that couldn't happen with the Milburn. As they began the steep descent, its dynamic braking relay would automatically have taken over and held the car back to a safe speed.

What if the dynamic braking resistor were burned out, and Alexander didn't know? Leaving the shed and going out on the level road, he'd have used the mechanical brake. That brake was adequate for general driving but would never have held the Milburn's weight on a really bad hill. With its heavy engine and batteries, the midget electric weighed a great deal more than one would think to look at it. Without that dynamic braking resistor, they'd be out of control and over the wall before they realised what was happening.

Nor was there any way Alexander could have tested the relay in advance. It only worked on steep downgrades, and there wasn't another on their route. He'd have been perfectly confident the mechanism was in perfect order because he'd given the Milburn a thorough overhaul just before he put it up for the winter. The shed was secure, he'd taken every possible precaution against dampness, mice in the wiring, or any other mishap. Nothing had ever gone wrong before. Why should it happen now?

The answer to that was plain enough. Somebody made it happen.

Sarah stuffed the few things she meant to take back with her into a tote bag and rushed out to the Studebaker. As she was starting the engine, she heard another vehicle churning up the drive in low gear. That must be Lomax. She'd have to wait, since two cars couldn't pass on that narrow lane.

'Hope you ain't been hangin' around on account o' me,' he called out when he saw her. 'I figured you'd be gone by now. Gettin' kind o' late.'

'I know it is,' she answered, 'and I should have left ages ago. I'm glad I met you, though, because there's something I want to ask you. When the policeman asked me about salvaging the Milburn I said not to bother, but now I've changed my mind. Do you think it's too late?'

'Gosh, I dunno. Tide was just about on the turn then, an' it's been goin' out ever since. Seems to me I wouldn't count on 'em findin' much by now if I was you. There's an awful strong undertow around them rocks.'

'Would they still make the attempt if I asked?'

'Don't cost nothin' to ask, I don't s'pose. Want I should stop down at the station an' talk to 'em?'

'No, I'll phone from a pay station along the way. You might as well stay here and do whatever needs doing. It seems to be turning colder.'

'Ayuh. Might get a freeze before mornin'. I'll drain them pipes real careful. You take it easy, Miz Alex. Sure you don't mind drivin' alone?'

'Yes, I mind dreadfully, but I might as well get used to it.'

That wasn't very nice of her, now she'd made the poor man squirm. Sarah swung out around the mangled station wagon and started for the Boston road, wondering if the Studebaker had been tampered with, too. Perhaps she'd soon be joining Alexander and Aunt Caroline. Right now, she didn't much care.

CHAPTER
SEVENTEEN

The last time Sarah had driven this road alone she'd been in no fit state to drive, either. At least tonight it wasn't raining. She coaxed the Studebaker along trying not to think of that trip or of anything else but finding a telephone. Lomax was not likely to be mistaken about the chances of salvaging the Milburn, still she had to try.

Oh, God, did she have change for the phone? Yes, Alexander always kept a couple of dimes in the first-aid kit for just such emergencies. Dear, darling, kind, thoughtful Alexander. Her eyes blurred again. She rubbed the back of her glove over them and kept going.

There was a filling station at the corner where the village road met the turnpike. She pulled in there, asked the boy at the pumps to fill her tank, and went to dial the police station.

'Hello, is Sergeant Jofferty there, please?'

'No, ma'am, he's gone off duty. Can somebody else help you?'

'I hope so. This is Mrs Alexander Kelling speaking. You—my husband—'

'Yes, Mrs Kelling. We were just talking about the accident, as a matter of fact. Are you still at Ireson's Landing?'

'No, I'm on my way back to Boston. I've stopped at the gas station. Sergeant Jofferty asked me what I wanted you people to do about salvaging the Milburn and I said not to bother, but now I'm wondering if it's too late to change my mind.'

'Gosh, Mrs Kelling, I'm afraid so, unless we manage to pick up something on the beach. We sent a couple of scuba divers down for the—when it happened—but they got banged around on the rocks so badly that they did what they had to and quit. We'll have somebody go down with a searchlight at low tide, and have a look around, but I can't honestly say there's much hope. The car pretty well disintegrated when it hit.'

'I was afraid of that,' said Sarah, 'but I was hoping we could rescue the motor. I've been racking my brain about what went wrong, and all I can think of is that the dynamic brake resistor must have burned out. You see, it was a direct-current series motor, like a trolley car, and—'

She must have sounded as if she were babbling. The policeman cut in.

'Yes, we know, Mrs Kelling. We thought of the dynamic brake relay, too. That's the most logical explanation.'

'Yes, but I want to find it and see why it didn't work.'

'With a car that age, anything could happen.'

'The Milburn was in absolutely top-notch condition. There's no earthly reason why the dynamic brake relay should have failed unless somebody tampered with it.'

'I see. Well, we'll do our best, and let you know if we come up with anything. Take it easy, Mrs Kelling.'

And that was that. He didn't believe her. He thought he was dealing with a hysterical widow, which he was. Sarah fished out her other dime and used it to put in a collect call to Edith. As she'd feared, the old retainer had already got news of the wreck and was in a taking because she hadn't been properly informed beforehand.

'You might at least have let me know. I almost had a heart attack, seeing it on the television like that.'

'This is the first chance I've had to get to a telephone,' Sarah replied as patiently as she could. 'The one at the house is shut off for the winter, as you must have realised. Do try to calm yourself, Edith. I'll be there as soon as I can. I suppose people have been calling.'

'Phone's been ringing every two minutes, everybody wanting to know where you are. I told 'em I didn't know because I hadn't heard from you.'

'That was rather unnecessary, wasn't it? You knew perfectly well where I must be. Is anybody with you?'

'Mr Jem,' the maid admitted grudgingly. 'He heard it on the news, too. Been here since half-past six, drinking up Mr Alex's scotch. He's in there talking to some reporters now.'

'Oh, good heavens! Well, tell him to hold the fort. I'll see you in half an hour or so.'

Sarah hadn't thought of the newspapers, but since the Kellings had already made the front pages once this week, it would be too much to hope they wouldn't pick up this new calamity. Uncle Jem could no doubt handle them a great deal more capably than she.

She was taking out her wallet to pay for the gas when another car, far newer and more sumptuous than hers, drove up to the pumps. The attendant deserted her abruptly.

'Hey, Max, how's it going? Been over to the house?'

'Where else? You're supposed to stop for bread on your way home if Eddie's still open. Go finish with your customer. Good Lord, is that you, Mrs Kelling?'

'Mr Bittersohn! Then you—belong around here?'

'Not really. I'm an immigrant from Saugus. This is my nephew, Mike Rivkin, whose old man owns the station and had the good taste to marry my sister.' He got out of his car and came over to her. 'I heard about the accident. I'm sorry.'

'It wasn't—' Sarah stopped abruptly. She'd been about to say, 'It wasn't an accident.' Why should she tell secrets to this man just because his nephew pumped her gas, and why would he believe her when the police didn't?

Bittersohn was looking at her keenly. 'Are you sure you feel up to driving?'

'I have to get back.'

'That wasn't my question. Look, Mrs Kelling, I'm on my way to Boston, too. Why don't you ride with me and let my nephew bring your car into town tomorrow morning? He goes to Boston University.'

'Thank you, I'd like to.'

Sarah was about to hand over the car keys when a disagreeable thought struck her. 'Perhaps I'd better not. It mightn't be safe.'

'Mike's a perfectly capable driver.'

'I'm sure he is, but I'm afraid there may be something wrong with the car.'

'Why do you say that?'

'Because I don't know. That's the awful part. I don't know!'

Bittersohn took her by the arm and shook her a little. 'Give Mike your keys and registration. He won't drive your car till his father's mechanic has given it a thorough checking. If it's not safe for him, it's sure as hell not safe for you. Come on.'

Sarah was all to pieces now. She let Bittersohn lead her to his elegant automobile and collapsed in a huddle on the gorgeous leather seat. He reached across her to the glove compartment, fumbled for a mangled box of tissues, and dropped it in her lap. Then he switched on the ignition and nosed out into the traffic. They drove for quite a distance before Sarah was able to say anything.

At last she managed, 'You're being very kind, the way my husband used to be. Alexander was the kindest man who ever lived.'

Once she'd got started, she found it natural to go on talking, about the times when Alexander would take her out walking on Sunday afternoons, the times they sneaked over to Bailey's for a strictly forbidden sundae with nuts and marshmallow and hot fudge sauce spilling over the sides of the dish and down on the little silver plate, the times innumerable they rode the swanboats and fed the greedy mallards that could pedal as fast as the boatman.

It was good to remember those happy times, a relief to share them with somebody so they wouldn't be lost and forgotten if anything happened to her. She cried most of the way but it was quiet crying, gentle tears that slid unnoticed down her cheeks and gave her ease. By the time they got on Storrow Drive, she felt spent but calmed—no longer torn to pieces with anguish for what she had lost, but filled with gratitude for the love she had known.

'I'll drop you at your house if you'll tell me how to get there. These one-way streets have me buffaloed.'

That was almost the first thing Bittersohn had said, except a word now and then to show he was listening. Sarah responded thankfully.

'I don't wonder you're confused. They wait till everybody gets the directions memorised, then turn all the arrows around.'

She explained how he could best thread the maze. 'I do hope it's not too much out of your way, and I do apologise for being such dreary company, but it was—I can't tell you.' She laughed a little. 'That sounds pretty silly, when I've been telling you my life's history.'

'Not the whole of it, I expect.' Bittersohn opened the car door and helped her out as if she'd been an old woman. 'Take it easy here. I can't understand why you people on the Hill don't make the city do something about these treacherous brick sidewalks.'

'You're talking sacrilege,' she told him. 'Oh, dear, I hope I didn't leave my door key with your nephew.'

'Isn't anybody in the house?'

'My uncle, I believe, and Edith, our maid. Aunt Caroline had to have someone around to do her hair and all that. You must be sick of hearing about our domestic concerns. Ah, here's my key. Goodnight and—and thank you. About those drawings, I don't—'

If Sarah had been in any condition to observe, she'd have seen an odd expression flicker across Bittersohn's face.

'I'm afraid I still have some explaining to do about that project, Mrs Kelling. Mind if I give you a ring sometime soon?'

'I wish you would. It would be a comfort.'

'Think so?'

'I hope so!' It was a strange reply to make, but Sarah had given up trying to make sense. She gave the man's hand a squeeze, unlocked the door, and let herself in.

Jeremy Kelling was ensconced in the front hall, bellowing into the telephone, scribbling on one of Aunt Caroline's note pads. When he saw his niece come in, he rang off abruptly and got up to greet her.

'Here you are at last. We've been wondering if you'd make it in one piece.'

Sarah dropped her coat and bag. 'Mr Bittersohn brought me home.'

'Who's Mr Bittersohn?'

'A relative of the people at the gas station. What's happening?'

'Damned phone's ringing off the hook. Everybody wants to know the gory details.'

'I wish I did. We're supposed to get hold of the undertaker and tell them to contact the police at Ireson's Landing. I don't suppose it's any use calling Wellingtons at this hour. It was Wellingtons we had for Daddy, and Great-uncle Frederick, wasn't it?'

'And their fathers and grandfathers and one hell of a lot of other Kellings before and after and in between. They ought to give us a cut rate. It's not all that late, I expect they've got somebody answering the phone. I'll give them a ring, shall I? Sarah, you look like the wrath of God!'

'How would you expect me to look? This hasn't been exactly a fun day, Uncle Jem. Where's Edith?'

'Off sulking, I expect. She was doing a Sarah Bernhardt all over the house, so I told her to go soak her head.'

'Good for you. I'm going to soak mine and see if it will work any better.'

'Have some scotch. Bring me another while you're about it.'

The phone shrilled. Sarah left her uncle to cope and went to bathe her face and comb her hair in the downstairs bathroom. She fetched her uncle's drink, asked if he wanted anything to eat and was told he damn well did, got him a plate of sandwiches, went down to check on Edith and found her full of port and lamentations, put the old retainer to bed, and was hoping to perform the same service for herself when the Lackridges blew in.

'We bumped into each other at the airport. Both of us came rushing back when we heard the news. They had it on CBS!'

Leila was keyed up, set to take charge. Harry looked half drunk and wholly crushed. Sarah made more drinks and sandwiches, put on a pot of coffee, tried to comfort Harry while his wife wrested the telephone from Jeremy Kelling and started taking calls with crisp efficiency.

Sarah soothed her uncle's hurt feelings, got straightened out with him about the undertaker, thanked him profusely and kissed him goodnight. Harry walked the old man home, detoured via the liquor store for a fresh supply of whisky on his way back, and was soon maudlin, sobbing that he wanted to sleep in dear old Alex's room for auld lang syne.

Sarah steered him to the third floor, changed the sheets, found clean pyjamas, and left him to manage as he could. She got Aunt Caroline's room ready for Leila; finally got the woman to stop talking and call it a night. By then it was nearly two in the morning. Sarah had expected to cry herself to sleep, but by then she was too far gone for tears.

CHAPTER EIGHTEEN

It would have done her good to sleep late, but from force of habit Sarah woke at seven, still exhausted, her head spinning with hideous recollections and thoughts of things that had to be done. The absolute number one priority was to get downstairs before Leila did, lest what might remain of Edith's morale be shattered at the one time when she might conceivably be of some real use. What was to be done with the old retainer? Alexander ought to have made some provision for her, but how could he when he had no money?

She shelved that worry for the moment, put on an old plaid skirt and a navy blue sweater, and ran down to put on the coffeepot. It hadn't begun to perk before the first call came in, an ancient second cousin of Aunt Caroline's wanting to know about funeral arrangements, train schedules, and his chances of free lodging. Sarah told him the funeral notice would be in the evening papers, he'd have to call the station about trains, and she'd furnish a bed if he didn't mind climbing three flights of stairs—knowing he'd mind a great deal.

The last thing she wanted was a houseful of relatives, but it soon became apparent that she was getting one, regardless. By the time Leila appeared clutching one of Caroline Kelling's crepe kimonos around her bean-pole form, Sarah had a sheaf of memoranda ranging from 'Sherry, cream, ham, butter, bread, lettuce' to 'Check enuf toil. ppr.' and 'Order wheelchair Aunt Em. flt. 426 Alleg. 3:17.'

'God, what a night!' The first of the self-invited guests slumped into a wooden chair and lit a cigarette. 'Where's Edith?'

'In bed, I suppose,' said Sarah. 'I hope she's able to function when and if she does get up. There's an enormous lot to do.'

'Don't let it throw you, Sarah. I'll cope.'

'You will not!'

Sarah surprised herself by the vehemence of her refusal, but didn't moderate her tone much. 'This is my house, and I'll manage my own affairs as I see fit.'

'How?' Mrs Lackridge took a scornful drag at her cigarette. 'You've never managed anything in your life.'

'Leila, you don't know that. You've never cared enough about me to notice what I do. We may as well have this out right here and now. You've been a wonderful friend to Aunt Caroline, and, of course, Harry and Alexander were close as brothers. You've both been tolerating me since Alexander and I got married because you had no alternative, and I've felt more or less the same about you. I hope we can maintain a pleasant relationship for old times' sake, but I have no intention of becoming involved in your affairs, and I'll thank you to stay clear of mine. Would you like some toast and coffee?'

For a moment Leila sat stock-still, her opaque brown eyes hooded like a snake's. Then she emitted a little snort of laughter.

'If that's the way you want it, Sarah. No toast, just coffee. I never eat in the morning. Shall I go up and rouse the sleeping beauty, or will you allow us to occupy your premises a while longer?'

'Let him sleep,' said Sarah. 'I'm not asking you to leave, I simply wanted to put things straight. I know this is an ordeal for you as well as myself, and I honestly would be grateful for your help if we can just keep things in their proper perspective. Perhaps you'd like to go over those messages you took last night?'

Leila stubbed out her cigarette in the saucer and went to fetch her notes. Together they went through the lot, adding to the list of things to do, interrupted by more phone calls that Leila scrupulously refrained from taking unless Sarah asked her to. She didn't seem to resent the scolding, and Sarah had no qualms about having delivered it. That was just one of the things that needed to be done. By the time Edith, puffy-faced and straggle-haired, stumped upstairs to the kitchen, Sarah had a sheet of instructions ready to hand her. She didn't even bother to look at it.

'I can't.'

'Yes, you can,' said her new mistress. 'Call up Mariposa and ask if she can give us some extra time. Never mind, I'll do it myself. Drink some coffee and pull yourself together.'

The old retainer turned to Leila for sympathy. Mrs Lackridge cast an eye at Sarah, shrugged, and went on checking her lists. Sarah found Mariposa at home, volubly sympathetic and ready to oblige. She breathed a sigh of relief and hung up.

'She'll be here in half an hour. She can start the downstairs work. Edith, you're to clear out Mrs Kelling's room and make the bed up fresh, and don't spend all morning at it. Shove her personal things in the dresser drawers and make a little room in the closet.'

'You're not putting company in *her* room!'

'What else am I to do, swing Aunt Emma in a hammock from the bathroom ceiling? Mr Lackridge is in Mr Alexander's bed. When he wakes up, give him coffee or whatever he wants, then straighten that room and change the bed for Cousin Mabel. Cousin Frederick will have to sleep on the library couch, but we can't do anything about that now. Get things set up for tea and keep an ear peeled for the doorbell. Have you a clean apron to put on?'

'Yes'm.'

That was the meekest syllable Edith had even been heard to utter. Even Leila was impressed.

'My God, Sarah, you are a tiger when you get going. What else would you like me to do?'

'Stay here, if you will, and answer that ghastly telephone while I run out for some groceries. I shan't be long. If Harry wakes up, ask him how I go about getting some money.'

'Do you need cash right now?'

'No, they'll let me charge down at the corner. Thank you, Leila.'

It was a relief to get out of the house for a while, but when Sarah struggled back with two great bags of provisions, she found another lot of messages waiting. The undertaker wanted to see her about the caskets and the minister about the service, and could she please be punctual because of his tight Sunday schedule? She ran upstairs, changed into a black-wool dress and coat of her mother's, and ran down again. Mariposa was there by then, dressed in a crisp white uniform instead of her usual insouciant garb. Like the Prodigal Son, Sarah fell on her neck.

'You're an angel to give up your Sunday. Don't do any heavy cleaning, just tidy around and make things presentable. I expect scads of people will start dropping in, and there'll be three staying overnight, so we'll have to get started on some food. Could you take telephone messages, do you think?'

'I can sure try, Miz Alex.'

'Good, then you're relieved, Leila. I expect you'll want to go home and change.'

'I can take a hint,' Mrs Lackridge replied with no apparent rancour. 'What about His Highness?'

'Let him sleep as long as he will. Surely he'll have come to by the time we need the room. You wouldn't care to meet Aunt Emma at the airport, I don't suppose, and come back for drinks and supper with the mob?'

'Why not? Anything else?'

'Probably, but I can't think of it just now. You're being

marvellous, Leila, and I do appreciate what you're doing. You understand, I hope?'

'Forget it. I'd feel the same, no doubt. See you later, then.'

'Right. I have to fly.'

Sarah flew. Ten minutes later she was in a place of subdued lighting and soulful Muzak, contemplating polished walnut and satin padding in the company of a black-clad dignitary who oozed understanding and quoted prices with hushed reverence; as well he might, considering what they were. The loved ones had arrived, he told her, but he was quite sure she'd prefer not to see them at this time. Under the circumstances, the whole problem of viewing was going to present difficulties. Sarah swallowed hard and said there would be no viewing.

Nor did she wish to select from a well-stocked wardrobe of available garb. Nobody was going to see the clothes, anyway. Aunt Caroline could wear the grey lace she'd always looked so regal in, and Alexander might as well get his money's worth at last out of that dress suit. Her darling would enjoy the joke, if he were somehow able to know.

Sarah began to cry, was enveloped in professional solicitude and gently led to put her mind on flowers. She decided on a blanket of white carnations for Aunt Caroline, red for her husband. Red for Ruby Redd. She changed her mind and ordered bronze chrysanthemums. She must get out of this place before she started to howl like a wolf.

'Thank you,' she babbled, 'I'll have the clothing ready for you. Call if there's anything else you need. If I'm not at home, somebody will take a message.'

'Yes, Mrs Kelling. Certainly, Mrs Kelling. You can rely on us, Mrs Kelling.'

She was eased gently out the door and rushed off to meet the minister in his study, trying not to take up too much of his time crying because he still had a wedding to perform and evening service to conduct. She made it back to the house by about half-past two. Edith answered the door, wearing her best black uniform and lace cap.

'I hope you've had your lunch,' was her cheery greeting.

'No, I haven't,' Sarah snapped. 'Make me a sandwich—I don't care what—and a cup of tea as quickly as you can. I have to get some things for the undertaker, then meet Mrs Cobble at Back Bay. Mrs Lackridge has gone to the airport. What's Mariposa doing?'

'Helping me peel potatoes.'

From the pristine condition of Edith's apron, it was obvious who was doing the work and who the heavy looking on. Sarah wasn't about to stand for that.

'You can finish them yourself. Tell Mariposa to bring my lunch and whatever messages she's taken, as soon as the tea's ready. I'm going upstairs for a minute, then I'll be in the library.'

She packed Alexander's dress suit and a white tie, along with fresh underthings and a stiff-bosomed shirt. Harry Lackridge was still snoring in her husband's bed which was probably a good thing since his presence made her less disposed to linger and weep. She went and got Aunt Caroline's grey lace and brought everything down to the front hall. She was warm with all the rushing about, but felt the need of a fire to take the chill out of her soul. The kindling was catching on nicely when Mariposa brought the tray into the library.

'My, don't that look cosy. I made you a cheese omelet instead of a cold sandwich, Miz Alex. I bet you haven't eaten anything all day.'

'I had some chowder. No, that was yesterday. Who's been calling?'

'Everybody, seems like.'

Mariposa pulled a sheaf of notes from her pocket. The spelling was creative, but the facts appeared to be straight. Sarah read them over while she toasted her toes and ate her omelet. This was the first moment's peace she'd had all day and was likely to be the last. She was still sipping her tea when visitors began to arrive.

From then on there was no letup. Harry roused himself and came downstairs, fortunately in time to go and meet Cousin Mabel's train at Back Bay since Sarah couldn't very well walk out on her guests. Edith hovered near the front door, hanging up coats and accepting condolences as if she were the chief mourner. Mariposa was everywhere, trotting about with trays of sandwiches and pots of tea, coping with the telephone, finally strong-arming Sarah upstairs for a brief rest before supper.

'Miz Alex, there are so many people in this house right now everybody's going to think you're in the other room talking to somebody else. You sneak up the back stairs and catch yourself forty winks, else you're going to fall flat on your face in the soup.'

By this time, Leila was back, looking rather handsome in dark grey wool with a high rolled collar, being a great success with friends and relatives who knew Leila Lackridge far better than they did this white-faced, hollow-eyed Sarah Kelling who wasn't Walter's little girl any more. She might as well do the hostessing for a while. Sarah slipped up to her room, took off her mother's dress, and lay down on the bed. She thought she'd barely shut her eyes when Mariposa was beside her saying folks were beginning to wonder about supper and what should they do?

'Start setting out the buffet. I'll be down in two minutes.'

Feeling a trifle better for the nap, Sarah ran a comb through her hair, put on the black dress she was learning to hate, and went down to her company. She'd forgotten to put on any makeup and looked ghastly without it, but nobody would expect her to appear otherwise.

The meal was excellent, partly because Sarah had planned a simple but generous buffet, and partly because it was not Edith but Mariposa who'd somehow found time to prepare most of the food. The old retainer was on hand to dish up and take full credit, however.

Sarah got through it as best she could, answering the same questions over and over like a talking doll. No, she hadn't had time to decide what she'd do about the properties. Yes, it was a shame to lose the Milburn on top of everything else. Yes, she'd have a tremendous adjustment ahead of her. No, she didn't suppose she'd quite taken it all in yet and would Cousin Mabel care for more ham?

It was an unspeakable relief when the visitors were gone, the house guests bedded down, and Sarah at last free to go to bed; but as soon as she woke on Monday, the whole thing started again. There was breakfast to get, lunch to plan, more shopping, more telephone calls, more petty annoyances, like springing a run in her last pair of panty hose and not having a dollar left to buy another.

Leila, unable to stay away from the eye of the cyclone, was at the house almost at the crack of dawn. She monopolised the telephone for half the morning reassigning various projects and committee obligations Caroline Kelling had been involved in, but Sarah didn't mind that. It was a relief not to hear the thing ringing every few minutes.

The doorbell was bad enough. It had been a mistake not to have visiting hours at the undertaker's. As it was, everybody who'd ever sat on a platform with Caroline Kelling felt free to pay his respects at the house. Most of the callers were total strangers to Sarah. Leila knew everybody, though, so the widow left her to play hostess again and went to keep the appointment Harry had made for her with the family lawyer.

He was inclined to pussyfoot. Sarah was in no mood to listen.

'Mr Redfern, I have a houseful of relatives to feed, a funeral to pay for, a great deal of money in trust, and not one cent in my pocket. I don't need words, I need cash, and I need it right this minute!'

Hysteria, she was finding, has its uses. After a little more backing and forthing, Mr Redfern decided there would be no serious impropriety in Sarah's continuing to draw the not very generous household allowance Alexander had been in the habit of drawing each week. Large bills, such as the undertaker's, could be sent to him for payment until such time as her estate was transferred to a different trustee.

Sarah didn't see why there had to be any trustee at all, but for the moment she must be satisfied with what she could get. She went to the bank and cashed the cheque he had given her, bought her panty hose and a fresh supply of loaves and fishes, and went back to feed the multitudes.

The funeral was set for three o'clock that afternoon. She had no time to sit brooding over her bereavement, which was perhaps a good thing. Mariposa had other commitments today so Sarah had to make do with Edith's help, which didn't amount to much. They'd barely got the luncheon dishes cleared away when it was time to make herself presentable before the hired limousine came to pick up herself, her house guests, and Edith, who could not in decency be left out of the cortege. Alexander would have deplored the extra expense, but how else was she to cope with Aunt Emma's rheumatics, Cousin Frederick's heart, and Cousin Mabel's general cussedness?

She was told afterwards that the church was crowded. She saw nobody. By keeping her mind absolutely blank and her face rigid, Sarah managed to get through the service. It wasn't until the graveside ceremony was almost through, and she had to realise they were actually going to bury her darling Alexander forever and ever, that she broke down.

Leila, who'd managed to get to the forefront, shook her savagely by the arm. 'For God's sake pull yourself together,' she hissed. 'You're making a public spectacle of yourself.'

'Oh, shut up!' Sarah screamed. 'He was my husband and I loved him, and I'll cry for him all I want. Anybody who doesn't like it can go to hell!'

Everybody heard, of course. A few gasped, one or two snickered. Jeremy and Dolph started to Sarah's side, but it was wizened old Cousin Frederick who threw his arm around her in a most uncharacteristic gesture of spontaneous affection.

'You tell 'em, Sadie. Alex was a man worth crying for. If that scrawny bitch had anything but gin and vinegar in her veins, she'd be crying, too.'

'Damn right, Fred,' bellowed Dolph. 'Furthermore, Sarah knows enough to stay home and attend to her family obligations, instead of jumping around like a whirligig, shooting her mouth off, and getting her name in the papers. Mabel, if you don't quit tugging at my coat-tails—'

The minister hastily pronounced the benediction. Cousin Dolph and Cousin Frederick, feisty as a pair of superannuated gamecocks, took Sarah's arms between them and got her back to the limousine before she could be driven to shrieking frenzy by overtaxed nerves and the sight of those two elegant mahogany coffins propped over those two six-foot-deep holes in the ground.

CHAPTER
NINETEEN

Sarah had been sustaining herself with the expectation that once the funeral was over everybody would go away, but it wasn't that simple. Old friends had to be asked back for a final glass of sherry, relatives fortified with cold beef and salad for their homeward journeys, luggage collected, rides arranged, parting speeches listened to, Cousin Mabel dissuaded from staying on a few days to be a prop and mainstay.

When the rest had cleared out, the Lackridges and Edgar Merton were still to be got rid of. The three of them haunted the library where they had spent so much time with Caroline and Alexander, looking as bereft as they must be feeling. Overnight Edgar had turned from middle-aged to old, his cameo features pinched and bleached, his small frame shortened by a stoop. Harry, in contrast, was redder and thicker, his waistline bloated, his high-bridged nose flushed with emotion and liquor. With loose skin hanging in wattles below his insignificant chin and that potbelly swelling out above those overly long, spindly legs, he looked like a plucked turkey. Sarah knew how they felt, but she did wish they'd go away. At last, when she'd all but fallen asleep in her chair, they did. Even then remained Edith and her litany of woes. At the old retainer, Sarah drew the line.

'You're absolutely right, Edith,' she said. 'This place will never be the same again. Nor do I intend to keep it up one day longer than I have to, so there's no earthly reason why you should feel duty-bound to stay on. As you know, Mr Alexander has been paying Social Security for you, and don't try to make me believe you're not old enough to collect. I don't know whether he's made any provision for you in his will, but I'll see that you get a reasonable pension, although candidly I don't know what you've ever done to deserve it. With that and what you've managed to salt away over the years, you should be able to live very comfortably, and you might as well start thinking right now about where you want to go.'

'I knew this would happen,' cried the maid. 'Before

they're cold in their graves, you're throwing me out in the street.'

'Edith, you can't have it both ways,' Sarah said wearily. 'Just now you were moaning that you couldn't bear to stay, now you're throwing a snit because I'm taking you at your word. I know these past days have been hard on you, but they've been no picnic for me, either. I'm going upstairs, and you may do as you please.'

What Edith chose to do was flounce down to the basement, pack everything she'd accumulated over the years into two enormous suitcases, a vast number of cardboard cartons and shopping bags and a nice old steamer trunk that had belonged to Sarah's grandmother, to which she had no right whatsoever. She then called her nephew from Malden to come and get her with his pickup truck, and sat down to compose a letter to Sarah, stating in haughty detail where to send the pension cheques.

Sarah stayed upstairs till all was over. She'd meant to go straight to bed, but there was no sense in that. Edith would be sure to leave lights blazing and doors unlocked. It would be quite in character for her to march up and deliver a valedictory blast, dragging, her nephew along by way of audience. If that happened, Sarah didn't want to be caught in her nightgown.

She puttered around the bedrooms, stripping off used linen and making the beds up fresh, though she couldn't think who was ever going to sleep in them again. What she'd told Edith was true, she knew now. She was definitely going to move out as soon as Mr Redfern would let her put the white elephant on the market.

Sarah was immensely relieved when the loaded pickup truck drove away with no disagreeable final scene. Then she realised that for the first time in her life, she was all alone in the house. And what if she was? Plenty of women lived alone. She went downstairs and started checking doors and windows, making sure everything was secure.

The basement, she found, had been stripped to the walls. Edith had taken everything but the cast iron cookstove. Perhaps the old retainer honestly believed the furniture was hers, she'd lived with it so long. More likely, she'd succumbed to the urge to grab what she could while she had the chance. Sarah didn't care, the stuff couldn't have been worth much anyway.

But what about Edith herself? Wasn't it stupid to let her go without at least making an effort to question her? Sarah was too tired to care any more about things that had happened in the past. The only death she could think about was Alexander's, and there was just no way Edith could have tampered with the Milburn. She'd been here in Boston, soaking her corns and drinking port.

Or had she? They'd never called the house until some hours after the so-called accident. For all Sarah knew, Edith could have been anywhere in the meantime, perhaps visiting that nephew in Malden, the one who'd just left here in a truck that had 'TV Repair' painted on the sides. A man who could cope with modern electronic devices must know all sorts of clever ways to short-circuit the simplest kind of electric motor.

Would any nephew, however devoted, do such a thing to oblige his dear old auntie? He might, if he thought Auntie was down for something handsome in her supposedly rich employers' wills.

Sarah's insides growled and she laughed with relief. Thank God for bodies! There was nothing like a clamorous stomach to quiet an anxious mind. Although she'd bought and cooked and served enormous quantities of food during the past couple of days, she couldn't recall having eaten much of anything herself. Part of this appalling hollowness she felt might be plain, old-fashioned hunger.

Edith had scooped out most of the leftovers as part of her loot, but Sarah managed to find some cold meat and a little salad. She made herself a pot of tea and ate at the kitchen table, not bothering to set a proper place. She was rinsing her cup under the tap when the telephone rang. Sighing, she picked up the extension phone and was surprised to hear the voice of Max Bittersohn.

'I thought you'd like to know my brother-in-law checked out your car and could find nothing wrong. Mike's going to bring it in to Boston tomorrow morning, if that's okay with you.'

Sarah was a little taken aback. 'To tell you the truth, Mr Bittersohn, I'd forgotten about the car. I ought to have got in touch with your people myself, but it's been absolutely wild around here. Yes, if you're sure he'd be safe, I'd love to have your nephew drive it in. Where should I meet him? As for the bill—'

'Forget it. They didn't do anything, just looked. And Mike may never get another chance to drive a Studebaker.'

'I ought to see that he does, after this. Really, you and your family are being much too kind to a—I was going to say a stranger, but we can't be that now, can we?'

'How about "colleague"? That's a fancy word I've always wanted to have applied to myself. Seen Lackridge, by the way?'

'Heavens, yes. He and Leila have been sticking like flies on honey. I just got rid of them a little while ago.'

Sarah realised what she was saying. 'Please forget that. It's only that I've been deluged with vistors, and it's been such a chore trying to look after them.'

'What about your maid?'

'What, indeed? I don't have her any more.'

'Why not?'

'We never had got along, and finally things came to a boil. I knew I'd have to do something about her sooner or later, though I must admit it came a bit sooner than I'd planned.'

'When did she leave?'

'About half an hour ago.'

'Then who's with you?' Bittersohn asked sharply.

'Nobody.'

'You can't stay there alone.'

'Why not? Don't you believe in liberated womanhood?' Sarah asked with a bravado she didn't feel.

'Look, Mrs Kelling, this is no time to be a heroine. You've been through one hell of an experience, and you're not used to being by yourself in a big house. If you can't find somebody to come in, you'd better clear out of there. Go to a hotel or something.'

'But I'd still be alone there, and it would cost a fortune. You're sweet to be concerned, Mr Bittersohn, but I'll be fine, truly I will.'

'Then at least do me a favour and write down this telephone number. Do you have a phone by your bed?'

'No, I wish I did. We just have the two on the first floor.'

She thought he swore, but what came through was, 'Got a pencil?'

'Yes, right here.'

He gave her the number, slowly and distinctly, then made her read it back to him to make sure she'd got it right.

'Okay. Now, no matter what time it is, call me for any reason at all—if you're scared, if you think you hear mice in the cellar, if you can't sleep and want to talk, if you need eggs for breakfast. I'm not far from you, and I can be there in a few minutes. I'd come now, but you'd probably be better pleased if I didn't.'

'I was planning to go to bed soon,' Sarah admitted.

'You don't take sleeping pills?'

'No, nothing like that. I don't have any and wouldn't use them if I did.'

'Good. Take a couple of aspirin if you need something to calm you down. They're about as effective and a damn sight safer. Could you make up a bed downstairs, near the phone?'

'I expect so. A cousin of my father's slept on the library couch last night, as a matter of fact, although I'm afraid he didn't find it very comfortable.'

'There are things more uncomfortable than a bumpy sofa.'

'Mr Bittersohn, are you by any chance trying to frighten me?'

'I'm trying to keep you from being frightened if I can,' he said. 'If I've picked the wrong way to go about it, I'm sorry.'

'Please don't be. I do appreciate your concern, and I'll certainly take advantage of your extremely kind offer if I have any occasion to call. Thank you again for taking care of the car.'

Sarah put the phone back on its holder and sat looking at the number she'd written down, memorising the digits without quite meaning to. Either Mr Bittersohn was simply one of the sweetest men she'd ever met, or else he knew something he wasn't telling. Would it be safe to phone him if she needed to, or would she be letting herself in for more trouble?

In any event, his urging her to sleep closer to a telephone

made sense. She was not about to torture her exhausted body on that lumpy old couch, but she might at least move to Aunt Caroline's room instead of cloistering herself on the third floor. Then she wouldn't be constantly reminded that Alexander was no longer up there with her. She was getting so that she could think of him without starting to cry, which was a help. What she ought to do right now was start clearing out Aunt Caroline's closets and drawers, and moving her own things downstairs.

The work was therapeutic though wearisome. Sarah lugged armloads of clothes down to the laundry room where they could be sorted out and got rid of, to charities or relatives. Caroline Kelling had never thrown anything away. Sarah found evening gowns that must have been part of her trousseau, bought, no doubt, to set off the Kelling jewels. They might fetch a tidy sum at the Bargain Box even now. She herself wanted none of the things, lovely as they were. How could she ever wear them, knowing what had happened to the man who paid for them?

Sarah went on with her search. She rooted through drawers crammed with embroidered crepe-de-Chine nightgowns, with lace-trimmed chemises and step-ins from the flapper era, with real silk stockings that had seams up their backs. She unearthed a mauve satin lingerie case containing some astonishing black panties and, to her ineffable relief, the neatly tagged key to the safe-deposit box.

By ten o'clock, Sarah couldn't have lifted another handkerchief. She found geranium-scented bath salts in the bathroom that was so much more luxurious than the one she'd shared with Alexander, and used them lavishly. After a hot soak, she felt drowsy enough to crawl into Aunt Caroline's massive bed and hope for sleep. It came.

Shortly before three o'clock, Sarah was awake again. She didn't know what had roused her, all she knew was that suddenly she was sitting up straight, straining her eyes and ears into the silent dark. For a moment it seemed impossible that she would ever move again, then she persuaded her hand muscles to reach out and switch on a light.

It was cold, astonishingly cold. She hadn't opened a

window when she had gone to bed—there was never any dearth of fresh air in this draughty old house. Yet she could feel a blast coming from somewhere.

Either burglars or a broken sash cord, she thought. More likely a sash cord. She was used to such mishaps. Boston was always damp, with the harbour in front and the river alongside. Cords rotted, releasing iron sash weights. Plate-glass windows with their heavy wooden frames fell with a crash, losing their panes as often as not. She'd better go stick something over it before she froze to death.

Sarah's bathrobe was still upstairs, so she wrapped Aunt Caroline's velvet-covered down comforter around her, shoved her feet into a pair of fur-trimmed satin mules she found, and padded out into the hall. Soot-laden wind was swirling down from the third floor.

It was coming from Alexander's room, and that was odd. The last sash cord that had let go was also in his room, also in the middle of the night, and he'd replaced both cords forthwith to make sure he didn't get another such rude awakening. That was only a few months ago. How could it happen again so soon?

She switched on the light. It was not one window, it was both, wide open from the top, their white curtains whipping out like dancing ghosts. More incredibly, the bed Sarah had made up fresh a few hours before was in total disarray, sheets and blankets dragged off on the floor as though a sleeper had waked feeling suffocated, flung off his bedding, and rushed to let in the night air.

In spite of her down comforter, Sarah began to shiver. It's only a burglar, she kept telling herself, only a plain flesh-and-blood burglar. And she must be out of her mind, standing here waiting to be pounced on. She slammed Alexander's door shut on the eerie scene, made a mad scramble for Aunt Caroline's room, and locked herself in. If he wanted the silver, let him take it and go in peace.

But if someone had come to steal the tea service, what was he doing on the third floor, tearing the beds apart? How did he get there? She'd locked everything tight, she knew she had. After that phone call from Mr Bittersohn, she'd even gone up to the attic and checked the skylight, in case anybody might take a notion to break in from the roof.

Could a thief have tied a rope to the chimney and swung down over the side of the house, jimmying open Alexander's windows to get in? But why both? Why choose the side that faced the street, instead of coming down the alleyway where he'd be less apt to be spotted?

Aunt Caroline's boudoir was directly under her son's bedroom. Sarah went in there and stuck her head out the window to see if she could spot a dangling rope. Something moved up there. She ducked back in a hurry, then realised it was only those thin white curtains billowing out in the wind. Nevertheless, she didn't want to look any more. She clutched the heavy draperies and pulled them over the glass, feeling those myriad French knots under her hands, like Braille.

God in heaven, it was Braille! All those hours when she'd shut herself in here alone with needle and thread, Aunt Caroline had not been aimlessly killing time. She'd been writing her diary.

CHAPTER
TWENTY

Sarah dropped the tapestry as though it had been the shirt of Nessus. To pry into somebody else's private writings was one of the most revolting breaches of courteous behaviour any decently bred person could commit.

And what if it was? Caroline Kelling had killed her own husband, had got rid of a murdered woman's body as coolly as if she'd been setting out the garbage, had somehow contrived the timely death of Walter Kelling, had almost certainly been sent to her own death along with her only son as a result of what had happened in the past. If there was any explanation of this ghastly chain of events anywhere, it had to be here. She picked up the cloth again, held it flat against the window frame, and began to sort out the letters with her fingertips.

'My little love,' those were the first three words she read and the ones that kept recurring. Caroline Kelling had a lover! It was for his sake she'd got rid of Gilbert Kelling.

She had intended to go away with this man, to share her life and her fortune with him as she had already begun sharing her body while her husband was alive. The French knots went into voluptuous detail. Sarah would never have believed Aunt Caroline capable of such erotic passion.

It was appalling to think of that ageing woman sitting here in black solitude, pouring out her soul in this almost eerie manner, reliving every moment of a love affair that must still consume her even though it had inevitably been blighted by the years and her growing incapacity. Probably, to Caroline Kelling, the passage of time had not been very real. Her little love was always young, always as handsome as adoring memory pictured him, although God alone knew what the man might look like by now.

The entries, if such they could be called, followed no logical order. When the brooding fit came over her, Aunt Caroline must simply have caught up a fold of the material, felt for a smooth place, and filled it in at random. Words were abbreviated, jumbled together without connectives, without punctuation, sometimes with no apparent sense. Reading was a puzzlement as well as an agony. Yet Sarah became wholly engrossed in piecing together the incredible revelations that emerged from those thousands upon thousands of meticulously worked French knots, forgetting that whoever murdered Caroline and Alexander might even now be in the house with her.

Caroline and her little love, whoever he might be, had been carrying on their tempestuous romance for some months before they came to the decision that Gilbert Kelling must be got rid of. It was the lover, she gathered, who first hinted at murder, but Caroline herself who worked out the plan that had succeeded so neatly in its objective, but ruined the hopes they'd had of enjoying Gilbert's fortune together.

Caroline had been vehement in taking all blame to herself. The man had been swept into tragedy by his wild adoration of her. He must be shielded at any cost. Even in her most incoherent rhapsodies, Caroline had been careful to avoid putting in any tangible clue to her lover's identity. The one fact that came out was that he'd been forced by circumstances to go through a form of marriage with somebody else, although his heart and his thoughts would always be with his beloved. Poor Aunt Caroline!

It was Ruby Redd who'd wrecked their lives, not Gilbert's murder or Caroline's affliction. Until the stripper entered the picture, the affair had been waxing hotter and heavier than ever. The rich widow and her little love still had every intention of getting married after a discreet interval had passed, no matter what the world might think of the match.

Was that a clue? Why should the world, or that minuscule portion of it whose opinion Caroline Kelling gave two pins for, have any objection to her marrying again unless the man was for some reason blatantly unsuitable? Some of the clan might indulge in a bit of cat about Gilbert's money going to an outsider, but most of them were of the opinion that their relative had given his beautiful wife a pretty raw deal. Sarah couldn't think offhand of anyone, except possibly Cousin Mabel, who'd have been spiteful enough to begrudge the family heroine a second husband who could give her the loving care she needed. Perhaps Caroline was being morbid about her afflictions here, picturing herself accused of trapping the man into being her nurse and depriving him of a normal wife's attentions.

Whatever her qualms, Caroline's little love had evidently kept insisting he wanted her under any conditions, until Ruby Redd showed up demanding blackmail. How a stripper from the Old Howard ever learned the pair had murdered Gilbert Kelling, or what the damning proof she held against them was, Caroline didn't say. Possibly she never knew. More likely, the proof would have pointed too clearly towards the man whom she was so determined to protect.

Ruby made her approach to the lover, but it was Caroline who paid. The man must not have had any real money of his own. That, Sarah thought cynically, could explain his unswerving devotion to a rich widow. Aunt Caroline herself might have had some inkling that once her fortune gave out his attachment would lessen. She didn't admit any such thing, but it was clear that she'd been thrown into panic by the speed at which Ruby was bleeding her of her funds. At last she'd put her foot down.

'I said no more . . . face her down . . . deny . . . forgery
. . . slander . . .'

That hadn't worked. Ruby demanded a confrontation,
forced the lover to bring her face-to-face with Caroline late
one night, when Alexander was off at a stag party and the
maids could be got rid of.

Caroline had planned the meeting herself, expected an
unpleasant scene, but the reality was beyond anything
she'd imagined. 'Here in this house . . . railing . . .
threatening . . . grinning sidewise at him with that
vampire's mouth as if they shared some obscene joke. Said
promised rubies . . . must have them or dreadful things . . .
kept yelling you promised . . . how could I . . . said
ridiculous . . . how did she know about rubies . . .'

Then it came out. Piecing the incoherencies together,
Sarah managed to understand that the lover had finally
been put in the position of having to explain that Alexander
had let himself be seduced by the creature who was
blackmailing them. Ruby had been stringing the infatuated
boy along so that she could pump him about the true extent
of his father's fortune. Alex had been a willing dupe.
Knowing her obsession with rubies, he'd bragged about the
family jewels, promised to let her wear the parure in return
for her disgusting favours.

Caroline went on and on about the appalling scene.
'Outrage . . . laughed at me . . . called me fool . . . stupid
. . . said I didn't know what . . . flaunted herself before his
eyes . . . twined her body . . . tried to make me think he
and she . . .'

The lover had repulsed the dancer's blatant sexual
advances, pushed her away in anger. Caroline seemed not
to have comprehended precisely what happened after that.
Ruby must have become enraged and tried to fly at her. To
save her life, the lover struck out. Suddenly Ruby was dead
on the hall floor and the man was protesting, 'I did it for
you. She was going to kill you!'

It was not a killing, it was sheer heroism; noble, justified,
no wrong at all. Yet they couldn't risk putting their case
before a judge. Again Caroline thought of a plan. They
must hide the body in the old family vault, soon to be part of
a historical site, never to be opened again.

Alexander wasn't meant to be involved, he simply happened to come home at the wrong moment. However, they immediately realised they could use him. Even while he was kneeling beside Ruby Redd's body, feeling for a pulse that wasn't there, the others were out in the kitchen, plotting.

The lover must get away by the back door. Caroline would go back and pretend she thought Alex had killed his paramour in a drunken quarrel. It served him right for having betrayed his mother. Obviously, Aunt Caroline had never felt the slightest compunction about laying such a dreadful punishment on her child, only exultation at having so valiantly shielded her little love.

For her, the tragedy was that the blackmailing didn't stop. Ruby, too, had betrayed them. She'd shared their secret with an accomplice who stood guard outside the house and saw what happened. Now they were more vulnerable than before. Again the lover got the threats. Again it was Caroline who paid.

That was where Gilbert Kelling's estate had gone, every cent of it, to save another man from disgrace and prosecution for murder. Caroline revelled in the sacrifice she had made, never caring that she'd robbed Alexander of his birthright. She actually seemed to think she'd done a mother's duty when she laced Walter Kelling's mushrooms with her eyedrops so that Alex could marry Sarah for her inheritance.

It was a horrible document. Yet Sarah read on until her fingertips were raw from fumbling over the hard knots, until her body was chilled through despite the down comforter. She stayed at the window until dawn cast its dirty coral glow over the rooftops. Then, as though she dared not let the sun see what she was up to, she crawled into Caroline Kelling's bed and went to sleep.

CHAPTER
TWENTY-ONE

This time it was the telephone that woke her. Sarah started downstairs still half asleep, felt the blast from those open windows on the third floor and decided she'd better shut them before she went down. By the time she got to the phone, there was nobody on the line. Fuming, she climbed back to her own room and put on some clothes.

Nothing up here seemed to have been disturbed. Even Aunt Caroline's pearls as well as her own modest strand and what remained of the money she'd got from Mr Redfern were lying on the dresser. Sarah went to take a closer look at Alexander's room. Here, too, except for the mess of bedclothes on the floor, there really wasn't much wrong. His studs and cufflinks were safe in the collar box along with Grandfather Kelling's massive solid gold watch and chain with the star sapphire set into the fob.

That scared her more than anything else. Sarah backed out of the room and was running down to check the dining room silver when she heard an almighty thumping on the front door. Whoever that might be, it was surely no ghost. Uncle Jem, perhaps, though he wasn't usually so energetic at this hour of the morning. She peeked through one of the narrow glass panels that flanked the doorway and saw Max Bittersohn, in what appeared to be a state of utter panic.

'Mr Bittersohn, what's the matter?'

'Why didn't you answer the phone?' he yelled back.

'I did but you hung up too fast.' She opened the door. 'Come in and help me hunt the burglars. I think there's been a break-in, though I haven't found anything missing so far.'

All at once Sarah was exhausted. 'Would you mind terribly if I went out to the kitchen and made some coffee first? I haven't had breakfast, and I feel a bit wobbly.'

'So do I. Why the hell didn't you call me?'

Sarah hunched her shoulders. 'Because I didn't have guts enough to come downstairs, if you want the truth. I'd moved into my mother-in-law's room on the second floor, thinking that would be close enough to the telephone, but it wasn't.'

'Want to tell me what happened?'

'I wish I could. All I really know is that sometime during the night, both windows in my husband's room on the third floor were opened from the top and the covers pulled off the bed.'

'That's odd. And you say nothing was taken?'

'Not that I could see. A valuable antique watch and some other things are still there, and my own room next to his wasn't disturbed at all, though I'd left my money and Aunt Caroline's pearls in plain sight. I haven't searched downstairs yet because I just got up. I locked myself in Aunt Caroline's room after I found the windows open and didn't get to sleep till daybreak. I hadn't realised what a coward I am.'

All he said was, 'Where do you keep the coffee?'

'Oh, please don't bother. I can manage the stove, if nothing else. Do you eat eggs? Those seem to be about the only thing I have in the house.'

'You don't have to get anything for me.'

'But I'd like to. I hate cooking for just myself.'

Sarah poked bread into the toaster. She felt weepy again; was that because she'd found a shoulder she could bawl on? Why was this strange man showing such concern, when her own family didn't mind leaving her to fend for herself? Egg box in hand, she turned and faced him.

'Mr Bittersohn, I'm going to ask an extremely rude question, and I hope you'll understand why I have to know. Does your benevolent interest in me have anything to do with the Kelling jewellery?'

To her surprise, he laughed. 'I was wondering when we'd get around to that. I can't afford to buy the collection, and I'm not planning to steal it, if that's what you're getting at.'

'But what about your book?'

'Forget it. Okay, I guess it's time I came clean. Remember my uncle, the pawnbroker?'

'You mentioned that you had one.'

'Well, back when I was in college, he got caught in a flimflam involving some stolen diamonds, and wound up in jail on manufactured evidence. That didn't worry him much, he said the hours were shorter and you met a nicer class of people. My mother, on the other hand, was very upset because it was a *schamde* for the neighbours. When my mother's upset, everybody's upset. This to me was a real problem. I was still living at home and working my way through school, which gave me little enough time to do my homework under the best of conditions. I had exams coming up, and I knew Ma would never shut up and let me study unless I managed somehow to get Uncle Herman sprung. So I started nosing around and happened by some miraculous accident to catch the crooks who set him up.'

'And you got your Uncle Herman out of jail?'

'I did. He's never forgiven me for making him look like a fool, and the neighbours are still talking. So's my mother. What can you do? Anyway, that was what you might call the turning point of my career. I switched to an art history major—which further upset my mother who was determined I should become a rich podiatrist—and started a little private practice tracking down stolen jewellery, objets d'art, antiques, and whatnot. After graduation I branched out into various other odd jobs like finding out who's painting the Rembrandts and Tintorettos these days. There's a great deal of theft and fraud in the art world that the police never get called in on. They haven't the time or the expertise to handle certain situations that come up, and often the client doesn't want any publicity. So that's what I do for a living. I don't carry any credentials because it wouldn't be a smart thing to do, and anyway, there's nobody who could give me any. But you're welcome to check some references if you want.'

He mentioned four impressive names that Sarah knew. One of them happened to be a member of the Kelling clan.

'So that's how Uncle Thaddeus got his Corots back. You should have heard the lies he told.'

'I've heard worse, no doubt. If you're cooking those eggs for me, would you mind flipping them over and letting them get brown till they're about the texture of asphalt shingles?'

'If I must.'

Sarah transferred her own two to a warmed plate and turned the others with a spatula. 'I hope you also want the yolks broken. I'm all thumbs this morning.'

'I don't wonder. Getting back to this visitation, or whatever it was, have you any idea when it happened?'

'I'd say it must have been three o'clock. I woke up suddenly—I suppose because I'd heard the windows banging down. Anyway, I felt this terrific draught and went to see where it was coming from. Surely these eggs must be hard enough now?'

'Great. Thanks.' Bittersohn attacked the leathery mess with enthusiasm. 'If you're such a coward, what made you go charging up there by yourself?'

'I thought a sash cord had broken. They rot out every so often. I suppose the truth of the matter is that I didn't think at all; I simply reacted.'

'Had you been asleep long?'

'Since about half-past ten, I think. After you called, I spent some time clearing out Auntie Caroline's room so I could use it, then took a hot soak and read William James for a little while.'

'Why William James?'

'He always puts me to sleep; don't ask me why. I've been trying to read that book for years and still haven't got beyond the fourth chapter. How did we get started on William James?'

Bittersohn helped himself to another piece of toast. 'Never mind, go ahead and talk. Say anything that comes into your head. Who knows, it could be important.'

'May I ask questions?'

'Sure, why not?'

'This—this reason you have for being interested in the family jewels. Was it anything to do with having my mother-in-law arrested?'

The man blinked. 'That's one I didn't expect. Is there any reason why I should?'

'Perhaps.'

'Care to explain?'

Sarah made her decision. 'Yes, I do. I've got to tell somebody, in case something happens to me. It's not right to just let this ride. Would you believe that if my Great-uncle Frederick hadn't been so down on his relatives, my husband and his mother would still be alive?'

'And where would you be? Go ahead, Mrs Kelling, start wherever you want and say whatever you please.'

'I hardly know how to begin.'

'Then let me ask you, when did you first learn that your mother-in-law was up to tricks with the jewellery?'

'It began that day my cousin and I found Ruby Redd's skeleton in what used to be our family vault. You know about that, you saw it on the news. Remember you started talking about it at the Lackridges', and Alexander didn't want Aunt Caroline to know?'

'How could I forget? He looked as if he were in shock.'

'I'm sure he was. He had good reason to be, as I found out later.'

'How did you find out?'

'I began to suspect something later that same evening.'

She told of the photograph that matched her sketch of the wall in the vault, of her decision to question Tim O'Ghee, of finding the old bartender dead, and of the scene Mrs Wandelowski and the self-styled doctor had staged to persuade her that he hadn't been murdered. She explained why she'd been in such a state that night Bittersohn met her at the coffee shop coming from Ireson's Landing. She told of the confrontation with Alexander, of how he'd seen his mother get rid of his father's medicine, how Caroline forced him to help her hide Ruby Redd's body, how she'd killed Walter Kelling and made Alexander marry Sarah to keep all three of them alive. Sarah explained how she thought the Milburn had been wrecked, and why. Lastly, she let Bittersohn know about that bizarre journal Caroline Kelling had left, and what it revealed.

When she got through he said, 'My God!' and held out his cup for more coffee.

That commonplace gesture put the final stamp of reality on the whole fantastic situation. Sarah got up from the table and reached for the coffeepot.

'I'm afraid it's gone cold. I didn't realise I'd been talking so long. Can you wait a moment till I heat it up, or would you rather I made a fresh pot?'

'Don't bother. My mother says I drink too much coffee anyway. Look, speaking of coffee, I don't know if you realised it, but that night when I met you at the coffee shop, you looked as if you'd been through the wars. After you left, I called my brother-in-law and asked him how to find your place at Ireson's Landing, just out of curiosity. I was almost there when I noticed a car making a left-hand turn out of the driveway, so I slowed down and opened my window, hoping to get a glimpse of the driver.

'Between the rain and the dark I couldn't see much, but I thought it was a man, and I had a hunch I'd know him if I could have got a better look. That was encouragement of a sort, so I went on up the drive, got out my flashlight, and started prowling. The ground was so soft that I had no trouble picking up tracks. I followed that path down to the wall and found a couple of places where you'd apparently skidded and fallen. That was a relief, at least I could assume you hadn't been beaten up by the guy. I didn't see any scraps of paper around, so it's entirely possible he did pick up the sketch you threw away.'

'But you can't say who he was?'

'I'm hoping it will come to me. I'm wondering now if it mightn't have been that man who posed as the doctor the day you found O'Ghee. He could have been tailing you—trying to find out if you'd swallowed the story about O'Ghee's committing suicide, and what you were going to do about it if you hadn't.'

'Yes, he could. He knew who I was and how to find me. Then it must have been he whom I saw that second time out there, too, the night before Alexander was killed.'

'No, I'm afraid that may have been my nephew Mike. A detective he isn't. I'd been uneasy about you after Dee mentioned at that asinine conference he put on that you and your husband were heading back to Ireson's Landing. I still couldn't figure out what had happened that other time, but I knew you'd had a bad experience of some kind. However, I had no special reason to connect that incident with the business about the Kelling jewellery. Frankly, it seemed more plausible to me at the time that your husband had killed Ruby Redd and bricked up her body in the family vault and was having problems with somebody who knew he'd been her boy friend. However, I was thinking in terms of blackmail, not murder. In any event, I'd committed myself to being in New York that night, so the best I could think of was to phone Mike and ask him to keep an eye on you while I was out of town, just on general principles. He did the best he could. I'm sorry it wasn't good enough. He's blaming himself like hell, poor kid, because he didn't think to check out the Milburn.'

'He mustn't do that,' said Sarah. 'He couldn't even have got at the car without breaking into the shed. I still can't imagine how anybody managed to tamper with the Milburn. Alexander would have spotted the damage if there'd been anything to see.'

'At least you can be darn sure Mike's gone over every nut and bolt on the Studebaker with a magnifying glass.' Bittersohn replied. 'It's good therapy for him. I might as well tell you that meeting you at the filling station as I did wasn't exactly an accident. I'd spoken with Mike late the previous night from New York, and he'd said everything was fine. I called him when I got back to Logan Airport, and he was all to pieces. He'd been hearing about the wreck on a local police scanner they keep at the station. So I hotfooted it out there, keeping my eyes peeled all the way for that old Studebaker. I stopped to ask Mike if he knew whether you were still at Ireson's Landing, and as luck would have it, you pulled in two minutes later. All I had to do was wait till you'd gone to phone, then drive back around to the front of the station and put on a little act.'

'I'm sure your kindness was no act,' Sarah told him. 'I can't tell you—'

'Forget it. Mind if I run through a couple of points again?'

'Not at all.'

'That conversation you had with your husband after you got home from the party—is it possible anybody overheard?'

'I don't see how. It was much too cold to have a window open, and I very carefully made sure Edith, our maid, wasn't within earshot because I knew she'd snoop if she knew anything was going on. She had her own sitting room in the basement, where she spent most of her spare time with the television blaring. Often she'd doze off in her chair. She's not a young woman, and she likes her port. That's what she was doing while we were talking. We'd had a fight in the kitchen when I had gone to fix a snack for Alexander, and she'd flounced off in a huff. Besides, he and I were in the library with the door closed, and it's a very tight fit. He put weatherstripping around the edges to keep out draughts from the hall.'

'Your mother-in-law wasn't with you? I don't suppose there's any possible chance Mrs Kelling could hear more than she led you to believe?'

'No chance whatever,' said Sarah positively. 'I couldn't have lived with her all these years and not known. Anyway, she wasn't in the house. She'd gone out to dinner with—oh, good heavens!'

'With whom?' Bittersohn prompted. 'Her little love?'

Sarah shook her head. 'I honestly don't know, but I wonder. His name is Edgar Merton, and everybody says he's been in love with Aunt Caroline for years and years. He's still quite a handsome man, and he isn't much bigger than I am. Aunt Caroline was tall, as you know. Edgar barely came up to her chin.'

'Has he got any money?'

'You'd think so from the way he lives, but I don't think he has a penny in his own right. Edgar's people got cleaned out in the Depression, so he married an heiress. Alice Merton was never an awfully clever woman. She started to become senile six or eight years ago and is completely noncompos now. Since she had to be hospitalised, Edgar's been showing Aunt Caroline a great deal of attention. I must admit I encouraged his visits because it gave Alexander a chance to breathe.'

She cleared her throat. 'Anyway, Edgar was at the tea and asked the three of us to go on with him to dinner at the Harvard Club. I told him Alexander wasn't up to it and suggested he take Leila Lackridge.'

'Why Mrs Lackridge?'

'Harry was off selling his books, and Leila was at loose ends. It was easier if she went along to help with the conversation and take Aunt Caroline to the ladies' room or whatever. I wanted Edgar to keep her out as long as possible so we'd have a peaceful evening. We were in bed before she got back.'

Bittersohn must have seen the pain that recollection caused her. He asked brusquely, 'What does this Merton do?'

'Nothing in particular. Visits his friends, plays bridge at

his club, goes off on a trip now and then. He's well past retirement age, though I don't think he had much to retire from. Edgar was supposed to be connected with one of the big brokerage houses, but he couldn't have worked awfully hard at his job. He and Alice always used to be travelling.'

'That so?' Bittersohn mulled over this information for a moment. 'Who else?'

'Who else paid attention to Aunt Caroline, you mean? My father, for one, after Mother died, but you can't count him since she killed him. Of course, there have been any number of people who've gone out of their way to be kind to her. She was a heroine, supposedly, and still a tremendously attractive, intelligent person to be with. My Uncle Jem—oh, that beastly phone! It never stops.'

She put her hand out to the wall extension, but Bittersohn grabbed it. 'Wait a second. Where's the other phone?'

'In the front hall, on a little stand in the far corner.'

'Stay here. Let it ring twice more before you pick it up.'

He hurried down the hallway. Puzzled, Sarah obeyed. When she answered, Harry Lackridge was on the line.

'Sarah, what took you so long? Is something the matter?'

'No, no problems,' she lied. The last thing she wanted was to have him and Leila galloping to the rescue again. 'I'm tired, but that's to be expected.'

'What are your plans for the day?'

'To get through it as best I can.'

'Might I interest you in lunch at the Ritz?'

'That sounds elegant, Harry, but I couldn't possibly. There's so much to do.'

'What, for instance?'

'I have to see Mr Redfern again.' She didn't actually, but that was the first excuse that popped into her mind.

'Why?' he prodded. 'Didn't you get squared away about the money on Monday?'

'Not to my satisfaction. Mr Redfern claims that ridiculous will of Father's is still in force, and all he can do is dole me out a measly housekeeping allowance until a new trustee is appointed. I'm thinking seriously of getting a different lawyer.'

'Now, Sarah, calm down. Don't be hasty, Alex wouldn't

want that. All that another lawyer would do is stall around and run up fees against the estate. If Redfern wants to talk to me about the trusteeship—'

'I can't imagine why he would,' Sarah snapped back, then realised how rude she was being. 'Harry, I know you're trying to help me for Alexander's sake, but you must realise that nobody could ever take his place, and nobody can live my life for me. I can't be relying on you or anybody else to manage my affairs, and right now I just want to get on with what I have to do. Surely you understand?'

'I'm not going to argue with you, at any rate. Sure you won't change your mind about lunch? Maybe another time?'

'That would be lovely.' Sarah rang off gratefully and went to see what her other self-appointed guardian was up to. She found him taking the telephone apart.

'Mr Bittersohn, whatever are you doing that for?'

'To see what's inside.'

He shook a tiny metal object out of the mouthpiece and showed it to her on the palm of his hand. 'Know what this is?'

'I haven't the foggiest idea. Not—not one of those bug things?'

'Nothing else but. Furthermore, this is practically an antique of its kind. Your phone must have been tapped for a good many years. Mind showing me where you and your husband were sitting when you had that talk?'

'In here.' Sarah led him into the library.

'Is this where you'd normally spend a good deal of your time?'

'Yes. It's cosier than the drawing room and has a better fireplace. We've always been big on open fires because there's all that free wood lying around out at Ireson's.'

In the daylight, the library looked shabby like the rest of the house. Yet there was still charm in the crowded bookcases that stretched from the parquet floor to the nine-foot ceiling, in the oriental rugs with their softened blues and crimsons, in the scuffed brown-leather armchair and sofa, in some oriental artist's quaintly stylised portrait of the merchant prince who founded the fortune that Caroline Kelling paid over to a blackmailer.

Max Bittersohn wasted no time absorbing the atmosphere. He got down on his knees and began pulling out books from the bottom shelves, prying off the ogee moulding that finished off the tops of the painted pine baseboards. Sarah started to ask what he was doing, but he motioned for silence. A second or two later, the man was holding up a length of snipped-off wire.

CHAPTER
TWENTY-TWO

'This is how you were overheard, Mrs Kelling. I'd say this room has also been bugged for a considerable length of time. See how the wire is discoloured and furred with dust?'

'I don't believe this,' she said through stiff lips. 'What you're trying to tell me is that every time one of us has used the telephone or entered this room, somebody has been hiding outside the window listening in on every word we've said.'

'No, I'm not saying that. What usually happens is that the wires are connected to a hidden tape recorder somewhere that may be kept running or, more probably, just gets switched on at certain times. Who are your next-door neighbours, do you know?'

'I haven't the faintest idea. These used to be all private homes, but now most of them have been cut up into apartments. People come and go.'

'I think we'll find somebody came and stayed. I'm going to have an electrican come in here and trace this wire, if you don't mind. You wouldn't have any recollection of electrical work being done in the house, I don't suppose? I'm just wondering when and how it might have been installed.'

'Edith's nephew,' Sarah gasped.

'Who?'

'Our maid,' she stammered, 'the one I was telling you about. She has a nephew who does television repairs. Wouldn't this sort of thing be in his line?'

'I don't see why not. Did he ever have access to the house?'

'Dozens of times. We often left Edith here to mind the house when we went to Ireson's, and told her she could have people in for company. The nephew used to come with his wife and children, and I'm sure she gave them the run of the place though she wasn't supposed to.'

'Ever meet this nephew yourself?'

'Once or twice. Not oftener than I could avoid. He's one of those smarmy little men with a moustache that looks as if it's pasted on.'

'Good-looking guy?'

'I suppose so, if you're fond of lizards. But surely you're not thinking about him and Aunt Caroline. He's much too young, aside from anything else.'

'He had a father, didn't he?'

'It wouldn't be the father. He was some kind of factory worker, and Aunt Caroline wouldn't have gone to such drastic lengths to protect his professional reputation. But there is some uncle or cousin or something who's a fairly well-known surgeon at one of the big local hospitals. Edith used to brag about him every chance she got. It's not so far-fetched to think of Aunt Caroline falling in love with a handsome but penniless young intern who had a brilliant future to jeopardise. That would explain what she wrote about marrying her little love no matter what the world might say. The family would certainly have said plenty if Gilbert Kelling's widow tied up with a relative of her housemaid. That might also be why Aunt Caroline kept Edith on when she got rid of the other servants. I never could understand why she kept the worst of the lot, but if Edith's been functioning as a go-between all these years—'

'Or as a blackmailer?'

'I wouldn't put it past her, but what would she have done with the money? Don't forget there was a very large fortune involved. If she got hold of it, why should she have stayed on here, whining and crabbing about being overworked?'

'Good question. Hey, don't you have an appointment with your lawyer?'

'Actually, no. I said that to get out of lunch with Harry because it was the first excuse I thought of. He and Leila are determined to be kind to the poor little orphan, and it's a bit more than I can take just now.'

'Nevertheless, you must have had the lawyer in the back of your mind, or you'd have thought of something else. What do you say we go anyway?'

'We can't simply waltz ourselves down to State Street and barge in on Mr Redfern!'

'Why not? He works for you, doesn't he?'

Sarah blinked, then managed to smile. 'I suppose he does. I must say I'd never have thought of Mr Redfern as my employee.'

'That's what gets these guys believing they're God Almighty. You go on in there, and if he tries to give you a hard time, just tell him, "Listen, Buster, if it weren't for clients like me, you wouldn't be eating."'

'I cannot imagine saying, "Listen, Buster," to Mr Redfern.'

'Then I'll say it for you. Get your coat.'

'Are you serious?'

'Never more so,' Bittersohn assured her. 'I want him to open that safe-deposit box Mrs Kelling would never let anybody get a look into, and find out exactly where we stand. There's no question of your being the lawful heiress, is there?'

'Oh, no. Everything comes to me. Alexander said so.'

'Is Redfern executor of the estate?'

'He must be. The Redferns have always handled all our family affairs.'

'Then he'd be apt to have a key to the box?'

'If he doesn't, I do,' Sarah replied. 'I found it hidden in one of Aunt Caroline's bureau drawers.'

'Okay, we're in business. Come on.'

'But doesn't the will have to be probated first, or whatever you call it?'

'No, it works the other way around. The box must be opened and its contents inventoried along with all other properties before probate can begin. If Redfern has both your husband's and your mother-in-law's wills in his possession, there's no reason whatever why we can't all three go straight to the bank and take care of it right now. If he balks, we'll sic my Uncle Jake on him.'

'Your uncle the pawnbroker?'

'No, my uncle the lawyer. He stands four-feet-eleven in his Alder elevator shoes, and he'd take on the whole American Banking Association with one hand tied behind his briefcase. Uncle Jake will know what to do if this Redfern starts giving you the runaround.'

'I'm not sure he hasn't already started. You heard what I said to Harry.'

Sarah explained about her father's overly cautious will and the trouble she was having getting money out of his estate.

'Does that sound reasonable to you?'

'It doesn't sound as though he's ready to go out on a limb for you, anyway,' Bittersohn replied. 'Come on, let's go.'

'Would you mind waiting two minutes? I'd better put some decent clothes on. If I turn up in blue jeans and a sweatshirt, he'll think I've gone soft as a grape.'

Sarah was not sanguine about this venture, but what difference did that make? The worst Mr Redfern could do would be to toss them out. Even that would be preferable to sitting around the house by herself, wondering what was going to happen next. That wiretapping was the absolute end. Finding out that her most intimate, most frightening, yet most precious conversation with her dead husband had been overheard in such a disgusting way was almost as bad as losing him again.

Bittersohn's discovery threw the possibilities wide open. Sarah had thought only Edith and Lomax knew in advance that the Kellings were going to Ireson's Landing for the weekend. Who else had heard Alexander calling up the caretaker, had listened in while they were making their plans, had been in a position to anticipate every move they'd be apt to make?

Whoever had been monitoring those tapes must know how rigid Aunt Caroline was about doing the same things in the same ways again and again and again, must have been aware that if the weather was even halfway decent, Alexander would take the Milburn out of its wraps and give his mother a ride along the shore road. The weather reports had promised the fog would lift around noontime that day, and it had. With the information he'd gleaned, the murderer could almost have pinpointed the moment when the Milburn was going to top the rise and fly out of control, could have planted a plausible witness down on the shore to make sure the fatal accident went off as planned.

Any eavesdropper would know about the old electric's dynamic braking relay. He, or she, must have acquired a vast library of tapes over the years with Alexander's dear, quiet voice explaining the Milburn's internal workings to anybody he could persuade to listen. Oh, if she could only hear them, too!

Sarah began to cry again, ran to the bathroom and dabbed water on her face. It wasn't fair to keep Mr Bittersohn waiting while she indulged her grief. However, when she ran downstairs a few minutes later in the black wool dress and coat, she found he'd made good use of the time.

'I've checked out your locks, which haven't been tampered with as far as I can tell. Also, you may be glad to know there's no bug in your kitchen phone.'

'I don't feel particularly glad about anything right now,' Sarah told him frankly. 'Shouldn't we check the rest of the baseboards, too?'

'The electrician can do that later, but I hardly think he'll find anything. Wiring the whole house would be a big job and a bigger risk. The library was ideal because that section behind the bookcases wasn't likely to be disturbed for years on end, and because you use that room so much. I assume most of your acquaintances would know your habits?'

'Oh, yes. We'd often serve tea or whatever in there because the fire was always going, and Aunt Caroline kept her backgammon board on that little table beside the window. For that matter, anybody passing by outside would have been able to see her there. She and Edgar would play for hours on end. And at night the lights would be on. She and Leila held some of their committee meetings in the library, too. Mr Bittersohn, you don't suppose this bugging could be in any way connected with politics?'

'Their political activities being mostly the sort of thing they were talking about that night at the Lackridges'?' He sounded amused. 'What do you think?'

'I've always thought it was a great deal of nothing,' Sarah

had to reply. 'I daresay I'm trying to make this thing less—personal.'

'That's natural enough. Feel like walking?'

'How else would we get there?'

'Skateboard, pogo stick, taxi.'

'Taxi? For that little distance? Mr Bittersohn, how could you?'

Sarah locked the door and set a brisk pace towards Brimstone Corner. If they were so foolhardy as to crash in on a prominent Boston attorney without an appointment, they might as well go and get the snubbing over with as quickly as possible.

CHAPTER
TWENTY-THREE

'I'm sorry, but I'm afraid Mr Redfern couldn't possibly see anyone right now.'

Miss Tremblay's voice held mingled regret and surprise. She was sorry to disoblige a young woman so suddenly and tragically widowed, but nonplussed as to why Sarah could think it feasible to visit Mr Redfern without an appointment.

Max Bittersohn reached over to Miss Tremblay's memo pad, wrote something on it, and handed her the paper. 'Give him this. I think you'll find he can fit us in.'

'But I—'

'Try.'

Pursing her lips, the elderly secretary tapped and entered the sanctum. She came out looking very puzzled indeed.

'Would you go straight in, please?'

Bittersohn didn't even look duly gratified, he merely ushered Sarah past the varnished oak door, seated her in the visitor's chair in front of the desk, and fetched another chair for himself.

The lawyer cleared his throat, put on his half-eye glasses, took them off, put them on again, and finally uttered.

'I wasn't expecting to see you again so soon, Sarah.'

'I don't see why not,' she replied. 'We didn't accomplish much on my last visit.'

'I was under the impression that we did.'

She wasn't about to bandy words. She sat looking straight at him, trying to remember that Mr Redfern was only a man who worked for her, until the lawyer was forced to speak again.

'And what brings you here today, may I ask? This is an extremely busy time for me.'

'It's a difficult time for me, too,' she snapped back, 'and I'll thank you to bear in mind that you're supposed to be protecting my interests. If you can't be bothered, I'll have to find somebody who can.'

'Now, now, Sarah. If it's about your father's will—'

'It's not. Not today, at any rate. I came to get a letter of permission or whatever I need to gain access to my mother-in-law's safe-deposit box at the High Street Trust.'

'And you shall have it in due course.'

'I want it now.'

'That's not possible.'

'Why isn't it? I don't want to take anything out, I just want to see what's in the box.'

'My dear Sarah, one doesn't simply barge in on people and make demands like a child in a tantrum. There are regular procedures that take place in an orderly fashion.'

Sarah turned to Bittersohn. 'Would your uncle agree with that?'

'I think Mr Redfern is aware that Jacob Bittersohn would act in the best interest of his client,' he replied. 'I question whether he'd compare her to a child in a tantrum. I believe he'd agree that you have the right to look at your own property. Furthermore, I don't see what the hell you're stalling about, Redfern. This is not a frivolous request. Mrs Kelling, who happens to be my client as well as yours, has learned, in going through her late mother-in-law's effects, that members of her family have been systematically victimised over an extended period of time. To make an effective investigation, we need to know exactly where she stands right now.'

'Can you substantiate that statement?'

'We can. We have documentary evidence. We don't

propose to show it to you until we're convinced that you yourself haven't been a party to fraud and maybe something worse. So far, your attitude leaves room for doubt.'

'That is a libellous suggestion!'

'Sue me. In the meantime, could we get on with what we came for? Mrs Kelling was told by her husband that she inherits whatever the estate consists of at the time of his death, and that this includes a collection of heirloom jewellery that was held by Caroline Kelling for her use during her lifetime but was, in fact, owned by her son. Is that correct?'

The lawyer squirmed. 'In substance, I believe that is the—er—general thrust. Sarah will also inherit the two properties.'

'Who's got the deeds?'

'Mrs Caroline Kelling also held those in her personal charge during her lifetime. Since she was not the owner, it would have been appropriate for her to leave them with us, but she chose not to do so.'

'Would they be in the safe-deposit box with the jewellery?'

'I have no way of knowing.'

'Then isn't that in itself a sufficient reason for opening the box? You've got to do it sooner or later anyway. Do you have the necessary documents at hand?'

'We do,' Redfern admitted.

'So what are we waiting for? Are you coming with us, or going to write us a letter?'

'My schedule is—' Redfern tried to look portentous, caught Bittersohn's eye, and was abruptly deflated. 'I'd better come with you.'

He took a felt hat and a beautiful black cashmere topcoat from a bentwood rack and came out with them. 'Miss Tremblay, I shall be out of the office for approximately forty-five minutes.'

'But, Mr Redfern! Yes, Mr Redfern.'

She was gazing after them in total stupefaction when they went out.

The bank wasn't far from the lawyer's office, and Mr Redfern lost not a moment in stating their business. Almost immediately the branch manager himself came out to meet them.

'This is remarkably good of you, Mrs Kelling. I didn't expect such a prompt answer.'

'To what?' Sarah asked him.

He looked surprised. 'Didn't you get my letter? I wrote immediately on learning of Mrs Caroline Kelling's death. The situation has been precarious for some time now, and—perhaps we'd better go into my office and sit down.'

'What situation?'

Sarah was glad to take the chair he offered her. 'You'll have to forgive me for not having the faintest idea what you're talking about. There's a stack of mail at the house I haven't got around to opening yet, and I presume your letter must be among the rest. We came because I need to see what's in my mother-in-law's safe-deposit box. Among other things, we have to find the deeds to the two properties.'

'Yes, of course, we shall certainly need those. Then you don't have them, Redfern? I naturally assumed she'd return them to you after she took out the second mortgages.'

'Second mortgages?' barked the lawyer. 'But the properties were owned free and clear, always had been. Verplanck, what are you talking about?'

The banker tilted back in his swivel chair. 'In nineteen fifty-two, if my memory serves me correctly, Mrs Kelling, as executrix of her husband's estate, took out mortgages on both the Beacon Hill house and the Ireson's Landing property. I'm surprised she never appraised you of that fact, Redfern. In any event, the interest was faithfully paid on both, but none of the principal. That in itself was surprising, but as the properties continued to increase in value, we weren't worried. Some five years ago, Mrs Kelling came in again and demanded that we issue second mortgages on the two properties. I may say that I took it upon myself to remonstrate.'

'How?' said Sarah.

'Why, I said—oh, you're referring to the problem in communication. She had her son with her. He was able to reach her by some method of hand signalling.'

'Alexander brought her? Then he knew all this?'

'Certainly. He'd have to, wouldn't he? He was no longer a minor, and the properties were legally his, as I understand it, even though his mother was still acting as executrix.'

'But that's impossible! Just a few nights ago we were talking about selling off part of the Ireson's Landing property, and he never breathed a word about mortgages.'

Mr Verplanck and Mr Redfern exchanged glances. Neither of them said, 'Husbands don't always tell their wives everything,' but it was plain they thought so. The banker went on in something of a rush.

'Be that as it may, we did, in fact, remortgage the properties since the dramatic rise in value appeared to warrant the extra risk, although I frankly was none too happy about the transaction and am considerably less so now.'

'Has anything been paid on the second mortgages?' asked the lawyer.

'Not one cent. The interest is now also in considerable arrears. We've been writing both to Mrs Kelling and to Mr Alexander Kelling, but have had no response. My letter to the—er—current Mrs Kelling deals, I regret to say, with the imminent necessity of foreclosure unless a settlement can be reached.'

'How much must I pay?' stammered Sarah.

Mr Verplanck named a sum that staggered her.

'Can I do it, Mr Redfern?'

The lawyer shook his head. 'Offhand, I don't see how.'

'Then I suppose we'll have to sell some of the jewellery. That must be what Alexander had in mind. He—oh, I just can't believe this! Please, can't we open that box now?'

'I think we'd better,' said Mr Verplanck.

He led them down a remarkably beautiful marble staircase, pressed a buzzer that got them admitted to the vault room, and gave Sarah's key to the young woman at the desk.

'Miss Mummerset, would you mind getting this box for us?'

'Sure thing, Mr Verplanck.'

She checked her file for the box number, took another bunch of keys from her desk, unlocked the steel gates that barred access to the tiers of boxes, and went like a homing pigeon to the right place.

'I had a hunch some of the family would be along after the funeral,' she remarked. 'I hadn't realised till we got to talking about the accident at coffee break yesterday that Mrs Kelling was a customer of ours. Miss Purlow was telling us how she used to come in wearing a mink coat and the most gorgeous hats you ever saw, to get out her jewels for the opera or whatever. Miss Purlow said everybody would just stop whatever they were doing and stare, as if she'd been a movie star.'

She giggled. 'I guess I shouldn't have said that. Anyway, I'm sorry about the accident. I just wish I could have met Mrs Kelling myself. She's never been to the box since I've worked here. Gosh, it's heavy. Careful, Mr Verplanck, don't drop the diamonds and rubies.'

'Thank you, Miss Mummerset,' said the bank manager repressively. 'Now what's the protocol, Redfern? Do you open it, or does your client?'

'Mrs Kelling gets the honour, I should think.' The lawyer looked doubtfully at the tiny booth Miss Mummerset was trying to usher them into. 'I don't know how we're all supposed to fit in that cubbyhole. Might as well do it right here on the desk, if the young lady doesn't object.'

'I'm dying to see them. Isn't this exciting!'

'Miss Mummerset leads rather a lonely life down here,' the manager said apologetically. 'Over to you, Mrs Kelling.'

Miss Mummerset was right, it was exciting. Sarah held her breath as she raised the painted metal lid and peered inside. The box was full. On top lay a sheaf of yellow, dog-eared foolscap, written over in faded clerkly copperplate. Yes, the deeds were here. She lifted them out.

The rest of the box was packed solid with smallish orange-red bricks. She would have known their shape and texture anywhere.

CHAPTER TWENTY-FOUR

'How did I get here?'

'Now, Mrs Kelling, you lie still and don't excite your-self.'

A kind-looking woman of fifty-odd was bending over Sarah, fiddling with a blanket that had been wrapped around her. 'I'm going to see if Mr Verplanck has any whisky in his office.'

'Strong tea or coffee with lots of sugar would be just as good.'

That was Max Bittersohn's voice. Sarah stretched out a hand to him.

'I've made a fool of myself again, haven't I?'

'You fainted, if that's what you mean.' He took the hand in his comforting grasp. 'Probably the most sensible thing you could have done.'

'I'm sure Mr Redfern doesn't think so. Where is he?'

'In a huddle with Mr Verplanck.'

'The owl and the panther are sharing the pie. I suppose they think Alexander took the jewellery.'

He didn't say anything.

'Do you?' she prodded.

'I'm trying not to think at all, till we get some more facts,' was his not very satisfactory answer.

The lady came in with a couple of Styrofoam cups on a tray. 'I brought you some, too, Mr Kelling.'

'Thanks.' Bittersohn took the cup without correcting her mistake. 'Have you been working here long?'

'Oh, yes. I'm one of the old-timers.'

'Then maybe you can tell us who used to work downstairs in the vault, say between ten and twenty years ago?'

'Oh, that would be Alethia Browne. She was here for ages and ages. I remember her as a middle-aged woman when I first came here straight out of Boston Clerical.'

'You wouldn't happen to know where she retired to?'

'She never retired anywhere. She didn't get the chance.'

'Why not?'

The woman glanced uneasily at Sarah. 'I don't want to

upset Mrs Kelling any more than she is already.'

'I don't think you could,' said Sarah. 'Please tell us what happened to Alethia Browne.'

'The Boston Strangler got her.'

'Are you sure it was the Strangler?' asked Bittersohn.

'Well, of course none of that was ever proved, but it was him all right. Same kind of crime as the rest of them, no sign of breaking and entering or anything. He just walked in and took one of her own nylons that she'd washed and hung on the bathroom rack to dry. Looped it around her neck and that was that. Mr Verplanck had to go over to the morgue and make the formal identification because she didn't have any folks of her own left around here, and boy, was he green around the gills when he got back! At least the Strangler didn't do anything to her, if you know what I mean. Not like some of those other poor women.'

'He didn't, eh? I suppose she lived not too far from here?'

'Yes, over on Myrtle Street. Alethia had a little apartment of her own, just one room and a bath and kitchenette, but she'd fixed it up real cute. We all felt terrible about Alethia. The customers just loved her. She knew them all by name, and she'd ask about their families and all.'

'Then she must have known my mother-in-law,' cried Sarah, 'and my husband, too. She'd have—'

'Take it easy,' said Bittersohn. 'Finish your coffee and let's get out of here.'

'But shouldn't she rest a while longer?' said the kind lady.

'I want to get her to a doctor.'

'Oh, yes, that's much the best thing to do. Shall I call you a cab?'

'We'll manage, thanks. It's not far. Would you mind telling Mr Redfern and Mr Verplanck that Mrs Kelling will contact them later?'

Sarah added her own thanks and got off the couch, grateful for Bittersohn's steadying hand. She did feel both wobbly on her legs and fuzzy in the brain, but when they got outside she told him, 'I'm not going to any doctor.'

'I didn't think you were. I just didn't want you telling that woman your life story. Feel like stopping for a bite of lunch?'

'No, really I couldn't,' she said. 'My insides are doing flip-flops. Mr Bittersohn, what am I going to do?'

'About getting the jewellery back?'

'About everything. I'm sure it's ridiculous even to think about the jewellery. That must have been all sold ages ago to pay the blackmailer.'

'I think you're going to find it's been sold quite a few times, always by the same person.'

'But how is that possible? Does he keep stealing the pieces back from the people he sells them to?'

'It's a little more subtle than that. What he does is to approach a prospect and show him, or more often her, an absolutely first-class antique necklace, ring, or whatever. He invites the prospect to have an appraisal made by any reputable jeweller. The pair of them go together and get a perfectly valid opinion that the stones couldn't possibly be any more genuine. The seller insists on knocking the appraiser's fee off the purchase price as a gesture of goodwill. The transaction is completed, always for cash on the barrelhead, and he fades gracefully into the sunset.

'Sooner or later, the mark finds out that what he bought wasn't what he wound up with. He's been stuck with a very good copy of the original, worth maybe a couple of hundred dollars. Maybe he, too, has a streak of larceny in his soul so, armed with that expert's appraisal, he fakes a robbery and gets his money back by bilking his insurance company. That's how I happen to be in on this business, too many people have been filing claims for the same pieces.

'Your ruby parure, for example, was stolen in Rome, Brussels, Hong Kong, Rio de Janeiro, Dallas, and Milwaukee before a very clever lady in Amsterdam managed to pull a double sneak and hang on to what she paid for. I'm afraid your chances of getting those rubies back at this point are just about nil, unless you can persuade a Dutch court to accept that Sargent portrait as evidence of ownership and are prepared to refund the purchase price, which was pretty high. I can't promise to salvage anything at all, but I'll do what I can. Right now, you'd better go home and get some rest. I'll come, too, if you don't mind.'

'You're going to get that man to trace the wires, aren't you?'

'Yes, and also fix up the phone so you can take it to bed with you.'

'Why bother? It looks as though I'll be moving out of the house any day now.'

'Don't worry about that till it happens. Say, hadn't we better stop for some groceries? I wiped out your larder this morning, the least I can do is buy you another pound of bacon.'

'You needn't do that, but you might help carry the bags. Alexander always used to—'

Sarah choked up and couldn't finish the sentence. Neither of them said much after that until they had left the supermarket on Cambridge Street and were trudging back up to Tulip. They were almost there when she mentioned what was on her mind.

'You knew the jewels would all be gone, then?'

'Yes,' Bittersohn admitted, 'I was pretty sure there'd been a clean sweep of the collection when I saw those genuine India pearls your mother-in-law was wearing the night I met her.'

'Why?'

'They're fakes.'

'Oh, good heavens! Do you think she knew?'

He shrugged. 'Would she have cared?'

'I don't suppose so, if they went to bail out her little love. It's absolutely incredible to me that Aunt Caroline was ready to kill Uncle Gilbert for his money, then give up every penny of it without a qualm to protect another man.'

'Who must have been some prize specimen if he was willing to sit back and let her do it,' Bittersohn agreed. 'I'd say your mother-in-law must have been the kind of woman who has to be the star in some real-life soap opera. You said she planned to cover herself with grease and glory by swimming the English Channel, but her parents squashed that fantasy. So she decided to become a society queen and married a man who had the cash but not the inclination. Then she found herself a red-hot romance, pulled her fake heroics to finance it, and wound up deaf, blind and a heroine. Since there wasn't much else left for her to do, she played the noble martyr to the hilt for the rest of her life. Whether she was genuinely devoted to that no-good bum, or infatuated with her own role as the beautiful woman who gave her all for the man she loved, is something I don't suppose we'll ever know.'

'I don't know why I keep thinking, "poor Aunt Caroline,"' said Sarah. 'She really was a monster, yet I can't help feeling a little bit sorry for her. She destroyed Alexander, but at least he had one real thing in his life, which is more than she did.'

'She and a lot of other people.'

There was something in Bittersohn's voice that made Sarah shy away from any further remark. They finished the distance in silence. When they got to the house he helped her get the groceries inside, said, 'I'll be back around two with the electrician,' and left.

Sarah put away the food and made herself a sandwich she didn't particularly want. Their breakfast dishes were still sitting there, so she washed them. What was it going to be like when there was only one cup, one plate, one knife, one fork, one spoon? She hurried out of the kitchen and went upstairs to finish transferring her belongings to Aunt Caroline's suite. She might as well enjoy it while she could.

Those hideous draperies in the boudoir would have to be taken down. What if somebody besides herself happened to notice what the embroidery stood for? The best plan would be to take them out to Ireson's Landing and burn them in the big fireplace.

It was a wonder Leila had never dicovered Caroline's secret diary, she'd been in the boudoir often enough. But did Leila read Braille? Perhaps she'd never bothered to learn, she was so adept at the hand signalling. Still, it would be easy enough for her to get hold of a chart and transliterate if she once caught on. If she did, she'd never be able to keep her mouth shut, and that would be total disaster for the whole Kelling clan.

Sarah was down in the cellar struggling with the heavy old wooden stepladder when Bittersohn came back with the electrician. She thought of asking them to take the ladder upstairs for her, then realised they'd no doubt need it for tracing the wires, which in fact they did.

The process was a great deal more tedious than she'd thought it would be. She answered questions, showed where things were, watched till it got too boring, then left the men to their tapping and prying and went back to her own chores. There were dozens of notes to be written. The sooner she got at them, the less depressing they'd be. She sat down at the Samuel McIntyre escritoire in the drawing room where she'd be out of the men's way, and had made a fairly impressive dent in the pile when Bittersohn came to tell her they'd finished.

'We had quite a time. The wire had been led down inside the wall all the way from the attic and carried over the roofs to a skylight three houses up. Now we've got to find out where it goes from there, which calls for a spot of fraudulent entry.'

'Can you manage that?'

'Sure. We'll put on our false whiskers and make believe we're from the phone company or something. Incidentally, Frank put a long cord on your telephone so it will reach upstairs.'

'That's marvellous. I can't thank you enough.'

'Why thank me at all? It's included in the service. Look, I don't want to press the issue, but can't you get somebody to come and stay with you, if only for tonight?'

'I'll ask my Uncle Jem.' Sarah was through being a heroine.

'Good. And keep that phone number I gave you handy just in case, eh?'

'Is that part of your job, too?'

Sarah smiled at him and he smiled back.

'Sure. I'll be in touch.'

He was gone and she was alone again, but not for long. Just about teatime, Edgar Merton came to call. Seeing that dapper figure on the doorstep, Sarah felt a surge of utter panic. She forced herself not to show it, though she couldn't manage much in the way of a cordial greeting. That was all right, he'd hardly expect a new widow to bubble over with enthusiasm. If he actually was Caroline's 'little love', he himself must be feeling a terrible sense of loss.

If he was, he didn't show it. He spoke of Caroline as a gallant lady whom he'd admired and respected. He was sorry she was dead, but clearly far from desolated. He was much more concerned about Sarah herself, how she was bearing up, what were her plans, whether there was some way he might make himself useful to her. On this last subject he became so importunate that Sarah began to simmer. Why couldn't he have made himself useful to Aunt Caroline when she'd spent all Uncle Gilbert's money paying off the blackmailers?

Then she remembered they hadn't yet proved Edgar was the man, and felt ashamed of herself for judging him.

'Sit still, I'm going to put the kettle on. You'd like tea, wouldn't you?'

'That would be delightful,' he replied in a somewhat puzzled tone, 'but doesn't Edith usually take care of culinary matters?'

How did she answer this one? Of course people would find out sooner or later that the old retainer was no longer here, but Sarah wasn't keen on having it known just now that she was alone in the house. She decided to say Edith wasn't feeling very well.

'Are you sure she's not just angling for attention?' he replied. 'I know this has been a shock to her, as it has to all of us, but this is no time for her to give way. She ought to be thinking of your convenience and comfort. Perhaps, as an old friend of the family, I might nip down and have a word with her? Ginger her up a bit?'

'She's not here,' Sarah had to tell him then. 'She's gone out to her nephew's.'

'Leaving you in the lurch? That's a fine thing, I must say! If she was well enough to travel—'

'He came and got her in his van. We all agreed it was the best thing to do. I forget, do you take cream or lemon?'

'Oh dear, have I made so little impression on your memory? Lemon, please, and just a speck of sugar.'

Sarah wished she hadn't offered tea, now she was stuck with him for at least another half-hour. Edgar's manner was really strangely frisky in view of the circumstances. Was he beginning to go soft in the head, like Alice? She gave him the stack of condolences to sort as a sobering influence, and took her time about fixing the tray. When she got back, he greeted her like a long-lost daughter.

Or would it be a daughter? Did daughters get their hands patted so often? Incredible as it seemed, she was forced to wonder if Edgar was, as Aunt Emma would say, making up to her.

'Yes, this is a terrible loss. I remember Caroline as a beautiful young woman. I myself was a child at the time, of course, though I trust I was never so ungallant as to remind her of the difference in our ages.'

'I trust you weren't, either,' Sarah thought, 'because you'd have been brought up short if you'd tried.'

What kind of fool did he think she was? He'd been at Harvard with Uncle Mortimer, who was Class of '26, and judging from Uncle Mort's reminiscences, Edgar had been no infant prodigy.

He wasn't being very clever now, laying it on so thick about her fortitude, courage, presence of mind, and how lovely she looked in her grief, which was an outright lie because she looked ghastly and knew it. At last he got down to business.

'Knowing you were accustomed to the companionship of a man whom I may venture to consider my contemporary, and being painfully aware that my own bereavement may take place any day now—'

This was too much! White to the nostrils, Sarah got up and began rattling cups back on the tray. 'I'm afraid you'll have to excuse me, Edgar, I didn't realise it was so late. I have to be somewhere soon, and I've barely time to change.'

He was too well-bred to do anything but get up and go, though not without a few more tender pressings and a fervent promise to call again soon. Was the old goat actually intending to offer a conditional proposal of marriage before the flowers were dead on Alexander's grave? Surely he wouldn't have the atrocious taste to go that far, but he must be paving the way for something.

One thing certain, he couldn't have cared any more for Caroline Kelling than he did for Alice Merton. That long hearts-and-flowers courtship had been nothing more than his way of keeping another possible meal ticket on the string in case the doctors' bills ate up Alice's money before she died. With Caroline gone, he was already trying to line up a substitute. Was this what Aunt Caroline had eaten her heart out for so many years? Could a woman of her mentality ever have been taken in by such a lightweight?

Probably, if she wanted to be badly enough, Sarah dumped the tea things in the sink and went to call Uncle Jem. Egbert was awfully sorry, Miss Sarah, but the boss was sick in bed with a cold he'd caught at the funeral, and there was no sense taking the phone to him because he'd lost his voice, which was one consolation from Egbert's point of view.

Sarah said, 'Oh, that's too bad. Give him my love and tell him to take care of himself,' and hung up. Now what? Who else might be willing to come on such short notice? Leila would, if she was around, but Sarah couldn't ask Mrs Lackridge to come and hold her hand after having delivered that blast about minding her own business, and she didn't want her, anyway. And everybody else was so old, or so far away.

She could drive out to Chestnut Hill and sleep over at Aunt Appie's or the Protheroes', but they'd want to know why Edith wasn't around and why Sarah was so squeamish about staying alone, and a lot of other whys that Sarah wasn't ready to talk about yet. She'd made her bed, she might as well go upstairs and lie in it.

CHAPTER
TWENTY-FIVE

It was far too early for that, though. Worn out as she was, Sarah knew she'd only drop off for a few hours, then wake up with a long, dark night ahead of her. She ought to eat some dinner, too, though she wouldn't be hungry for a couple of hours now that she'd had tea. She might as well get back to her thank-you notes, work till eight or thereabout, then fix herself a snack and take another good soak in that elegant pink tub of Aunt Caroline's. After that, one could always fall back on William James.

She turned on the radio for company and made herself concentrate on writing. The music on WCRB was soothing,

but it soon gave way to news and Sarah found that listening
to other people's tragedies was too harsh a reminder of her
own. She tried switching stations, got more of the same,
switched off the set. She looked at her pile of notes, decided
she couldn't stand the sight of one more kind word,
slammed down her pen, went around drawing the shades,
found herself pacing through the empty house like the
tigress at Franklin Park Zoo she and Alexander used to feel
so sorry for.

This was horrible! She'd almost rather see Edgar Merton
back than endure any more of her own depressing
company. She was on the verge of calling Anora Protheroe
to beg a night's lodging and brave the inquisition when the
doorbell rang again. It was Bob Dee, with a flat white
pasteboard carton and a brown paper bag.

'I hope you're in the mood for pizza and beer. I couldn't
think what else to bring.'

'You didn't have to bring me anything, but what a lovely
idea. Come in, Bob. I was just thinking I must do
something about dinner, and now I shan't have to. Why
don't we eat in here in front of the fire? I'll get some plates
and glasses.'

'Hey, you don't have to bother. At the pad we eat with
our fingers and drink out of the cans. Saves washing up.'

'I'm afraid several generations of Kellings would turn
over in their graves if I tried that. Put on another log, will
you, Bob? I'll only be a minute.'

Pizza in the drawing room with an unattached male might
not be the height of propriety for a woman in her
circumstances, but at least it was a change. Bob Dee might
be a nincompoop, but he was cheerful and forgiving. And
young. Sarah ate the soggy, stringy, spicy pastry, drank her
beer, and let him prattle.

For a while she rather enjoyed herself. One of the tall
cans was all the beer she could manage, though, and Dee
was obviously not about to let the rest of the six pack go to
waste. The more he drank, the louder and sillier he got.
When she dropped a hint that the party was over, he
horrified her by turning amorous.

'Hey, the night is young and you're so beautiful. How
about it, beautiful?'

'Bob, would you please bear in mind that I've just lost my husband?'

'I'm bearing, I'm bearing. What do you think I came for? Off with the old, on with the new, like it says in Shakespeare. Don't try to kid me, Sarah. The guy was old enough to be your father, and there's a very naughty name for screwing around with your old man. I'm sure you wouldn't do anything naughty. No,' he wrapped an arm around her and puffed beer in her face. 'You're going to be nice. Aren't you, Sarah?'

She wrenched her body out of his clutch and snatched up the poker. 'I'm going to beat your ears off if you don't get out of here and leave me alone. I was stupid enough to think you came simply out of kindness, but I shan't make that mistake again. If you bother me any more, I'll tell Harry Lackridge exactly what sort of person he has working for him.'

For some reason, Dee thought that was pretty funny. 'Okay, Sarah, if that's the way you want to play it. Don't say I didn't warn you. Thanks for the use of your john.'

Sarah slammed the door behind him and put the chain up. She was relieved he hadn't turned ugly, but thoroughly disgusted with herself for having been such a fool as to let him in. That session with Edgar Merton should have warned her. Everybody thought she was about to fall into a huge fortune. She was going to be a target for every wolf in Boston.

That safe-deposit box full of bricks might turn out to be a blessing in disguise, at that. Once the word got around that Sarah Kelling was flat broke and about to be foreclosed on, at least she wouldn't be bothered by the likes of Bob Dee. She thrust the empty pizza carton into the fireplace and took a savage pleasure in watching it burn. She gathered up the rest of the litter, took it out to the kitchen, filled the sink with hot water and detergent, and conducted a rite of purification. Getting the dirty dishes out of the way made her feel one degree less soiled herself. A hot bath did more.

Those dreadful curtains she'd meant to get rid of were still hanging in the boudoir. She'd have to attend to that tomorrow, and find some to hang in their place. Bare windows at the front of the house would look awful. Some of Aunt Caroline's old pals would be sure to notice and wonder why the young widow was in such a hurry to change things. The less attention she attracted, the better for her.

If one were going to stay in the house, it might be fun to redecorate the boudoir for a sitting room. Then she could rent the rooms on the other floors and keep this suite for herself. It would be a way of getting money to pay the mortgage, and there would be people around.

Sarah turned the idea over in her mind. With half a dozen lodgers and what she could make out of free-lance illustrating, she just might be able to scrape through. She'd need a certain amount of capital for mattresses, linens, things of that sort. Perhaps she could sell some of the furniture she wouldn't be needing any more. There were still a number of good pieces in the house, probably because Aunt Caroline hadn't dared get rid of them for fear people would start asking too many questions about the jewellery. That escritoire might fetch a decent sum. Perhaps Mr Bittersohn would know how to market it so she wouldn't get skinned.

And how did she know Mr Bittersohn himself wouldn't skin her? She musn't start thinking of him as Sir Galahad just because he hadn't yet made a pass at her. Why should he? He knew she didn't have any money. Sarah whacked at her pillows to plump them up, and reached for William James.

That incident with Bob Dee must have left her even more shaken than she realised. She read a full twelve pages before she managed to get to sleep. Punctually at midnight, she was awakened by the telephone on the night stand beside her bed. When she picked it up and said hello, nobody answered, but she could hear heavy breathing. Some drunk who'd got a wrong number, no doubt. She slammed down the receiver and tried to get back to sleep.

Fifteen minutes later to the second, the phone rang again. Again there was no voice on the line, only that same breathy sound. When it happened a third time at half-past twelve, she realised she was being deliberately harassed. She picked up the receiver to break the connection and put it back without answering.

This must have been what Bob Dee had in mind when he said, 'Don't say I didn't warn you.' It was exactly the sort of spiteful nonsense he'd think was funny. She'd take the receiver off the hook, set the phone outside her door so she wouldn't have to listen to the telephone company making noises on the line, and let him entertain himself getting a busy signal.

But what if Mr Bittersohn took it into his head to check up on her, and went into another swivet because he couldn't get through? Late as it was, she'd better call and explain why the phone would be out of commission. Sarah turned on the light, read off the number he'd dictated to her, and dialled. To her relief, he answered right away.

'This is Sarah Kelling,' she said. 'I hope I didn't wake you.'

'No, not at all. I was sitting here reading. What's up?'

'Nothing, really. Some pest is calling up every fifteen minutes and breathing at me. I'm going to take the receiver off the hook, but I thought I should let you know in case you tried to call for any reason.'

'How long has it been going on?'

'Since midnight. He's done it three times so far.'

'How do you know it's a he?'

'I don't. It's just that I had a—a rather silly experience with our mutual friend Bob Dee this evening, and I thought it might be his notion of a practical joke.'

'Mrs Kelling, I don't think you ought to take anything for granted, and I don't think it's a good idea to tie up your telephone. I'd like to come over, if you don't mind, and be on hand when the next call comes in. Wait five minutes, then come downstairs and turn on the outside light. Don't open the door till you make darn sure you know who it is. I'll give five short rings. Okay?'

Sarah started to say, 'If you really think—' realised he'd already rung off, and started putting on her bathrobe and slippers.

But what if it was Bittersohn himself who was making the calls so that she'd give him an excuse to come over—as she'd just done? Why on earth would he do a thing like that? She mustn't get paranoid. She mustn't be stupid, either. She wouldn't go down there in her nightgown, and she would keep that poker handy, just in case.

Sarah put on slacks and a sweater, shoved her feet into woolly slippers because the floor was cold, and padded silently downstairs. It wasn't five minutes yet, but her nerves wouldn't let her sit up there cold-bloodedly watching the clock hands inch around.

A cup of hot coffee mightn't be a bad idea. She was so wide-awake already that a little caffeine wasn't going to make any difference. Not bothering to turn on a light because she knew the way so well, Sarah went out to the kitchen and was about to put the pot under the faucet when she heard a noise.

Of course one was always hearing things in the city: trucks and fire engines going by, students whooping it up on the sidewalk, drunks being sick in the alley. This noise was none of those. It sounded as if somebody was trying to take the cellar door off its hinges.

She didn't know what put that notion into her head, but it was simple enough to check. The back entry was directly below the kitchen window. Thankful that she hadn't put on a light or made any racket herself, she flattened her nose against the pane and looked down.

Yes, there was somebody, hard at work. She could see a dull gleam from the shaft of some long tool he was using, probably a big screwdriver. She thought it must be a man because he appeared to be working with no great effort, and it must take real strength to budge those rusted-in screws. All she was actually able to make out was a large dark blob and a couple of whitish oblongs perhaps ten inches high sitting on the pavement beside him. Were those his tool boxes? Why more than one?

Whatever they were, he'd better get them out of there fast. Moved by exasperation to recklessness, Sarah ran boiling hot water into a pail, eased the window open, and dumped the bucketful square on his head.

It must have burned, it certainly shocked. Whoever was there dropped whatever he had and took off like the proverbial scalded cat. She was filling the kettle again in case he came back for his tools when the doorbell rang five quick tings.

Before she cracked open the door on its chain, she made very sure it was Bittersohn. Even then, she wasn't ready to let him in.

'Turn around slowly under the light so I can get a good look at your coat.'

'If you want,' he said in surprise. 'Any special reason?'

'I want to see if you're wet. I just poured a bucket of hot water on somebody who was trying to break in from the alley.'

'My God, woman, you're dangerous! No, fortunately, I'm dry. I hope you're not going to try any assault and battery on me.'

'Don't push me, then. I threatened Bob Dee with a poker this evening.'

'Too bad you didn't let him have it. What did he do?'

'I'd rather not say.'

'Okay, you don't have to. What happened to the burglar?'

'He ran away. He left something, though, so he may have come back to get it by now.'

'Come on. How do you get downstairs?'

'I'll show you.'

Sarah switched on the hall lights and led Bittersohn down through Edith's deserted lair. The alley door was sagging half off its hinges; she'd been none too quick with her bucket. Bittersohn pushed it open. Those whitish oblongs were still sitting outside, in a steamy puddle. He picked one up, and sniffed at the top.

'The son-of-a-bitch! He was going to burn the place down. Smell that.'

He thrust what turned out to be a plastic jug under Sarah's nose.

'It smells like paint thinner,' she said.

'It is paint thinner. A gallon or so of this and a book of matches are all any competent arsonist needs.'

'Then those phone calls—'

'Probably to make sure you were in the house and keep you busy so you wouldn't go roaming around.'

'But I might have burned to death!'

'I don't want to upset you any more than you've been already, Mrs Kelling, but I'd say that was the general idea, that and getting rid of whatever evidence might be in the house.'

'Those draperies of Aunt Caroline's! But why not just break in and take them down?'

'Because whoever wants to get rid of anything incriminating doesn't know what to look for. You haven't told anybody but me about them, have you?'

'No, not a soul. I see what you mean. Anybody who knew Aunt Caroline very well for a long time must have recognised that theatrical streak in her and guessed she wouldn't be able to resist leaving some kind of diary about her great romance, but who could ever dream she'd choose the way she did?'

'Did you get a good look at the torch?'

'The what?'

'The guy with the jugs. The arsonist.'

'Oh. No, I'm sorry to say I didn't. I thought it was a man, but I couldn't be sure. Actually it was just a shape in the dark.'

'Big or little?'

'Big. Biggish, anyway. How tall are you?'

'Five eleven and a whisker. Say six feet with my shoes on.'

'Then I'd say this person was also about six feet and more heavy-set than you, though one can't be sure in cold weather because people bundle up in extra clothes. I honestly didn't believe it was you, I was just being overly careful because I'd made stupid mistakes about two other men this evening.'

'That's okay, I don't blame you a bit. Do you think you scalded the guy?'

'I hope so. It would serve him right.'

'It'll also provide a means of identification if we can get to him before he heals. Let's leave these jugs here and I'll watch for a while to see if he comes back for them, though I doubt if he'd be fool enough to do that. There's no way they could be traced because you can buy the stuff at any hardware or paint store, and I'm sure he wore gloves. You go back to bed. I'll stick around down here, just in case.'

'Would you like some coffee? I was going to make some.

That's how I happened to be in the kitchen and hear him working at the hinges.'

'I'm surprised he kept at it once you turned on the light.'

'I didn't. I've gotten into the habit of going about the house in the dark a lot, I suppose because everything was arranged for a blind person's convenience. I can make a pot of coffee in the dark, fix it any way you like, and bring it down to you without spilling a drop. Want me to?'

'Just don't break your neck.'

'I shan't. Right now I'm mostly concerned to save it.'

CHAPTER
TWENTY-SIX

Edith had made such a clean sweep of the basement that there wasn't even a chair left for Bittersohn to sit on. Sarah unearthed a folding leather campaign chair that Alexander's Great-uncle Nathan had nursed his gout in at San Juan while Teddy Roosevelt and the Rough Riders were storming the hill, and took it down to the cellar along with a pillow and an afghan.

She saw no reason to stay with the man, and he didn't want her to. Still, she couldn't face the thought of going back to bed. She compromised by curling up on the library couch with the velvet comforter from Aunt Caroline's room, and napped fitfully until the traffic outside and the lumpiness of her improvised bed drove her to rouse herself.

Poor Mr Bittersohn, what sort of night had he put in? Sarah took a shower to revive herself as far as possible, got into clean clothes, and went down to see if he'd survived his vigil. She found her guest sprawled in the campaign chair with his head bobbing backwards over the top and his legs tangled strangely in the afghan. He was emitting an occasional choking snort, as well he might. When she touched him on the shoulder he jerked upright and said crossly, 'I wasn't asleep.'

'I'm sure you weren't, but you must have been wretchedly uncomfortable. Did anything happen?'

'This damn chair folded up on me twice, and a mouse ran

up inside my pantleg. Otherwise, it was a restful night. Are the jugs still there?'

Sarah took away the stick of wood he'd used to prop up the half-dismantled door and peered out. 'Yes, still here. Oh, look, he's taken off the alley door, too. I wondered how he got over the wall.'

Like so many of its Beacon Hill counterparts, the Kelling house had a tiny bricked courtyard behind it surrounded by a high brick wall with a wooden door that led to the alley behind. This door, which had been securely bolted the last time she saw it, was also off its hinges and lying on the pavement. She walked over and kicked at it.

'I wonder why he bothered? This door is so rickety all he'd have to do would be to push in a panel and reach around to the bolt. Alexander was intending to put on a new one next spring.'

Bittersohn came up beside her and studied the peeling wood thoughtfully. 'That's a good question. I've met only one crook in my life whose hobby is taking doors off hinges. That could be how the Milburn was got at. Tell me, Mrs Kelling, you wouldn't happen to know a middle-aged man who's about my size but more heavy-set, with a sallow complexion and noticeable liver spots on his forehead? He's bald, has an unusually thin nose, small greenish eyes set close together, and an odd way of lifting the left-hand corner of his mouth when he talks. I doubt if you'd meet him socially, but he may have come to the house as a repairman or something of the sort.'

'We've hardly ever had repairmen,' Sarah said. 'Alexander did most of the odd jobs. Still, the description does ring a bell. Oh, I know! But he wasn't bald, he had thick grey hair.'

'Who?'

'That man who called himself a doctor. I remember the thin nose and the blotches on the forehead.'

'You're positive?'

'Yes, I am. The room was so small that I was standing practically nose-to-nose with him. I noticed the hair particularly because it was so handsome, and the rest of him wasn't. It looked too good to be true.'

'No doubt it was,' said Bittersohn. 'Well, we'd better put

these doors back up, though I'm afraid he's wrecked them prying to get at the hinges. Got a hammer and nails and some scrap lumber?'

Together, they propped up the doors and Sarah held boards across while Bittersohn whacked in the nails. He made a thorough job of it before he put down the hammer.

'There, that's not very fancy but it ought to hold till you can get a carpenter to do the job right. Now, I'm going to make a quick dash to my place for a shave and shower, then I'll come back with the car and we'll take a look at the area where you say you saw this guy. Think you can find the house again?'

'How could I forget? If you like,' Sarah ventured shyly, 'you could go up and use Alexander's razor. There's a bathroom on the third floor with his things still in it. I could be getting us a bite of breakfast while you're freshening up, which would save some time. Unless you'd rather go home?'

'No, that's okay. You sure you wouldn't mind?'

'I don't think so. I've already had to put company in his room for the funeral. There's no sense in being sentimental.' Sarah dabbed at her eyes. 'It's on the third floor. You'll find everything you need, I think, except that I'm afraid I can't offer you a change of linen.'

That would be carrying common sense one step too far. She didn't know what she was going to do with the clothes she'd mended so often for her lost darling, but no stranger was going to see those careful darns. She put another pot of coffee on to perk, started bacon frying, and began to section the grapefruit she'd bought yesterday. By the time Bittersohn came down, looking a good deal less shopworn in spite of his wilted shirt, she had a meal ready. They ate without paying much attention to the food and then walked down to the Underground Garage.

'Over Arlington to Broadway, then straight across to Dorchester Avenue and take a right?' he said as he switched on the ignition.

'I should think that's the best way.'

Sarah found she was perched on the extreme edge of the leather seat, her fists clenched as if she were going into battle. She forced herself to lean back and take deep breaths to relax the tightness in her solar plexus. The closer they got to where they were going, the harder she had to breathe. She was getting dizzy from hyperventilation when Bittersohn said, 'We must be getting close to where we turn.'

'Yes, just up the street, by that drugstore.'

'Any place close to the house where we might be able to pull up and keep watch without being spotted?'

'I'm afraid not. It's a sort of cul-de-sac. Perhaps we could leave the car somewhere and—oh, look, here she comes! The woman in the green coat and the snakeskin boots. She's going into the drugstore.'

'To buy some burn ointment, maybe?' Incredibly, Max Bittersohn was smiling. 'So that's Mrs Wandelowski.'

'Do you know her?' Sarah gasped.

'You might say we've met. She once tried to part my hair with a ceremonial sword from the Knights of Phythias.'

'For goodness' sake, why?'

'Because, as Hillary said about Everest, it was there. She was a little upset with me at the time. She's probably pretty annoyed with you right now for getting Abelard's rug wet.'

'Abelard is her husband, then?'

'Or not, as the case may be. Abelard and Madeleine, two minds with but a single thought—and that one pretty nasty. So they're both wearing wigs now. They always were a dressy pair.'

'Who are they?'

'Odd-jobbers. They do whatever the higher-ups don't have the time or the inclination to tackle personally. I always thought they must have a home base somewhere. So Madeleine's been running a boarding house in her spare time. That figures.'

'What else does she do?'

'Changes sheets in a motel, clerks in a supermarket, whatever suits the purpose of the moment. She never stays anywhere long, and she seldom gets caught. Madeleine has the advantage of being about the most nondescript woman you'd ever run across. Change the wig, leave off the makeup, put her into a waitress's uniform instead of that flashy getup she's wearing now, and you'd never believe she was the same person. Her part is usually to gather information, plant something on somebody, intercept a letter, some small job of that sort. Abelard, being a much more noticeable sort of person, lurks in the background until it's time to do his specialty.'

'Such as impersonationg a doctor or burning down a house.'

'Or being the telephone repairman with a bug in his box, or the mechanic who screwed up the brakes on your Milburn. Abelard's clever with his hands.'

'Then he was the one who killed Mr O'Ghee, I suppose?'

'I honestly don't know, Mrs Kelling. Until this business came up, I'd never have figured Abelard for a hit man, although I don't doubt he was the one who got rid of the body. Well, I guess we've seen what we came for. Shall I take you back to the house?'

'I'd be rather glad if you would,' Sarah replied. 'I don't know why, but I'm anxious to put my hand on that letter Mr Verplanck wrote me. I can't think why I didn't see it because I worked for several hours yesterday trying to get the correspondence straightened out. Also, he claims he wrote to Aunt Caroline and Alexander any number of times, and I didn't see those letters, either.'

Bittersohn made a small noise in his throat.

'I don't mean that Alexander didn't let me read his mail, I just mean picking up the envelopes the postman pushed through the slot. That was a little job I generally attended to because the mail's apt to come at a time when Alexander would be out somewhere with his mother. I'd sort it out, so I knew who was writing to whom. Also, I handled Aunt Caroline's correspondence for her, more or less. She'd write letters in Braille and get me to type them up. If she'd suddenly started getting a spate of letters from the bank and never sending any answers, I think I'd have noticed. Don't you?'

'It's worth thinking about, anyway. All right, Mrs Kelling, let's go look for your letter.'

Getting back to the Hill was simple enough, but parking was another matter.

'Oh, dear,' Sarah moaned, 'I should have suggested we leave the car at the garage and walk up. It's always impossible around here.'

'I'll find a place,' said Bittersohn. 'Why don't you go on in and start looking for your letter? Sure you won't mind being alone in the house for a few minutes?'

'Of course not. Why should I?'

She hopped out fast because the driver behind them was using abusive language, and let herself in. Without bothering to take off her coat, she began shuffling through the piles of mail she'd left on the escritoire. She knew perfectly well there was no envelope from the High Street Trust among them, and there wasn't.

Had Edith been pinching the mail as well as the furniture? It was tempting to blame her, but not very sensible to jump to conclusions. There were other possibilities. Edgar Merton, who'd spent so much time here playing backgammon with Aunt Caroline; Edgar to whom she'd given this same collection of messages to sort out for her only yesterday. The more she thought about Edgar, the less she liked what came to her mind.

In any event, she'd better call Mr Verplanck and tell him she couldn't find the letter. At least it might buy her a little more time to straighten things out. After being passed through a secretary or two, she got him on the line.

'This is Sarah Kelling. I want to apologise for my ridiculous behaviour yesterday and also to thank that extremely kind lady who took care of me. Perhaps you'd be kind enough to give me her name so I can drop her a note?'

The bank manager made appropriate responses.

'I also wanted to tell you that I can't find that letter you say you wrote me. I've been through all my mail, and it's simply not in the house.'

'Why, naturally it wouldn't be, Mrs Kelling,' he replied in the tone one might use to a not very bright child. 'It was directed to your post office box, as usual.'

'What post office box? We don't have one. Why should we?'

'Oh, dear.' His sigh was audible over the phone. 'Apparently this is another of your mother-in-law's little mysteries. At the time she took out those first mortgages, she instructed me to address all communications regarding that and any other bank matters to Box 2443 at the Back Bay Postal Annex, and that's precisely what we've always done. Obviously, since she never informed you of this fact, you have not checked the box. Perhaps it would help to clarify matters if you did.'

'I certainly shall,' said Sarah. 'I'll do it right away. Mr Verplanck, you must realise that I'm in a state of utter confusion. I'll get things straightened out with you as soon as I know where I stand. Box 2443, you said?'

'That's correct, Mrs Kelling. Then I'll look forward to hearing from you or Mr Redfern by the end of the week.'

He hung up with a smart little click. Mr Verplanck wasn't concerned with Sarah Kelling's problems, only with the bank's money. It looked as if she'd soon have a conclusive answer for all those relatives who kept pestering her about what she was going to do with the properties. She already had the answer to why Alexander had never told her about the mortgages. He had never known about the post office box, either.

Then who had impersonated him at the interview with Mr Verplanck? She dialled the bank's number again.

'Mr Verplanck, I'm sorry to be a pest, but could you please tell me what Alexander Kelling looked like when you met him?'

'Really, Mrs Kelling, I—'

'Please! I know it sounds crazy, but it's terribly important.'

'Well,' he evidently made up his mind that he might as well humour this madwoman and get her off his ear, 'he was—er—tall.'

Sarah's heart sank a little. 'Tall? Are you positive? How tall? As tall as his mother?'

'To the best of my recollection, he was at least half a head taller.'

'Oh, no!' How could that be? 'What else do you remember about him?'

'Mrs Kelling, it's been quite some time, and we had only the one meeting. You can hardly expect me to recall one face out of the many I see every day.'

'But you ought to. Almost anybody who'd ever set eyes on Alexander would never forget him for a specific reason, and you should be able to tell me what it is.'

'Are you referring to a birthmark or some such thing?

I'm sorry, but I can't recall anything outstanding about him except his height. He seemed an agreeable enough man, but he didn't say much. Now that I think of it, I believe he had hay fever or something. He kept his handkerchief up to his face a good deal of the time. He also had dark glasses on because he found the allergy was affecting his eyes. To tell the truth, I don't think I ever did get a good look at him.'

'I'm sure you didn't, Mr Verplanck,' said Sarah with unutterable relief. 'My husband didn't have hay fever, and he'd never have been rude enough to keep his dark glasses on while he was talking to you. You'd have remembered him for the same reason everybody else always did. Alexander was the handsomest man you'd ever have seen in your life.'

'Good God, Mrs Kelling, are you trying to tell me I negotiated those mortgages with a pair of imposters?'

'No. With Caroline Kelling and one imposter.'

'Then who was the man?'

Sarah was wondering how to answer, when she heard footsteps somewhere in the house. Was it the arsonist, back to try again? What should she do? Rush out to the sidewalk and wait for Bittersohn? Call the police? Make a noise herself in the hope of scaring him off? That would be pretty crazy. Best lie low.

Hastily she said, 'Mr Verplanck, I'll have to call you back,' and tried to replace the receiver without a sound. In her nervousness, she knocked the phone off the stand. It fell with a mighty crash.

At once, to her mingled relief and fury, an all-too-familiar voice called out, 'Edith, is that you?'

CHAPTER
TWENTY-SEVEN

'Harry, you scared the life out of me! No, it's Sarah. Edith isn't here. However did you get in?'

'Through the door, naturally.'

'How could you? It was locked.'

'No, it wasn't,' said Lackridge. 'When I rang the front

doorbell and nobody answered, I thought Edith might be down in her lair with that damned television blaring away as usual, so I went around through the alley and found both doors ajar. You ought to be more careful about keeping the place locked up, Sarah. Anybody could barge right in.'

'But, Harry, that's not possible. Mr Bittersohn nailed them shut.'

'What the hell for? What's Bittersohn doing around here, anyway?'

Sarah was almost demoralised enough to tell him, but not quite. She had no right to let the publisher know that his supposed author was really a detective using him for cover. Luckily, Harry answered his own question.

'Figures if he can't get at the family jewels one way, he'll try another, eh? You watch out for that chap, Sarah. You know what those people are like, give them a toe in the door and the next thing you know, they're trying to crawl in bed with you.'

'Yes, I had a little lesson in that regard from your lad Bob Dee,' Sarah couldn't resist telling him. 'By the way, Harry, how did he know Alexander and Aunt Caroline and I were going to Ireson's Landing for the weekend? He mentioned it at that meeting we had, and I don't recall having told anybody.'

Lackridge looked blank for a moment. Then he said, 'Where else would you have been going? Speaking of beds, what the hell's going on around here, anyway? I came to look for a little notebook I've misplaced. It has all my appointments for the next two months, and I'm lost without the thing. It occurred to me that I might have left it in Alex's room that night Leila and I slept here. That's why I came this morning. Since nobody was around, I decided I might as well go straight upstairs and look for it. The place is a mess. I know you're in no fit state to function yourself, but couldn't you get Edith to straighten things up?'

Sarah shook her head, trying to clear her mind. 'I told you Edith's not here. The rooms were in order when I left the house a couple of hours ago. The problem is, somebody's been breaking in and trying to burn the house down.'

'You're crazy!'

Lackridge caught himself. 'Sorry, Sarah, I didn't mean that. But Leila and I were talking. We realise you've been under an intolerable strain, and we think it might be a good idea if you were to go away for a while.'

'I thought I'd made it clear to Leila that I prefer to make my own plans,' Sarah snapped back. 'If you're hinting that I ought to be committed for observation, I suggest you leave that decision to Uncle Jem or Cousin Dolph. It's kind of you to be concerned, but I do have a family.'

'Sarah, be reasonable. All this talk about people breaking in and setting fire to the place—'

'You've seen the evidence, haven't you? You say the bedrooms are torn apart. You say the basement door was open when Mr Bittersohn himself can tell you he nailed it shut.'

She wasn't convincing Harry Lackridge, she could see that. He wasn't bothering to hide his sneer. Alexander would never have sneered. It was odd how unlike the two friends had been, yet so very like in superficial ways. Harry's voice was harsher than Alexander's but his diction was as impeccably Phillips and Harvard. The height, the thinness, the well-worn Brooks Brothers tweed suit, all were Alexander's without the elegance. In this ill-lit hallway, even the aquiline features were not all that dissimilar at first glance. Years ago, when Harry's skin was still fresh and his eyes clear, when his teeth were unyellowed and his grin hadn't yet become a twisted sneer, he'd sometimes been taken for one of the Kelling clan. If anybody in the world could have impersonated Alexander Kelling and got away with it—perhaps she really was going crazy. Sarah thought of a way to find out.

'Harry,' she said, keeping her voice from shaking as best she could, 'when you came through the basement, did you notice anything different about Edith's sitting room?'

He blinked. 'How do you mean, different? How should I know? I hadn't been down there in years. Anyway, it was rather dark and I couldn't find the light switch.'

'But you had to walk through the room to get to the kitchen stairs. Weren't you afraid you'd break your neck on the furniture? You know what a packrat Edith's always been.'

Lackridge hunched his shoulders. 'I'd forgotten about that. I damn near did kill myself, if you want to know. I slipped on a rug, and barked my shin on something or other. A rocking chair, I believe it was.'

'That was remarkably clumsy of you, Harry,' Sarah told him quietly, 'considering that Edith moved out of here night before last, and took the rugs and every stick of furniture with her. The basement rooms are bare to the walls, and you couldn't have helped noticing. You didn't come through there at all, you came in the front door with the keys Aunt Caroline gave you back when you were having your red-hot love affair. And you weren't looking for any appointment book, you were trying to find her diary.'

'Then she—don't be ridiculous, Sarah! How could Caro keep a diary?'

'You'd be surprised. I certainly was.'

'You found it?' He wasn't bothering to keep up his act any more.

She hadn't really taken it in until that moment that Harry Lackridge intended to kill her. Incredibly, the realisation did not frighten her at all.

'Oh, yes,' she replied quite calmly. 'You must have realised Aunt Caroline wouldn't be able to resist dramatising her great romance. I must say it was pretty raw of you to murder the woman you were supposed to be madly in love with, after you'd milked her of everything she owned and a lot more that she didn't.

'I was very fond of Caroline. If you hadn't started throwing your weight around and making trouble—'

'Stop it, Harry. You killed her and Alexander because you knew Mr Verplanck was about to start foreclosure proceedings on those two mortgages you were supposed to have been paying the interest on. Not even a blind fanatic could have gone on covering up for you once the bank came to put us out in the street. Don't try to make me believe you gave a rap about Aunt Caroline. You don't have one scrap of human feeling for anybody but yourself. I can't imagine what she ever saw in you.'

'She saw what she was looking for, and she got it.'

'The beautiful Mrs Kelling and a nasty little boy straight

out of prep school? It does sound incredible, especially when I look at you now. Her little love!'

'She wrote that?' He grabbed Sarah's shoulders and began shaking her violently. 'You're lying! Caro swore she'd never tell.'

'No, Harry, she didn't call you by any name but that. She kept faith with you, even though you betrayed her in every way you possibly could. But it wasn't hard to figure out who her little love must be. Who but you could have staged that scene with Ruby Redd when Aunt Caroline got tired of forking out money to that imaginary blackmailer you'd invented so you could get your grubby hands on Uncle Gilbert's fortune? You knew Alexander was seeing Ruby, you were the one who got them together in the first place. You knew the girl would help you put on your little act if you promised her the ruby parure as a reward. Promising wouldn't cost you anything. I'm sure you'd planned from the beginning to start that fake quarrel as an excuse to murder her. Aunt Caroline would never be able to refuse another of your blackmail demands after you'd supposedly saved her life by killing somebody else. Having your so-called best friend walk in just at the right moment to be stuck with the blame and have his whole life ruined was a stroke of luck you hadn't counted on, wasn't it?'

'That's a pretty story, Sarah. Where did you say you heard it?'

'Harry, I'm telling you, it's all in the diary. You'd explained to Ruby Redd that Aunt Caroline was deaf, but you forgot to mention that she could lip-read. Ruby was shooting her mouth off right and left, shouting about how you'd promised her the parure, and so forth. You tried to explain that away by saying it was Alexander who'd promised, but there were still parts of the dialogue Aunt Caroline didn't understand because it never dawned on her in all those years that you were the one who'd rigged the performance. It's perfectly obvious to me, now that I know what you are.'

Lackridge was smiling, the same yellow-toothed grin he put on when he was playing the buffoon in his wife's drawing room. 'That must be quite a document. What else did she write?'

'She told how you put her up to killing my father so that she could coerce Alexander into marrying me and getting them both an income after you'd swindled her out of Uncle Gilbert's estate. And, of course, there was the part about how Uncle Gilbert was got rid of, which I already knew. I don't have to tell you that, do I? You must have heard Alexander telling me on your bugging apparatus. That doesn't work any more, by the way.'

'That doesn't matter. I shan't be needing it,' Lackridge said in a tone that was appalling because it was so matter-of-fact. 'How did you find the bug? That couldn't have been mentioned in the diary.'

'No, and neither was the safe-deposit box full of bricks, or the fact that you strangled the bank attendant who knew you had access to the box, although I'm sure she never realised what you were up to. Aunt Caroline never found out about that particular murder, I don't suppose, or the swindle you worked all over the world with the Kelling family heirlooms when you were supposed to be off peddling books. You might at least have left a set of copies in the box so that I could see what the jewellery would have looked like if I'd ever got to inherit it.'

'Sorry, Sarah, I try not to mix sentiment with business unless I have to. It leads to complications, as you've so clearly pointed out. Where is Caro's diary?'

'Why should I tell you?'

Why, indeed? Sarah had thought she wanted to die and be with her husband. Now she knew she wanted to stay alive, and her one hope of survival lay in keeping up this mad conversation until, God willing, Mr Bittersohn managed to find a parking space.

'I don't think you'll ever find it, Harry,' she said. 'It's a shame your odd-job man failed in his attempt to burn down the house last night, isn't it?'

'And who is my odd-job man?'

'His name is Abelard and he lives over near Andrew Square with a woman named Madeleine, who may or may not be his wife. She calls herself Mrs Wandelowski and claims to run a rooming house. That was where either you or they murdered Tim O'Ghee, who used to bartend at Danny Rate's Pub, as you so well know. I suppose the old man thought he could put the screws on you a bit when Ruby Redd's body turned up. That was a bad mistake. He should have remembered how you hate to pay anybody for anything. When I think of all the times Alexander broke his back doing photography for you, and you begrudged so much as buying him a roll of film, after you'd robbed—'

She mustn't let herself get maudlin. Sarah gulped down the tears and tried to keep her voice level.

'Telling Abelard to fix the Milburn so it would go out of control and smash must have broken your heart. Think what you could have got for it from an antique-car collector. Of course, you'd have had a hard time stealing it back and selling it over again, as you did with our ruby parure until that woman in Amsterdam got the better of you.'

'How did you know about the woman in Amsterdam?'

Now she'd gone too far. Lackridge wasn't going to stand for any more goading.

'Sarah,' he insisted, 'where did you get this information?'

She was terrified now, but she wouldn't back down. 'I haven't the slightest intention of telling you, Harry.'

'You're going to be an extremely sorry young woman if you don't.'

'Do you think you can hurt me any worse than you have already?'

'In a word, yes.'

He was too tall and too fast. Before she could back away, he grabbed her left arm and twisted until the big bone snapped just above the elbow. He let go and the limb flopped useless at her side.

'Now do you understand that I want an answer, Sarah, or shall I make my position a little more clear?'

The pain was making her want to vomit. She spoke through clenched teeth.

'Clever of you to break the left arm instead of the right, Harry. That must mean you have some more free artwork lined up for me to do.'

He twisted the arm again, spinning her back against the console. 'Frankly, Sarah, I never did care for you. This isn't going to bother me one bit.'

As he raised his hand to slash across her face, the doorbell rang. Sarah sucked in every ounce of breath her lungs would hold, and let it out in one mighty scream.

One second later, a body crashed through the library window and into the hall. Max Bittersohn was on top of Harry Lackridge, pounding him into the floor while Sarah stood and watched, perhaps from the identical spot where Caroline Kelling had watched her little love strike down Ruby Redd so many years before.

CHAPTER
TWENTY-EIGHT

'You'll need somebody to look after you for a while.'

Sarah had given her statement to the police from a bed in the emergency ward at Massachusetts General, but insisted on being taken home as soon as her broken arm was X-rayed and set. Uncle Jem and Egbert had stayed with her overnight as a pair of most unlikely nursemaids, but fled delightedly back to Pinckney Street when Max Bittersohn showed up the next morning and invited the patient to lunch.

Since the distance was short and the day was fine, he and she had walked down to the Hampshire House. Sarah was still having a lot of pain, but after two bourbon manhattans and her fair share of a bottle of Pouilly-Fuissé, she wasn't feeling it much.

'I know I'm making a mess here,' she replied, struggling to get the last forkful of chicken divan off her plate. 'Do forgive my horrible manners.'

'You're doing fine, Mrs Kelling. Sure you feel all right?'

'I'm alive, that's the main thing. Harry did mean to kill me, you know.'

'I never doubted it for one minute. Anyway, he's safe in the jug now. I only wish I'd been able to ditch that damned car in time to save you from getting hurt.'

Sarah dipped the corner of her napkin in her water glass and scrubbed cheese sauce off her chin. 'In a way, it's probably just as well you didn't. If it hadn't been for my arm, we might never have got the police to believe such an insane story about a solid citizen like Harry Lackridge.

There's something awfully convincing about a compound fracture of the humerus. Have they arrested Bob Dee, do you know?'

'Booked him on suspicion. I don't know what will come of that, though he has been identified as the eyewitness who just happened to be on the spot, by a very curious coincidence, when the Milburn was wrecked. He'd given a false name, which isn't going to help him any.'

'I hope it won't. And what about Abelard and Madeleine?'

'Abelard's singing like a scalded nightingale. With their police records and your evidence about how they bumped off old Tim O'Ghee, they wouldn't dare refuse to co-operate. I have to go and speak my piece to the grand jury tomorrow morning first thing.'

'Am I expected to testify, too?'

'No, your statement is going to be allowed as evidence for the purpose of indictment, although you'll undoubtedly be key witness for the prosecution when Lackridge comes to trial. You and your mother-in-law's draperies, that is.'

'Oh, no! I meant to burn those ghastly things before anybody else could read them.'

'Good thing you didn't, otherwise you might be liable to a charge of obstructing justice. The draperies have already been impounded. You'll be getting a receipt, no doubt. A Braille expert will be called in to prepare a transcript of Mrs Kelling's fancywork, but you'll be asked to identify the actual embroidery and testify that you saw her doing it.'

'That's no problem. I've watched her making those zillions of French knots any number of times. So has Edith, and Leila, and Harry himself, for that matter. Won't he be livid! After he'd gone through that performance of sneaking in and throwing things around, in the hope of scaring me away from the house so that he'd have a clear field to hunt for the diary, when it was hanging right there in plain sight all the time. I'll bet the reason he didn't kill me right away was that he had some scheme in mind to get himself appointed my trustee and scoop up Father's money along with everything else.'

'That's entirely possible. People like Lackridge always think they can have anything they want for the taking. He still doesn't believe we're going to nail him, you know. Don't be surprised if he puts on quite a show in court.'

'The relatives are going to love the trial, all those passionate outpouring of Aunt Caroline's getting into the papers.'

'It's not your fault.'

'You'll never convince my Cousin Mabel of that. She'll be telling everybody I need a keeper instead of a trustee.'

'I think Redfern's being an old woman about that trusteeship,' Bittersohn grunted. 'Maybe we'll have to get Uncle Jake to drop in for a talk with him. Care for some dessert?'

'My financial position being what it is,' Sarah tried to joke, 'I'd better take all the free food I can get, hadn't I'? Mousse au chocolat would be lovely. Mr Bittersohn, do you honestly think I'll ever get back any part of what Harry stole?'

'I hope so. Hey, that reminds me, we've traced that wiretap. The wires ran over to a one-room basement apartment that's supposed to have been rented for the past several years as a *pied-à-terre* by a nice lady from Shrewsbury.'

'Madeleine in yet another wig?'

'You called it. Her fingerprints were all over the place, along with Abelard's, Lackridge's, and even a few of Bob Dee's. I expect whichever of them happened to be available would drop in and monitor the tapes. The recorder ran on a timer from four to six in the afternoon and eight to ten in the evening.'

'That would be when we were most apt to be sitting in the library,' said Sarah. 'Harry knew our habits so well. I don't suppose you happened to find any tapes with Alexander's voice on them?' she added wistfully.

Bittersohn shook his head. 'I'm afraid not, Mrs Kelling. There'd be no point in keeping the tapes around once they'd been checked. We did find a box under a loose floorboard that held some diagrams of what could be jewels from the Kelling collection. Madeleine and Abelard were probably the go-betweens in getting the duplicates made. Lackridge wouldn't be apt to trust them with the originals, so they'd have worked from notes and drawings.'

'I wonder whom Harry got to do the artwork,' Sarah mused. 'Too bad I wasn't born a little sooner, I might have got the job. But you didn't find any of the actual pieces?'

'Only a couple of Victorian trinkets that wouldn't be valuable enough to copy. One is a gold ring in the shape of a pair of clasped hands that pull apart to reveal a heart. The other is a brooch, a blue-enamelled bird with a baroque pearl dangling from its beak.'

'The bluebird that carries the sky on its back,' Sarah cried. 'That must be Granny Kay's pin. She was Alexander's grandmother, not mine. I never knew her, but she must have been a darling. He adored her and was fascinated by that brooch she always used to wear, ever since he was a tiny boy. Once when he was about four, she quoted that line of Thoreau's about the bluebird carrying the sky on its back. Being too young to understand the metaphor, he took her literally and assumed Thoreau was talking about the brooch. He told me it seemed perfectly reasonable to him that Granny Kay's bird should be the one that got to hold up the sky. He often wondered what had become of the bluebird after she died, but nobody seemed to know.'

She wiped her eyes. 'I don't know anything about the ring. It may have been another of her keepsakes. Aunt Appie said once that Granny Kay had been in love with somebody else when she was young, but her parents forced her to marry Alexander's grandfather because he was a better match. Girls were brought up to be dutiful in those days. I'm afraid it wasn't a happy marriage. He was another cold fish like Uncle Gilbert. Anyway, I hope I get to keep the bluebird. Alexander would like me to have Granny Kay's brooch.'

'You'll get it if I have to steal it for you myself,' Bittersohn promised, 'although I expect the jewellery, as well as the sketches, will have to be presented as evidence at the trial. Some of your older aunts could identify the pieces, couldn't they?'

'Oh, yes. Aunt Appie could, and Aunt Emma and several others. I can give you a list of names and addresses if you want. Will the sketches help us to get back any of the more valuable pieces, do you think?'

'They may, but I shouldn't count on it too much if I were you. We know some of Lackridge's victims, but we don't know who got to keep the genuine stuff, except for that parure we've already discussed. It would be nice to think he still has a cache somewhere, but the odds are he's lost the other pieces one by one as he did the parure. He wouldn't always find it easy to make the switch after the sale, and Lackridge was never one to push his luck too far. That's why he managed to keep ahead of the police as long as he did. You may be in better shape with the real estate. I should think those mortgages could be declared invalid by reason of fraud, although you can be sure the bank won't give up without a struggle. Verplanck has to answer to his shareholders, after all. He may take the position that Mrs Kelling was acting within her rights as executrix, regardless of how she went about it. You could wind up in a court fight before you're through.'

'I'll fight if I have to,' said Sarah. 'I can't honestly say I'm all that keen to be stuck with two white elephants, but I'm not going to be done out of them by Harry Lackridge. He's taken everything—' she thought of Alexander and the bluebird, and drank some coffee to steady herself.

'I was never fond of Harry, but who could have dreamed he'd turn out to be such a—a vampire? And for what? He came from a decent family, went to the right schools, married into a flourishing business, although I suppose he's run it into the ground by now. There was no earthly reason for him to become a thief and a murderer.'

'He didn't become crooked, Mrs Kelling, he was born that way. If Lackridge had been the richest kid in the world, he'd still be a crook. He does what he does because he enjoys it.'

'Then he's insane,' said Sarah. 'How did you ever come to suspect him in the first place? Harry's always so ultra-respectable.'

'I know. That's what tipped me off. Let me tell you another little bit of my life's history. Back when I was a freshman at college, I worked part-time in a drugstore over on Commonwealth Avenue. One night a guy driving a brand-new Mercedes double-parked outside the store and ran in for a pack of cigarettes. He was in a great flap, poking bills at me and wanting change for the phone, claiming I'd given him too much, then too little, switching the money back and forth till I didn't know where I was at. It didn't dawn on me till he'd gone out that I'd been victimised by a quick-change artist. As he drove off, I managed to catch the number of his car, and tracked him through the registry.'

'And it was Harry.'

'To make a long story short. You know, Mrs Kelling, that shocked me as much as anything that's ever happened to me. I simply could not figure out why a man in his position would bother to stick a kid like me for six dollars and twenty-seven cents. I never forgot it. After I went into business for myself, I ran into a couple of odd little incidents where Lackridge seemed to be hovering vaguely in the background. I could never get anything on him, but I kept hoping. Then I got put on this insurance case, learned that the Kellings, who supposedly owned the ruby parure, were bosom buddies of Lackridge and his wife, and figured I was in business at last.'

'You were clever to think of writing that book.'

'Not really. It was such an obvious ploy that I couldn't believe Lackridge would fall for it, until he did. What hooked him was the size of the grant I claimed to be getting from my backers to underwrite the publication. He couldn't resist the chance to chisel off a wad for himself by cheating on the production costs. Besides, a flashy book like the one I was proposing would be good cover. He had to publish something occasionally to protect his reputation. I only hoped I could nail him before I actually had to sit down and write the damn thing. Thanks to you, I did.'

'No thanks to me.'

Sarah put down her spoon, unable to finish her mousse. 'I can't help wondering how much of what happened was my fault. If I hadn't mentioned old Mr O'Ghee that night at the Lackridges', he mightn't have been dead in the morning. If I hadn't talked Alexander into spending the weekend at Ireson's Landing—'

'Mrs Kelling, you know better than that. If O'Ghee was living with Madeleine, you can be sure it wasn't because she made good coffee. An old man like him must have come in handy lots of times. He'd never be noticed hanging around waiting to pass on a message or pick up a package. But he must have known all about Lackridge's tie-up with Ruby Redd, so once her body turned up he'd be too dangerous to keep alive. As for your husband and his mother, I'd say Lackridge had written them off the day he quit keeping up the mortgage payments, and you know how long ago that was. My guess is that he had the scheme with the Milburn all worked out some time ago, and if you hadn't given him a chance to put it into action, he'd have made one for himself.'

'How?'

'Easily enough, I should think. Couldn't he pull his old buddies act and suggest that you all go down to your summer place with him and his wife? Wouldn't your mother-in-law have gone big for that?'

'Yes,' Sarah admitted, 'she'd have jumped at it with both feet.'

'Then when the rest of you were nicely on the spot, Lackridge could have been held up at the office or something and had himself an alibi until after Abelard managed the accident with the Milburn. Once your husband was dead, the state of the family finances would have to come out. Lackridge would then start a rumour that Kelling had actually committed suicide in remorse for having mismanaged his father's estate, and taken his mother with him so she wouldn't have to suffer.'

'Which is exactly the sort of garbage some people would believe,' said Sarah bitterly.

'Lackridge is a clever man, Mrs Kelling. There's no way you could have kept him from doing what he did because you had no idea what sort of person you were up against. Neither did I, if you want the truth. Until you told me your story, I had no reason to think of Lackridge as anything but a first-class society con artist, and it's always been my experience before that swindlers of his calibre avoid any kind of violence. Now it looks as if we may be able to tie him to at least six murders besides the ones you know about, and you can bet he'd have gone right on killing if you hadn't helped to stop him.'

'But it's so totally insane! You say he likes to do it. How can he?'

'How can a hunter enjoy slaughtering some beautiful wild animal that's never done him or anybody else any harm? It's his way of showing what a great, big he-man he is. Gives him the means to stroll into a casino and throw a wad of G-notes on the blackjack table, makes him feel important.'

'That's what he did with Alexander's money?'

'That and other things. He owns a big spread outside Fort Worth, a villa on the Côte d'Azur, has his twin-engine Cessna, and his unpretentious little forty-foot yacht—all under assumed names, of course. He doesn't get to use them much because he has to keep coming back to Boston and being respectable Harry Lackridge, putting up a noble fight to keep the fine old family business afloat, but what the heck? They don't cost him anything. He runs them on other people's money.'

'Do you think Leila knows?'

'Offhand, I'd say she hasn't a clue. As far as he's concerned Mrs Lackridge is probably just part of the window dressing, although she must have come in handy as Mrs Kelling's watchdog. I'm afraid this is going to put a crimp in her political activities.'

'Poor Leila,' Sarah sighed. 'I suppose I ought to go and see her, though I dread the thought.'

'Finish your coffee. Right now she's probably down at Station One getting the third degree. You'd better be thinking about what you're going to do for yourself.'

'Uncle Jem has that all arranged. He called his sister Emma and she's invited me to stay with her till my arm is better. She lives out near Springfield, which is far enough from Boston so people won't be pestering me all the time. Also, Aunt Emma has maids who can help me dress and so forth while I'm stuck in this ridiculous cast.'

'What about your own place?'

'Mariposa, my guardian angel, is moving in to keep an eye on things till I get back. I asked if she'd be scared staying alone, but it turns out she's bringing her dog and her boyfriend, and she says they both turn pretty mean if anybody tries messing around with her. So everything's under control but me. I really must go home and pack a few things.'

'Look, if you need a ride out to Springfield—'

'Thank you, but Aunt Emma is sending her chauffeur. You've been absolutely wonderful, Mr Bittersohn. I only wish there were something I could do for you in return.'

Bittersohn took the hand she held out to him. 'I wish so, too, Mrs Kellings. But I guess there isn't, is there? Come on, I'll walk you up the Hill.'